BEST SF: 1968

BEST SF:
1968

edited by
HARRY HARRISON
and
BRIAN W. ALDISS

G. P. Putnam's Sons
New York

COPYRIGHT © 1969 BY HARRY HARRISON

Library of Congress Catalog
Card Number: 68–18178

PRINTED IN THE UNITED STATES OF AMERICA

Contents

Acknowledgments

"Budget Planet," by Robert Sheckley, copyright © 1968 by Mercury Press, Inc.; reprinted by permission of Harold Matson Company, Inc.

"Appointment on Prila," by Bob Shaw, copyright © 1968 by the Condé Nast Publications, Inc.; reprinted by permission of the author.

"Lost Ground," by David I. Masson, copyright © 1968 by David I. Masson; reprinted by permission of the author and Messrs. Faber and Faber.

"The Rime of the Ancient SF Author, or Conventions and Recollections," by J. R. Pierce, copyright © 1968 by Ultimate Publishing Co., Inc.; reprinted by permission of the author.

"The Annex," by John D. MacDonald, copyright © 1968 by John D. MacDonald; this story, which first appeared in *Playboy,* is reprinted by permission of the author.

"Segregationist," by Isaac Asimov, copyright © 1968 by Isaac Asimov; reprinted by permission of the author. Reprinted from *Abbottempo,* published by Abbott Laboratories.

"Final War," by K. M. O'Donnell, copyright © 1968 by Mercury Press, Inc.; reprinted by permission of the author.

"2001: A Space Odyssey," by Lester del Rey, copyright © 1968 by Galaxy Publishing Corp.; reprinted by permission of the author and Scott Meredith Literary Agency, Inc.

"Review of 2001: A Space Odyssey," by Samuel R. Delany, copyright © 1968 by Mercury Press, Inc.; reprinted by permission of the author and Henry Morrison, Inc., his agents.

"2001: A Space Odyssey Review," by Ed Emshwiller, copyright © 1968 by Mercury Press, Inc.; reprinted by permission of the author.

"Apeman, Superman—or, 2001's Answer to the World Riddle," by Leon E. Stover, copyright © 1968 by Leon E. Stover; reprinted by permission of the author.

"The Serpent of Kundalini," by Brian W. Aldiss, copyright © 1968 by *New Worlds*; reprinted by permission of the author.

"Golden Acres," by Kit Reed, copyright © 1968 by Kit Reed (re-

BEST SF: 1968

INTRODUCTION

It has been a good year for science fiction, which is a pleasant and exciting change. If, as some people suggest, science fiction is the wave of the future, it has been dashing itself into foam upon the shore, without much result, for the past forty-odd years. But now there seems to have been a sudden and almost dramatic change. For example:

Science fiction shambled to life in the crumbling yellow pages of the pulp magazines. If SF stories appeared in more respectable journals they were considered not to be science fiction. This attitude is gone—along with the pulp magazines themselves. The SF magazines of today are anything but pulp, and at least two of the editors are much-sought-after public speakers. John W. Campbell of *Analog* is a frequent visitor to the universities, and numbers among his friends and acquaintances many of the leading scientists of today—and tomorrow. Frederik Pohl of the *Galaxy* group flies from coast to coast lecturing to business groups about their possible futures. Science fiction magazines are respected.

From time to time, up to World War II, mainstream

publishers would bring out the occasional SF book—being careful not to label it as such. After the war a few gallant, and occasionally crooked, souls published the Real Stuff on a shoestring basis. For the most part these firms eventually failed, just at the time the established publishers began to dip tremulous toes into the murky waters of this kind of fiction. Now these major publishers are glad to put the correct label on SF. There is even a science fiction book club, and the presses of the paperback publishers roar until there is SF in every supermarket, drugstore, and bookshop across the land.

The motion picture. With a few outstanding exceptions, such as *Things to Come*, the cinema screen has flickered luridly with evil monsters, mad scientists, space-going boobs in cardboard rocketships, and all the flimsy hardware and plasticine animals of the low budget film. This has, perhaps, been changed drastically by a single motion picture; *2001: A Space Odyssey*. Its multimillion dollar finances alone demand attention. Also its slightly unusual ending. (Some of the better reviews of the film are included in this volume, and may help to clarify the varying opinions about that ending!)

The Establishment. They are slowly being seduced—for the most part by members of their own groups. The ivory tower dwellers of literature still ignore the existence of the exciting medium of science fiction, so book reviews appear seldom, if ever. But the universities are enthusiastically aware of SF. Manuscript collections are being built up in the libraries at California State College at Fullerton, the University of California in Berkeley, Syracuse University, and others. Courses in science fiction are now taught at the Illinois Institute of Technology, Fullerton, and Clarion State College in Pennsylvania.

All of which is of absolutely no importance to the reader who comes to science fiction for relaxation and enjoyment. Or is it? I firmly believe that it is. None of the early science fiction writers ever predicted that the greatest benefits to be derived from rocket projects would be the spin-off of new materials and methods. The spin-off from the awakening interest in SF is more writers, better writers, better stories—and more enjoyable ones. The older, established writers have been lured back, and newer writers are developing. There are more—and better—books to choose from. There are better stories. There is even a clash of factionalism as proponents of the "new wave" struggle with the die-hard defenders of the old. I wish I could join sides in this battle, having always enjoyed a good fight, but I am afraid I cannot.

There is no new wave, save in the eye of the beholder. Some writers are experimenting with new forms in SF, but some writers have always experimented with new forms. Some writers have written dirty words in SF, but dirty words are neither new nor interesting most of the time. Some writers have written confused, dense, impressionistic and bad prose—and this certainly has been with us since the dawn of creation. One of the foremost writers in the "new wave" admitted that my own writing fits into both camps. So do the stories anthologized in this present volume. Those who care to assign categories may do so by putting NW or OW before each entry on the title page. I refuse to do so. My only yardstick is quality—and these are the best stories that could be found that had been published during the year 1968.

I have not been alone. Hovering behind me has been the stern and critical spirit of James Blish, who established certain standards for an anthology of this kind in last year's volume. I have attempted to follow his credo. The contents are all science fiction, as best as I can define that slippery term. The book is all fiction—with the exception of a brief poem and a handful of reviews that I felt were germane to the field as a whole. I hope that he will excuse this lapse. And, once more, no restrictions have been placed on choice of story. These are the stories, and all the stories that I wanted to have in this anthology. Period. The only aid and advice in selection that I received was from Brian W. Aldiss, whose name you will note on the cover and title page. Brian, the best of friends, is also the best of critics, and he has scouted the British publishing scene for this book. His help is happily acknowledged and greatly appreciated. In addition to unearthing some choice items, he has also written an afterword that takes a synoptic look at the past year in science fiction.

I enjoyed reading these stories. May you do the same.

HARRY HARRISON

BUDGET PLANET

ROBERT SHECKLEY

Robert Sheckley has the kind of metabolism that we all envy: he can eat three or four sturdy meals a day without adding an ounce of fat. His intellectual metabolism works in the same way. There is no fat in his stories, even though the reader is quickly made aware that vast amounts of material have been ingested. He writes satire, and is one of the two or three SF authors who can write it well. Here he proves himself a practitioner of what might be called neo-Menippean satire or, if that frightens you— this is the story of Genesis as told from a con man's point of view. It forms a chapter in the author's recent book, Dimension of Miracles, *which contains—happily—much more of the same.*

"So this is it, eh, Orin?" Maudsley said.

"Yes sir, this is it," Orin, the man on his left said, smiling proudly. "What do you think of it, sir?"

Maudsley turned round slowly and surveyed the meadow, the mountains, the sun, the river, the forest. His face betrayed no expression. He said, "What do *you* think of it, Brookside?"

5

Brookside said, in a tremulous voice, "Well sir, I think that Orin and I did a nice job. A *really* nice job, if you take into account that it was our first independent project."

"And do you concur in that judgment, Orin?" Maudsley asked.

"Certainly, sir," Orin said.

Maudsley bent down and plucked a blade of grass. He sniffed it and threw it away. He scuffed the dirt beneath his feet, then stared for several moments full into the blazing sun. In a measured voice, he said, "I am amazed, truly amazed. But in a most unpleasant way. I ask you two to bu'ld a world for one of my customers and you come up with *this!* Do you really consider yourselves engineers?"

The two aides did not reply. They had stiffened, like boys awaiting the birch rod.

"Engineers!" Maudsley said, getting almost fifty footpounds of contempt into the word. " 'Creative but practical scientists who can build the planet where and when you want it.' Do either of you recognize those words?"

"They're from the standard brochure," Orin said.

"That is correct," Maudsley replied. "Now, do you consider *this* a good example of 'creative, practical engineering'?"

Both men were silent. Then Brookside blurted out, "Well sir, yes sir, I do!

"We examined the job specs very carefully. The request was for a Type 34Bc4 planet with certain variations. And that's exactly what we built. This is only a corner of it, of course. But still—"

"But still, I can see what you did and judge accordingly," Maudsley said. "Orin! What kind of a heating unit did you use?"

"A type 05 sun, sir," Orin replied. "It fitted the thermal requirements nicely."

"I daresay it did. But this was a budget world, you will remember. If we don't keep the costs down, we don't make a profit. And the biggest single cost item is the heating unit."

"We are aware of that, sir," Brookside said. "We didn't at all like to use an 05 type sun for a single-planet system. But the heat and radiation requirements—"

"Haven't you learned anything from me?" Maudsley cried. "This type of star is entirely superfluous. You there —" He beckoned to the workmen. "Take it down."

The workmen hurried forward with a folding ladder. One man braced it and another man unfolded it, ten times, a hundred times, a million times. Two other workmen raced up the ladder as fast as it went up.

"Handle it carefully!" Maudsley called up to them. "And be sure you're wearing gloves! That thing's hot!"

The workmen at the very top of the ladder unhooked the star, folded it into itself and put it into a padded box marked STAR: HANDLE WITH CARE.

When the lid fell, everything went black.

"Hasn't anyone any sense around here?" Maudsley asked. "Damn it all, let there be light."

And just like that, there was light.

"OK," Maudsley said. "That 05 type sun goes back into storage. On a job like this we can use a G13 type star."

"But sir," Orin said nervously, "it isn't hot enough."

"I know that," Maudsley said. "That's where you have to use your creativity. If you move the star closer in, it'll be hot enough."

"Yes sir, it will," Brookside said. "But it'll be emitting PR rays without enough space to allow them to dissipate harmlessly. And that might kill off the entire race that's going to occupy this planet."

Maudsley said, very slowly and distinctly, "Are you trying to tell me that G13 type stars are dangerous?"

"Well, no, I didn't mean it exactly *that* way," Orin said, "I meant to say, they *can* be dangerous, just like anything else in the universe, if proper precautions are not taken."

"That's more like it," Maudsley said.

"The proper precautions," Brookside said, "involve in

this case the wearing of protective lead suits weighing some fifty pounds each. But this is impractical, since the average member of this race only weighs eight pounds."

"That's their lookout," Maudsley said. "It's not our business to tell them how to live their lives. Am I supposed to be responsible whenever they stub their toe on a rock I put on their planet? Besides, they don't have to wear lead suits. They can buy one of my optional extras, a Solar Screen that'll block out the PR rays."

Both men smiled nervously. But Orin said timidly, "I believe this is a somewhat underprivileged species, sir. I think perhaps they can't afford the Solar Screen."

"Well, if not right now, maybe later," Maudsley said. "And anyhow, the PR radiations aren't instantly fatal. Even with it, they'll have an average lifespan of 9.3 years, which ought to be enough for anyone."

"Yes sir," the two assistant engineers said, not happily.

"Next," Maudsley said, "what's the height of those mountains?"

"They average six thousand feet above sea level," Brookside said.

"At least three thousand feet too high," Maudsley said. "Do you think mountains grow on trees? Pare them down and put what you have left over into the warehouse."

Brookside took out a notebook and jotted down the change. Maudsley continued to pace around, looking and frowning.

"How long are those trees supposed to last?"

"Eight hundred years, sir. They're the new, improved model Apple-oak. They give fruit, shade, nuts, refreshing beverages, three useful fabrics; they make excellent building material, hold the soil in place, and—"

"Are you trying to bankrupt me?" Maudsley roared. "Two hundred years is entirely long enough for a tree! Drain off most of their elan vital and store it in the lifeforce accumulator!"

"They won't be able to perform all of their designed functions, then," Orin said.

"Then cut down on their functions! Shade and nuts is plenty, we don't have to make a damned treasure chest out of those trees! Now then, who put those cows out there?"

"I did, sir," Brookside said. "I thought it would make the place look—well, sort of inviting sir."

"You oaf," Maudsley said, "the time to make a place look inviting is before the sale, not after! This place was sold unfurnished. Put those cows into the protoplasm vat."

"Yes sir," Orin said. "Terribly sorry, sir. Is there anything else?"

"There're about ten thousand other things wrong," Maudsley said. "But you can figure out those for yourselves, I hope. What, for example, is this?" He pointed at Carmody. "A statue or something? Is he supposed to sing a song or recite a poem when the new race arrives?" Carmody said, "Sir, I am not part of this. A friend of yours named Malichrone sent me, and I'm trying to get home to my own planet—"

Maudsley clearly did not hear what Carmody was saying. For, while Carmody was trying to speak, Maudsley was saying, "Whatever he is, the job specs don't call for him. So stick him back in the protoplasm vat with the cows."

"Hey!" Carmody shouted as workmen lifted him up by his arms. "Hey, wait a minute!" he screamed. "I'm not a part of this planet! Malichrone sent me! Wait, hold on, listen to me!"

"You really ought to be ashamed of yourselves," Maudsley went on, oblivious to Carmody's shrieks. "What was that supposed to be? One of your interior decorating touches, Orin?"

"Oh no," Orin said. "I didn't put him there."

"Then it was you, Brookside."

"I never saw him before in my life, chief."

"Hmm," Maudsley said, "You're both fools, but you've never been liars. Hey!" he shouted to the workmen. "Bring him back here!"

"All right, pull yourself together," Maudsley said to Carmody, who was shaking uncontrollably. "Get a grip on yourself, I can't wait around here while you have a fit of hysterics! Better now? All right, would you mind explaining just what you're doing trespassing on my property and why I shouldn't have you converted into protoplasm?"

"I see," Maudsley said, after Carmody had finished explaining. "It's an interesting story, though I'm sure you've overdramatized it. Still, here you are, and you're looking for a planet called—Earth?"

"That is correct, sir," Carmody said.

"Earth," Maudsley mused, scratching his head. "This is most fortunate for you; I seem to remember the place."

"Do you really, Mr. Maudsley?"

"Yes, I'm quite sure of it," Maudsley said. "It's a small green planet, and it supports a mono-morphic humanoid race like yourself. Am I right?"

"Completely right!" Carmody said.

"I have rather a memory for these things," Maudsley said. "And in this particular case, as it happens, I built Earth."

"Did you really, sir?" Carmody asked.

"Yep. I remember distinctly, because in the course of building it, I also invented science. Perhaps you will find the story amusing." He turned to his aides. "And *you* might find the tale instructive."

No one was going to deny Maudsley the right to tell a story. So Carmody and the assistant engineers assumed attentive postures, and Maudsley began.

THE STORY OF THE CREATION OF EARTH

I was still quite a small contractor then. I put up a planet here and there, and I got to do an occasional dwarf star. But jobs were always hard to come by, and the customers were invariably capricious, faultfinding, and slow in their payments. Customers were hard to please in those days; they argued about every little detail. *Change this, change that, why must water flow downhill, the gravity's too heavy, the hot air rises when it ought to fall.* And so forth.

I was quite naive in those days. I used to explain the esthetic and practical reasons for everything I did. Before long, the questions and the explanations were taking longer than the jobs. There was entirely too much talk-talk. I knew that I had to do something about it, but I couldn't figure out what.

Then, just before the Earth project, a whole new approach to customer relations began to shape itself in my mind. I found myself muttering to myself, "Form follows function." I liked the way it sounded. But then I would ask myself, *"Why* must form follow function?" And the reason I gave myself was, "Form follows function because that is an immutable law of nature and one of the fundamental axioms of applied science." I liked the sound of that, too, although it didn't make much sense.

But sense didn't matter. What mattered was that I had made a new discovery. I had unwittingly stumbled into the art of advertising and salesmanship, and I had discovered the gimmick of great possibilities: Namely, the doctrine of scientific determinism. Earth was my first test case, and that is why I will always remember it.

A tall, bearded old man with piercing eyes had come to me and ordered a planet. (That was how your planet began, Carmody.) Well, I did the job quickly, in six days I believe, and thought that would be the end of it. It was another of those budget planets, and I had cut a few corners here and there. But to hear the owner complain, you'd have thought I had stolen the eyes out of his head.

"Why are there so many tornadoes?" he asked.

"It's part of the atmosphere circulation system," I told him. Actually, I had been a little rushed at that time; I had forgotten to put in an air circulation overload valve.

"Three quarters of the place is water!" he told me. "And I clearly specified a 4 to 1 land-to-water ratio!"

"Well, we couldn't do it that way!" I said to him. I had

lost his ridiculous specifications; I never can keep track of these absurd little one-planet projects.

"And you've filled what little land you gave me with deserts and swamps and jungles and mountains."

"It's scenic," I pointed out.

"I don't care from scenic!" the fellow thundered. "Oh, sure, one ocean, a dozen lakes, a couple rivers, one or two mountain ranges, that would have been fine. Dresses the place up, gives the inhabitants a good feeling. But what you gave me is *shlock!*"

"There's a reason for it," I said. In point of fact, we couldn't make the job pay except by using reconstituted mountains, a lot of rivers and oceans as filler, and a couple of deserts I had bought cheap from Ourie the planet-junker. But I wasn't going to tell *him* that.

"A reason!" he screamed. "What will I tell my people? I'm putting an entire race on that planet, maybe two or three. They'll be humans, made in my own image, and humans are notoriously picky, just as I am. What am I supposed to tell them?"

Well, I knew what he could tell them, but I didn't want to be offensive; so I pretended to give the matter some thought. And strangely enough, I *did* think. And I came up with the gimmick to end all gimmicks.

"You just tell them the plain scientific truth," I said. "You tell them that, scientifically, everything that *is* must be."

"Huh?" he said.

"It's determinism," I said, making up the name on the spur of the moment. "It's quite simple, though a bit esoteric. To start with, form follows function; therefore your planet is exactly as it should be by the simple fact of *being* at all. Next, science is invariable; so if anything isn't invariable, it isn't science. And finally, everything follows definite rules. You can't always figure out what those rules are, but you can be sure they're there. So, it stands to reason that no one ought to ask *why this instead of that?* Instead, everyone ought to ask *how does it work?*"

Well, he asked me some pretty tough questions, and he

was a pretty smart old fellow. But he didn't know crap
about engineering; his field was ethics and morals and
religion and spook-stuff like that. So of course, he just
wasn't able to come up with any real objections. He was
one of these types who loves abstractions, and he started
repeating, "That which *is* is that which *must be.* Hmm, a
very intriguing formula and not without its patina of
stoicism. I shall incorporate some of these insights into the
lessons I give to my people. . . . But tell me this: how can I
reconcile this indeterminate fatality of science with the free
will I plan to give to my people?"

Well, the old boy almost had me there. I smiled and
coughed to give myself time to think, and then I said,
"The answer is obvious!" Which is always a good answer,
as far as it goes.

"I daresay it is," he said. "But I don't perceive it."

"Look," I said, "this free will you're giving your people, isn't that a kind of fatality also?"

"It could be considered as such. But the difference—"

"And besides," I said hastily, "since when are free will
and fatality incompatible?"

"They certainly seem incompatible," he said.

"That's only because you don't understand science," I
said, performing the old switcheroo right under his hooked
nose. "You see, my dear sir, one of the most basic laws of
science is that chance plays a part in everything. Chance,
I'm sure you know, is the mathematical equivalent of free
will."

"But what you're saying is quite contradictory," he
said.

"That's how it goes," I said. "Contradiction is one more
of the fundamental rules of the universe. Contradiction
generates strife, without which everything would reach a
stage of entropy. So we couldn't have any planet or any
universe if things didn't exist in an apparently irrecon-
cilable state of contradiction."

"Apparently?" he said quickly.

"Right as rain," I said. "Contradiction, which we can
define provisionally as the existence of reality-paired op-

posites, isn't the last word on the subject. For example, let's posit a single isolated tendency. What happens when you push a tendency to the limit?"

"I haven't the slightest idea," the old guy said. "The lack of specifics in this sort of discussion—"

"What happens," I said, "is that the tendency turns into its *opposite*."

"Does it really?" he asked, considerably shook up. These religious types are something when they try to tackle science.

"It really does," I assured him. "I've got the proofs in my lab, though the demonstrations are a bit tedious—"

"No, please, I take your word," the old guy said. "After all, we did make a Covenant."

That was the word he always used for contract. It meant the same thing, but sounded better.

"Paired opposites," he mused. "Determinism. Things becoming their opposites. It's all quite intricate, I'm afraid."

"And aesthetic as well," I said. "But I didn't finish about the transformation of extremes."

"Kindly go on," he said.

"Thanks. Now then, we have entropy, which means that things persist in their motion unless there is outside influence. (Sometimes even when there is outside influence, in my experience.) But so, we got entropy driving a thing toward its opposite. If one thing is driven toward its opposite, then all things are driven toward their opposites, because science is consistent. Now you get the picture? We've got all these opposites transforming themselves like crazy and becoming their opposites. On a higher level of organization, we have groups of opposites going through the same bit. And higher and higher. So far so good?"

"I suppose so," he said.

"Fine. Now, the question naturally arises, is this all? I mean, these opposites turning themselves inside out and then outside in, is that the whole ball game? And the beauty-part is, it's not! No sir, these opposites flipping around like trained seals are only an aspect of what's really happening. Because——" And here I paused and spoke in a very deep voice. "——because there is a wisdom that sees beyond the clash and turmoil of the phenomenal world. This wisdom, sir, sees through the illusory quality of these real things and sees beyond them into the deeper workings of the universe, which are in a state of like great and magnificent harmony."

"How can a thing be both illusory and real?" he asked me, quick as a whip.

"It is not for me to know an answer like that," I told him. "Me, I am a mere humble scientific worker, and I see what I see and act accordingly. But maybe there's an ethical reason behind it."

The old boy mused on that one for a while, and I could see he was having quite a tussle with himself. He could detect a logical fallacy as fast as anyone, of course, and my reasons had been shot through with them. But like all eggheads, he was fascinated with contradictions and he had the strong urge to incorporate them into his system. And all the propositions I had proposed—well, his common sense told him that things couldn't be *that* tricky, but his intellectuality told him that maybe things did indeed seem that complicated, although maybe there was a nice simple unifying principle underneath it all. Or, if not a unifying principle, at least a good solid moral. And finally, I had hooked him all over again just because I had used the word *ethics*. Because this old gent was a perfect demon for ethics, he was supersaturated with ethics; you could call him Mr. Ethics, make no mistake. And so, quite accidentally, I had given him the idea that the whole bloody universe was a series of homilies and contradictions, of laws and inequities, all leading to the most exquisite and rarefied sort of ethical order.

"There is a greater depth here than I had considered," he said after a while. "I had planned to instruct my people in ethics only and to direct their attention to morally imperative questions such as how and why a man should live instead of what constitutes living matter. I wanted them to be explorers plumbing the depths of joy, fear, piety, hope, despair, rather than scientists who examine stars and raindrops and form grandiose and impractical hypotheses on the basis of their findings. I was aware of the universe, but considered it superfluous. Now you have corrected me."

"Well, look," I said, "I didn't mean to cause trouble. I just thought I should point out this stuff. . . ."

The old man smiled. "By causing me trouble," he said, "you have spared me greater trouble. I can create in my own image, but I will not create a world peopled with miniature versions of myself. Free will is important to me. My creatures will have it, to their glory and their sorrow. They will take this glittering useless toy which you call science, and they will elevate it to an undeclared Godhead. Physical contradictions and solar abstractions will fascinate them; they will pursue knowledge of these things and forget to explore the knowledge of their own heart. You have convinced me of this, and I am grateful for the forewarning."

I'll be frank, he got me a little nervous just about then. I mean, he was a nobody, he didn't know any important people, and yet, he had the grand manner. I had the feeling that he could cause me one hell of a lot of trouble, and I felt that he could do it with a few words, a sentence like a poisoned dart lodged in my mind and never to be removed. And that scared me a little, to tell the truth.

Well sir, the old joker must have been reading my mind. For he said, "Do not be frightened. I accept without reservation the world you have built for me; it will serve very well, exactly as it is. As for the flaws and defects which you also built into my world, I accept those, not entirely without gratitude, and I pay for those, too."

"How?" I asked. "How do you pay for errors?"

"By accepting them without dispute," he said. "And by turning away from you now and going about my business and the business of my people."

And old gentleman left without another word.

Well, it left me pretty thoughtful. I'd had all the good

arguments, but the old boy left somehow with the last word. I knew what he meant; he had fulfilled his contract with me and that ended it. He was leaving with no word for me personally. From his point of view, it was a kind of punishment.

But that's only the way *he* saw it. What did I need with his word? I wanted to hear it, of course—that's only natural—and for quite a while I tried to look him up. But he didn't care to see me.

So it really doesn't matter. I made a pretty nice profit on that world, and even if I bent the contract here and there, I didn't break it. That's how things are; you owe it to yourself to make a profit. You can't get too worked up over the consequences.

But I was trying to make a point out of all this, and I want you boys to listen carefully. Science is filled with a lot of rules, because I invented it that way. Why did I invent it that way? Because rules are a great assistance to a smart operator, just as a lot of laws are a great help to lawyers. The rules, doctrines, axioms, laws, and principles of science are there to help you, not to hinder you. They're there in order to provide you with reasons for what you do. Most of them are true, more or less, and that helps.

But always remember—these rules are there to help you explain to the customers what you do *after you do it,* not before. When you have a project, do it exactly as you see fit; then fit the facts around the event, not the other way around.

Remember—these rules exist as a verbal barrier against people who ask questions. But they should *not* be used as a barrier by you. If you've learned anything from me, you've learned that our work is inevitably inexplicable; we simply do it, and sometimes it comes out well and sometimes not.

But never try to explain to yourselves why some things happen and why other things don't happen. Don't ask, and don't imagine that an explanation exists. Get me?

The two assistants nodded vehemently. They looked enlightened, like men who have found a new religion. Carmody would have bet anything that those two earnest young men had memorized every one of the builder's words, and would now proceed to elevate those words into—a rule.

APPOINTMENT ON PRILA

Bob Shaw

I have never seen reference to "soft" science fiction, but hard science fiction may be described as SF that adheres to known fact and respects the logical and scientific processes. It is also fascinated with the hardware of science. Mr. Shaw, who will be remembered as the author of "Light of Other Days"—which contained an absolutely new science-fictional device, slow glass—writes a story filled with gleeful detail that could almost have been written by van Vogt during his golden period.

Candar waited for seven thousand years before he saw his second spaceship.

He had been little more than a cub when he saw the first, but the picture was still clear in his mind. It had been a warm, moist morning and his mother and father had just begun cutting through a village of the two-legged food creatures. Candar was quietly watching their great gray bodies at work when he became aware of the ship. It came low, and was traveling so fast that the damp air was compressed into opaque gray clouds inside the shock waves created by its blunt nose. The clouds swirled round

19

it like a tattered cloak so that the ship skipped in and out of visibility, and Candar wondered how anything could move at such a speed and not make any sound.

It was not until after the ship had passed overhead that the sound came, leveling the food creatures' flimsy huts even more efficiently than mother and father could have done. The ship banked sharply, halted high in the morning air and suddenly Candar and his parents were lifted into the sky. Candar deduced that he was caught in some kind of a force field. He measured its frequency, wavelength, intensity, and even discovered that his brain could produce a similar field of its own—but he could not get away. He and his parents were rushed upwards to where the sky turned black and Candar could hear the stars and, then, some time later, his mother and father were released. They vanished in a few seconds and Candar, already adapting to the new environment, realized that his parents had been steered into a course which terminated in the Sun. Judging by their agonized struggles as they dwindled from view, his mother and father had performed the same calculation.

The sun shrank, became a star, then much later a double star blossomed and became two egg-shaped suns courting each other in a binary ritual. Ten miles above a planet of black rock which wobbled a precarious orbit between the suns the spaceship let Candar drop. Only by converting his body into miles of springy, hair-thin organic wire did he survive the fall, and by the time he had re-formed his sense organs the ship was gone.

Candar knew that he had been imprisoned. He also knew that on this world which could carry no trace of food he would eventually die, and there was nothing to do but wait.

His new world made its painful run between the two suns every year; each time the black rock melted and ran like mud and nothing survived unchanged but Candar—and it was seven thousand years before he saw his second spaceship.

The thing Surgenor detested most about high-gravity planets was the speed at which beads of sweat could move. A trickle of perspiration could form on his brow and, with a rush like an attacking insect, be down the side of his face and under his collar before he could raise a hand to defend himself. In sixteen years of survey work he had never become used to it.

"If this wasn't my last trip," Surgenor said quietly, "I'd refuse to do any more."

"Can I have time to think about that one?" Voysey, who was on his second trip, kept his eyes on the survey module's controls.

"You've *got* time," Surgenor said. "Everybody on this job has time." He decided to talk about something else. "I'll bet you ten stellars we see the ship from the top of this hill."

"Already!" Voysey became alert and started setting verniers on the range-finder panel.

Already, Surgenor thought. It felt like centuries since the mother ship had set its six survey modules down at the black planet's south pole and ghosted back into the sky to do a half circuit and landing at the north pole. The ship would have completed the journey in half an hour—the men in the modules had had to sweat it out under three gravities for twelve days as their machines zigzagged along the planet's surface. Had there been an atmosphere they could have switched to ground-effect and travelled twice as fast, but even as it was they had made good time.

The car reached the top of the rise and the horizon, which was the line separating starry blackness from dead blackness, dropped away in front and Surgenor saw the clustered lights of the *Sarafand* down on the plain about five miles from them.

"You were right, Dave," Voysey said and Surgenor grinned at the note of respect in his voice. "I think we're going to be first back, too. I don't see any other lights."

Surgenor nodded. Strictly speaking, all six modules should have been exactly the same distance out from the *Sarafand* in their respective directions, ranged in a per-

fect circle. During most of the journey the vehicles had
adhered rigidly to the search pattern so that the data they
were transmitting to the mother ship always reached it
from six equally distant, equally spaced points. Any devi-
ation from the pattern would have caused distortion in the
planet map being built up in the ship's computer deck.
But each module had an awareness radius of five hundred
miles, with the result that when they got to within half
that distance of the mother ship the remaining territory
was being mapped six times over, and the job was well
and truly finished. It was an unofficial tradition that the
last two-hundred-and-fifty-mile leg of a survey was an
out-and-out race for home, with champagne for the win-
ners and an appropriate salary deduction for the losers.

Module Five, which was Surgenor's vehicle, had just
skirted a low but jagged range of hills and he guessed that
at least two of the others would have had to go over the
top and lose time. Somehow, in spite of all the years and
light-years, he felt some excitement. It might be nice to
finish his career in Cartographical Service with champagne.

"Here we go," Voysey said as the vehicle gathered
speed on the downward slope. "A shower, shave and
champagne—what more could you ask for?"

"Well, even if we stick to the alliteration," Surgenor
replied, "there's steak, sex, sleep . . ."

He stopped speaking as the voice of Captain Aesop on
board the *Sarafand* boomed from the radio grill.

"This is *Sarafand* speaking to all survey modules. Do
not continue your approach. Cut your motors and remain
where you are until further notification. This is an order."

Before Aesop's voice had died away the radio silence
that had been observed during the race was broken as
startled and angry comments from the other modules
crashed from the speaker. Surgenor felt the first cold
feather-flick of alarm—Aesop had sounded as though

something was seriously wrong. *Module Five* was still churning its way downward into the blackness.

"It must be some kind of mistake," Surgenor said, "but you'd better cut the motor anyway."

"But this is crazy! Aesop's crazy! What could go wrong?" Voysey sounded indignant. He made no move to touch the motor controls.

Without warning, an ultralaser burst from the *Sarafand* splintered the night into dazzling fragments and the hillside lifted skywards in front of *Module Five*. Voysey hit the brakes and the vehicle slid to a halt on the glowing edges of the ultralaser scar. Falling rock hammered on the roof in an irregular, deafening frenzy, then there was silence.

"Aesop's gone mad," Voysey said numbly, almost to himself. "Why did he want to do that?"

"This is the *Sarafand*," the radio blared again. "I repeat. No survey module is to attempt to approach. I will be forced to destroy any other module which fails to obey this order."

Surgenor pressed the button which put him on the air.

"This is Surgenor in *Module Five,* Aesop. You'd better tell us what's going on."

There was a pause, then Aesop spoke again. "Six cars went out on this survey—seven have come back. I need hardly point out that this is one too many."

With a sudden spasm of alarm Candar realized he had made a mistake. His fear stemmed not from the fact that the strangers had deduced his presence, or that they had reasonably potent weapons, it came from the knowledge that he had made such a simple error. The process of deterioration must have gone much further than he had realized.

The task of reforming his body to look like one of the traveling machines had been a difficult one, but not so difficult as the vast cellular reorganization which enabled him to survive when the two suns were overhead. His mistake had been to allow the machine, whose shape he had copied, to come within range of the scanning device aboard the largest machine. He had allowed the small machine to draw away from him while he went through the agony of transformation and then, when he went after it, had become aware of the pulsing spray of electrons sweeping over him. He should have deduced in advance that creatures with the feeble sense organs he had perceived would have striven for something to widen their awareness of the universe. Especially creatures who would take the trouble to build such complicated vehicles.

Candar's alarm faded away as he picked up the currents of fear and bewilderment stirring in the minds of the beings in the machines nearest to him. Minds like these could never present any serious problem—all he had to do was await his chance. He crouched on the cracked surface of the plain, most of the metallic elements in his system transferred to the periphery of his new shape, which was now identical to that of the travelling machines. A small part of his energy was going into producing light which he beamed out in front, and occasionally he emitted bursts of radio waves at frequencies based on the strangers' speech patterns.

He was Candar, the most intelligent, talented and dangerous single entity in the universe; and all he had to do was wait.

The standard intercom speakers fitted in geodesic survey modules were, in spite of their small size, very good. Surgenor had never heard one overload before, but immediately following Aseop's announcement effective communication was lost in a crashing, skidding roar as every module reacted in surprise or disbelief. A defense mechanism caused him to stare at the speaker grill in mild wonderment while another part of his mind assimilated Aesop's news.

A seventh module had appeared on an airless world which was not only uninhabited but, in the strictest clinical sense of the word, sterile. Not even the toughest

known virus could survive when Prila I ran the gamut of
its double sun. The cacophony from the speaker quieted
abruptly as Aesop came on the air again.

"I am open for suggestions regarding our next move,
but they must be made one at a time."

The hint of reproof in Aesop's voice was enough to
damp the noise level to a background rumble, but Surgenor could sense a growing panic. The trouble was that
operating a geodesic survey module had never become a
profession—it was too easy. It was a big-money job that
smart young men went into for two or three years to raise
capital for business ventures, and when signing on they
practically demanded a written guarantee that there never
would be any interruption in the profitable routine. Now
something had gone wrong and they were worried.

Surgenor felt a flicker of anger at his teammates, then
remembered that he, too, was getting out. He had joined
up seventeen years before, along with two of his space-
struck cousins—they stayed for eight years before quitting
and going into the plant-hire business. Most of his accumulated salary was in the business with them, but now
Carl and Chris had reached the end of their patience. He
had to take an active part in the running of the firm or be
bought out, which was why he had served notice of resignation. At the age of thirty-six he was going to settle down
to a normal life, do a little fishing and golfing, and probably get married. Surgenor had to admit the prospect was
not unpleasant. It was a pity that *Module Seven* had had
to crop up on his last trip.

"If there is a seventh module, Aesop," Gillespie in
Three spoke quickly, "another survey ship must have been
here before us. Perhaps an emergency landing."

"No," Captain Aesop replied. "The detectors rule that
possibility right out. Besides we are the only scheduled
crew within three hundred light-years."

Surgenor pressed his Talk button. "Have you checked
for some kind of underground installation?"

"The world map is not yet complete but I have run a

computor check on all the geognostic data. Result negative."

Gillespie in *Three* spoke again. "I take it that this new module hasn't tried to communicate with the *Sarafand* or with any of the crews. Why is that?"

"I can only surmise it is deliberately mingling with the others to get near the ship. At this stage I can't say why, but I don't like it."

"Well, what do we do?" The question was asked simultaneously by several men.

There was a long silence before Aesop spoke. "I ordered all modules to halt because I do not wish to risk losing the ship, but I realize now that a certain amount of risk must be taken. I can see only three modules and because the search pattern was broken over the last two hundred miles I cannot identify any of you by compass bearing. I will permit all modules to approach the ship to a distance of one thousand yards for visual inspection. Any module attempting to come closer will be destroyed. No warnings will be issued. Commence your approach now."

When *Module Five* drew to a halt a thousand yards from the *Sarafand* the only sign of other vehicles was one distantly wavering light on the plain beyond the big ship. Surgenor watched the light draw near wondering if it was—he hesitated, then applied the label—the enemy.

"I wonder is that it," Voysey said.

"Who knows?" Surgenor replied. "Why don't you ask it?"

Voysey sat motionless for several seconds. "All right. I will." He pressed his Talk button. "This is *Module Five,* Voysey speaking. We are already at the ship. Who is the second module now approaching?"

"*Module One,* Lamereux speaking," came a hearteningly familiar voice. "Hello, Victor, Dave. Good to see you— that's if it *is* you."

"Of course. Who do you think it is?"

Lamereux's laugh sounded slightly unnatural. "At a time like this I wouldn't even like to guess."

Voysey jabbed down on his Talk button, then changed his mind. "I hope Aesop spots a difference and blows this *Seven* to shreds without any talk. Before it makes a move."

"What if it doesn't make a move? It might be happy to do nothing but mix us up." Surgenor unwrapped a sandwich and bit into it—he had planned that his next meal would be a steak on board the mother ship, but it looked as though dinner might be a little late.

"What do you mean about not making a move?"

"Well, even on Earth there are birds that imitate men's voices, monkeys that mimic their actions—and they haven't any special reason for doing it. That's just the way they are. This thing might be a supermimic. Maybe it just turns into the same shape as any new thing it sees without even wanting to."

"An animal that can mimic a forty-foot long machine? I believed you about the Drambons, Dave, but this is too much."

Surgenor shrugged and ate more sandwich. He had seen the Drambons on his hundred and twenty-third survey, wheel-shaped creatures on a high-gravity planet who were the opposite of humans and most other beings in that their blood remained stationary at the bottom of the wheel while their bodies circulated. He always had trouble convincing new survey men that Drambons really existed—Drambons and a hundred other equally weird species. That was the trouble with the Instant Distance drive—it was the first form of travel which didn't broaden the mind. Voysey was five thousand light-years from Earth, but because he hadn't done it the hard way, hopping from star to lonely star, he was mentally still inside the orbit of Mars.

Slowly the other vehicles made their appearances on *Module Five*'s viewscreen until there were seven ranged in a circle around the black pinnacle of the *Sarafand*. Captain Aesop had remained silent during the approach manoeuvers, but comment from the various crews crashed continuously from the radio grill. Some of the men, finding themselves still alive and unharmed as minute after minute went by, began to relax and make jokes. The jokes died away as Aesop finally spoke from the lofty security of the ship's operations level, two hundred feet above the surface of the plain.

"Before we listen to such suggestions as may be available," he said calmly, "I wish to remind all crews of the standing order not to approach the ship to within one thousand yards. Any module doing so will be destroyed without further warning. You may now," Aesop concluded pleasantly, "proceed with the discussion."

Voysey snorted with resentment. "Coffee and cucumber sandwiches will be served presently! When I get back on board I'm going to take a fourteen-pound hammer to Aesop and smash his . . . He just doesn't *care*."

"Aesop does care," Surgenor said. "He simply isn't demonstrative."

The confident, reedy voice of Pollen in *Module Four* was the first to break the radio silence that had followed Aesop's announcement. This was Pollen's eleventh survey and he was writing a book about his experiences, but had never allowed Surgenor to see the manuscript. Surgenor suspected that it was because he, Surgenor, appeared in it as a laughable, Oldest-Member figure.

"To me, the problem we have here," Pollen began. "appears to take the form of a classical exercise in logic."

"Turn it off, Pollen," somebody interrupted angrily.

"All right, all right. But the fact remains that we can think our way out of this one. The basic parameters of the problem are these: We have six unmarked and identical survey modules and, hidden among them, a seventh machine . . ."

Surgenor pressed his Talk button. "Correction," he said quietly.

"Was that Dave Surgenor?" Pollen said. "As I was saying, there is a seventh machine . . ."

"Correction."

"That *is* Surgenor, isn't it? What do you want, Dave?"

"I just want to help you be logical, Clifford. There isn't a seventh machine—we've got six machines and a very special sort of animal."

"An animal?"

"Yes. It's a Gray Man."

For the second time in an hour, Surgenor heard his radio fail to cope with the demands made on it, and he waited impassively for the noise to subside. He glanced sideways at Voysey's exasperated face and wondered if he, too, had looked like that the first time he had heard. The stories were not wide-spread, but here and there they cropped up, on worlds where the native racial memory reached far enough into the past. There were distortions upon distortions, but always the theme of the Gray Men and the battle they had waged with and lost to the White Ones. Neither race had left any tangible traces of its existence to be picked up by Earth's belated armies of archaeologists, but the myths were still there. And the most significant thing, to one whose ears were in tune, was that—no matter what the shape of the storytellers or whether they walked, swam, flew, crawled or burrowed—the name they applied to the Gray Men was always their own name for members of their own species . . .

"What's a Gray Man?" It was Carlen in *Two*.

"It's a big gray monster that can turn itself into anything it wants," Pollen explained. "Surgenor never travels anywhere without his. He's had it all over the galaxy— that's what started all those old stories."

"It can't turn itself into anything it wants," Surgenor said. "It can only assume any external shape it wants. Inside it's still a Gray Man." There was another roar of disbelief in which Surgenor distinguished the words "Ancient Mariner" several times. "All right," he said with deliberate and typical stolidity. The best way to convince Pollen was to let him convince himself. "You don't have to accept my word, Clifford."

"I know, Dave—the Gray Man will vouch for everything you say!"

"Ask Captain Aesop to go through the xenological data stores and estimate the probability of the existence of the Gray Men in the first place, and also the probability that *Module Seven* is a Gray Man." Surgenor noticed that this time there was no laughter and was relieved because, if he was right there was no time for irrelevancies. In fact, there was probably no time at all. The bright double star, which was this world's parent sun, was hanging low in the sky beyond the dim bulk of the *Sarafand* and the distant black hills. In another seventeen months the planet would be threading its way between those two points of light and Surgenor wanted to be far away when that happened—but so did the multi-talented super beast hidden in their midst.

Candar was astonished to find himself listening to the food creatures' mental processes with something approaching interest.

His race had never been machine-builders—they had relied instead on the strength, speed and adaptability of their great gray bodies. On top of this instinctive disregard for machinery, Candar had spent seventy centuries on a world where no artifact, no matter how well constructed, could survive the annual passage through the binary hell. Consequently he was shocked to realize how much the food creatures depended on their fabrications of metal and plastics. The discovery which most intrigued him was that the metal shells were not only a means of transport, but they actually supported the lives of the food creatures while they were on this airless world.

Candar tried to imagine entrusting his life to the care of a complicated and fallible mechanism, but the idea filled him with a vast, unfamiliar dread. He pushed it aside and concentrated all his ferocious intelligence on the problem of getting close enough to the spaceship to seize the minds within. In particular, it was necessary to immobilize the

one they called Captain Aesop before the ship's weapons
could be brought into play.

Gently, delicately, controlling his hunger, Candar
prepared the attack.

Surgenor stared at his hand in disbelief.

He had decided to drink some coffee to ease the dryness
in his throat and had begun to reach for the supply tube.
His right hand had risen perhaps an eighth of an inch then
had dropped back on to the armrest.

Surgenor's instinctive reaction was to bring his left hand
over to assist the other, but it, too, refused to move—and
the realization came that he was paralysed.

The mindless period of panic lasted perhaps a full
minute, at the end of which Surgenor found himself exhausted from the conflict with his locked muscles. Serpents of icy sweat were making savage downward rushes
over every part of his body. He forced himself to relax
and assess the situation, discovering as he did so that he
still had control of his eye movements.

A sideways glance showed him that Voysey had been
caught, too: the only sign of life being a barely perceptible
tremor of the facial muscles. Surgenor guessed the phenomenon was new to Voysey. It was the first time Surgenor
had ever experienced it at first hand, but he had been on
many worlds where animals of prey were able to surround
themselves with a blanket field capable of suppressing the
grosser neural activities in other creatures. The deadly
talent was most often encountered on high gravity planets
whose predators were likely to be as sluggish as their
victims. Surgenor tried to speak to Voysey but, as he had
expected, was unable to direct air through his vocal
chords.

He suddenly became aware that voices were still issuing
from the communication speaker, and listened for a while
before the full significance of the fact dawned on him.

"There isn't much to worry about," Pollen was saying.
"This is the sort of exercise in pure logic which is right up
your street, Aesop. I would suggest that you lead off by

calling out the module numbers in rotation and commanding each to move back a hundred yards. In that way the
original six machines will be separated from the seventh,
or on one of the commands *two* machines will . . ."

Surgenor swore mentally at his inability to reach his
Talk button and cut Pollen off before it was too late, but
then the other man's voice was lost in a shrill, discordant
whistle of interference. The noise continued with no sign
of abating and Surgenor knew with a pang of relief, that
Module Seven had stepped in. Surgenor tried to relax and
found himself thinking clearly. Pollen had been loudly
and confidently signing their death warrants by making
the, in this case fatal, mistake of confusing the map with
the territory.

The situation on the black airless plain glimmering in
the viewscreens bore a superficial resemblance to the classical identification problem, and treated on that level Surgenor could see several solutions. Apart from Pollen's
standard juggling-with-numbers technique, a more empiri-
cal approach would be to have Aesop fire a low-powered
burst from a laser rifle at each module in turn. Even if a
Gray Man were able to withstand that sort of treatment
without flinching, spectroscopic analysis of the light produced would show up compositional differences. Another
solution would be to order each module to unship its little
inspection-and-repair robot. Surgenor doubted if the alien
could cope with a simulation task which involved splitting
itself in two.

The deadly flaw in all those solutions was that they
employed a process of *elimination*—which was something
Module Seven would never permit. Any attempt to narrow down the field would only trigger off the final calami-
ty a little earlier. The real-life solution, if one existed,
must be capable of instantaneous application, and Surgenor was not at all optimistic about his chances of finding
it.

From sheer force of habit he began reviewing the situation, processing his data, then realized the significance of

the voices from the communication speaker. Pollen and several others were still able to talk, which probably meant they were out of *Module Seven*'s range.

The discovery gave him a momentary lift and Surgenor examined the viewscreens, wondering just how many minutes, or seconds, were left. It was difficult to assimilate the discreet images properly, but he saw that there were two modules not far away to the right, which meant that his own vehicle was part of a loose cluster of three. All the others were much farther away on the opposite side of the circle and as he watched one of them began flashing its lights in a hesitant attempt at Morse. Surgenor ignored it, partly because he had long forgotten the code and partly because he was concentrating on the two nearer machines, one of which would be *Module Seven*. High up on the *Sarafand* lights flickered against the background of stars as Aesop responded in crisp, high-speed Morse. Surgenor almost wanted to laugh—trust Aesop to have the ancient code down pat.

The continuing screech of radio interference was making thought difficult but Surgenor kept doggedly at it. At first he was not sure why it was worth the trouble, then the dim outlines of an incredible idea began to emerge. There seemed to be something inconsistent about . . .

Voysey moved his right hand forward to the control console and started the engines.

For an instant Surgenor thought they had been freed but he found himself still unable to move. Voysey's face was chalk-white and immobile, saliva glistening on his chin, and Surgenor realized he had acted merely as a human servomechanism, controlled by *Module Seven*. Surgenor's mind began to race. This must be it then, he thought, the big moment. The only reason the alien could have for making Voysey activate the motors was that it was planning to move the vehicle to create a distraction for Aesop. Surgenor went numb at the idea—Aesop was not easily distracted, nor would he have any hesitation in vaporizing the first module to cross the invisible thousand-yard line.

Voysey's left hand released the brakes and the vehicle shifted slightly on the uneven ground.

Surgenor made another frantic useless effort to move. But what was *Module Seven*'s plan? Its radius of control was limited and it was about to create a diversion, which implied that it was going to get closer to the *Sarafand*. But that meant . . .

The truth seemed to bathe Surgenor's mind in an almost physical brilliance, then new vistas of danger unfolded. I know the truth, he thought, but I mustn't think about it because a Gray Man is telepathic and if I think about it . . .

Voysey's hand thrust hard against the throttle levers and the module dipped forward.

. . . The Gray Man will know that—No, think about anything else, think about the champagne I'm not going to taste ever again; think about the Drambons rolling in their self-contained pools of blood; but don't think about . . . I almost did it . . . I almost thought about . . . I can't help it . . . AESOP!

The distance separating Candar from the spaceship was one that, in a more efficient form, he could have crossed in two bounds. It might take slightly longer this way, but he knew he was too fast to be stopped by anything. He gave full rein to his hunger, letting it drive him on as he leaped forward. Behind him, rather slower than he had expected, the two machines he had taken under control rolled toward the spaceship. One of the food creatures was vainly trying to suppress a thought but there was no time to study its meaning. Changing shape as he went, Candar got safely within control distance and exultantly struck with his brain into the spaceship.

Nothing!

An ultralaser beam hit him with a violence which would have destroyed any other creature in a matter of microseconds, but Candar could not die so easily. The pain was greater than he could ever have expected, but even worse than the agony was his sudden clear look into the minds of the food creatures—those bleak, cold, alien minds.

For the first time ever, Candar felt fear.

Then he died.

The champagne was good, the steak was good, and sleep—when it finally came—would be even better.

Surgenor leaned back contentedly, lit his pipe, and gazed benignly at the group round the table on the *Sarafand*'s operations level. During the meal he had reached a decision, and he knew with a comforting glow in his belly that, for him, it was the right decision. He had made up his mind that he *liked* being an Oldest Member figure. Smart young men could go on putting him in their books, his cousins could buy him out of their plant-hire business—he was going to stay with the Cartographical Service until he dropped. It was his life, and he wasn't giving it up.

At the other end of the table, Pollen was making out his notes of the trip.

"The way you see it then, Dave," Pollen said, "is that the Gray Man was simply incapable of understanding the machine building philosophy?"

"That's right. A Gray Man, because of his special physical properties, would have no use for a machine at the best of times. And thousands of years on a planet like Prila I—where a machine couldn't exist anyway—would have conditioned his mind to the point where our machine-orientated lives would have been incomprehensible to him."

Surgenor drew on the fragrant smoke and looked out through the viewscreens to where the brilliant double star hung low in the sky, and he felt an unexpected surge of sympathy for the massive alien being whose remains still lay on the black rock of the plain. Life would have been very precious to a Gray Man, too precious for him ever to consider entrusting it to anyone or anything but himself. That, basically, was why he had made the mistake of trying to control the entity the *Sarafand*'s crew thought of as Captain Aesop.

Wondering how the Gray Man had felt in that last moment of discovery, Surgenor glanced at the discreet identification plate on the ship's central computing installation—that vast artificial intelligence into whose keeping they delivered their lives at the beginning of each survey. The plate said:

A.E.S.O.P.

Surgenor had heard the crewmen guess that the letters stood for Automatic Electronic Spaceship Operating Plant —but nobody was absolutely sure. Human beings, he suddenly realized, tend to take a lot for granted.

LOST GROUND

DAVID I. MASSON

"Lost Ground" is really a groundbreaker, a fascinating story by a fascinating man. Mr. Masson is a rare-book librarian and linguist, who has only recently begun to write science fiction. Here he speculates on the nature of time travel in an entirely new way, in a work of fiction that is multi-level and entertaining. Critical overenthusiasm in the past has discovered too many bright new lights of authors—who become darkened cinders after emitting only a handful of photons. This will not be true of Masson. We will hear much more from him. Read this and you will see why.

"Eat up your bacon now, May," said Miriel. "Daddy's ready to run you up—don't keep him waiting." May, humming irrepressibly to herself, picked up her fork and began toying with the crisp fragments. "May!" said Miriel sharply again. The ten-year-old's brown curls tossed, but she fell to. Philip, his dark eyes scanning the faces of his mother and sister with the air of an anxious dog, spooned in his porridge. He was only in his third year. Roydon, shifting about a little in his chair, was hidden behind the

37

paper, uneasily aware of its sour biscuity odor in the sun.
"STRIKE DUE TO LAST BITTER SPELL?" read one of the
headlines. "LATE RAGE-STORMS STALL OHIO," said another.
Roydon frowned, inserted a tiny earphone into one ear
and switched on the minitape recorder which he had set
to the last forecast.

"A system of depressions and associated troughs will
follow one another in quick succession over Scotland and
the north," it said. "Insecure, rather sad feeling today and
tomorrow, followed by short-lived griefs, some heavy,
some stormy, with cheerful intervals. By midweek griefs
will be dying out, rather sooner in the south. Drives
weak to moderate, veering creative to instinctive. Temperament chillier than normal for the rest of the week, but
serene; however, some early morning fear in the latter half
of the week is expected to form in low-lying areas, dispers-
ing slowly each day."

Roydon snapped off the recorder and removed his ear-
plug. "Better give May a slow pep pill before she goes.
The forecast's a bit gloomy; I shouldn't be surprised if
there were griefs on and off this afternoon, too."

"O.K. Here you are. May; swallow that with your tea,"
said Miriel. "And *you* might as well have one yourself,
darling. I can give Phil a quick quarter-dose if he goes out
to play."

"Oh *need* I, Mummy?" from May. "The school's O.K.,
and they always pass the stuff round at break."

"Yes, May—I think Miss Weatherbridge is a bit careless about these things; she has a lot of other things to
think about, after all."

"Oh, all right!"

Roydon dumped a singing May from his little city-car,
the green one. The pep pill was already lifting his spirits,
protected as they were by the car aerosol. He had to check
himself from chanting rowdily and dodging about in the
workwards traffic. "I should have waited till lunch-time
and had a quick one," he thought. "Miriel coddles me—
and I take it from her." The vision of her brown oval face
old-fashionedly curtained in the straight fall of soft dark

hair hovered between him and the traffic for an instant. After eleven years it was still a mystery and an enchantment to him. He opened the draught and let the sadness seep in for a little. A few of the school children waiting to cross at the next school were in tears. "Feckless parents," he thought. They would be all right after a minute in the air-conditioned school.

In the studio office all was bustle and confusion. Panset, the chief, was in and out constantly, mood-weather bothered him comparatively little, except that in periods of unusually warm temperament he usually had to take a tranquilizer outside. The pep aerosols were functioning nicely all over the building. The night's programme of current affairs was beginning to take shape, but must rest in a half-cooked state till late that afternoon, when Roydon would leave it in the hands and mouths of the studio people. He rang up Miriel at lunchtime to say he might be later than usual, the way things were running.

"Are you coming out for lunch, Vic?" he called to his mate across the table, fixing him unconsciously with a characteristically searching gaze under his thick brows; "I'm getting sick of the canteen stuff."

"Better pep yourself up again, then, Royo, there's a nasty grief outside," said Ken Mattock, coming in, breathing deeply and erratically through pinched nostrils.

"Oh, the corner place will do us. That's not far, we'll survive it, eh, Vic?"

"I'll take a quick booster first, if you don't mind. I'm a bit low this morning," said Vic, helping himself from his pharma-pouch. "Right—that'll fix me, I'm ready now."

That night, a rather disturbed May eventually persuaded to bed, Miriel broached the subject of school precautions again. "You know," she said, "I don't care for the way they hand out their peps and tranqs—much too rough and ready. I delivered May after lunch in the red city car: she was quite upset coming in. I had a word with the head. I'm going to keep her carefully drugged up and the school will have her for lunch in future. That means she won't be so easily exposed."

"You coddle her too much," said Roydon.

"No, Roy, I can't have her education going to pieces because of all these ups and downs. It may be all right for some parents, but not for us. We have her future to think of."

Roydon gave way. He sighed for the Golden Age of his parents' memory, when the world's atmosphere had nothing worse than true weather and a little fallout for men to contend with. A feature item on the chaos in Africa and India, scarcely mitigated by pharmacological aid, underlined his thoughts. The Indians and Africans were trying to ride out griefs by hectic dance sessions on the lines of the old Mediterranean tarantella-remedy, and angers and fears by great choral chants but these folk remedies were naturally very chancy. Only the most advanced nations had been able to meet the new emotional influences in the air with air-conditioning and with drugs subtle enough to act quick enough or slow enough and without seriously affecting judgment or the body's reactions. His own "World-Day" programme came through and he watched it dutifully and critically. It was followed by a Men-of-Science interview with a microdiathesiologist.

"You see," explained the pundit, "the mood-climate differs not only from country to country, but from place to place, from street to roof, from valley to slope, and often in quite spectacular ways. Take the corner of a high building or the top of a cliff. This sort of site is subject to great turbulence. While the general mood-weather round it may be gloomy one day or one hour and optimistic the next, the mood at the *acron,* as we call it, is often switching minute by minute from despair to ecstasy and back again. Hence the semi-mystical nature-loving joy one moment and the suicide leap the next."

"But such violent changes are not met with in other places, are they?"

"Not commonly. Indeed the micro-sentiment at many spots is more stable than that of the general mood-weather at man-height. The surface of marshes is nearly always depressed and fearful. Those of a park or a well-kept garden are warm, friendly, serene. And of course there is a third class of micro-diathesis which varies on a twenty-four hour cycle. A wood or a lake at noon is usually gay and serene, at midnight amorous in moonlight but hostile and intensely fearful in darkness. The nature of the cycle in this case depends on the illumination."

Roydon, yawning ostentatiously, switched the set off at this point. Details of this sort were rather beyond him, his yawn implied. But his heartbeat was accelerating. Programmes like this one he found disquieting. The world was dangerous enough without *these* local effects. He preferred not to know. The shelter of Miriel's arms and hair blotted out the world and its perils.

Three years later it happened. Roydon, now in the studio team of World-Day, and normally working from 3 to 11 p.m., was rung at the studio one March afternoon at 5.

"I thought I told you not to ring me at night—it's far too hectic here!"

"Roy, Roy, it's Phil! He—he—"

"He had an accident!" shouted Roydon. He recalled that Phil was usually brought home by some rather older children from infant school. Sobbing, Miriel told him that Phil and his friends had run into an unexpected pocket of terror in a dip in the road coming home. They had scattered, Phil darting insanely across the road, it seemed, and straight under a car. It was all over in a moment.

After the funeral, which ironically took place on a gay, serene morning, Miriel, who had kept herself on a tight rein, seemed to go to pieces. She refused all drugs, scarcely roused on the most cheerful of days, and gave herself up to a sort of resentfulness of sorrow. Roydon's parents, who had stayed on for some days, took May under their roof not far off, and for the rest of term were to fetch her to school and back. Roydon managed to secure leave and took Miriel west to a wild part of the country neither of them had seen before, which she could not associate with Philip. They left the two city-cars behind and hired a runabout. Gradually she began to pick up, but there was a ghostly something about her look, an air of looking through or past Roydon, which worried him. It was a fine spring and the mood-weather was optimistic, with only the occasional grief. Roydon let the griefs wash over Miriel when they were out walking, and sometimes over himself, as he felt they would help to purge the emotional load.

The first Sunday they went to church. The rather meagre congregation huddled in the cool Early English interior. The sermon was uninspiring. But there was a soothing quality about the gray-green gloom and the thin arches. The motor of the tranquilizer-cordial hummed gently in the silences. Afterwards Roydon was rather sorry they had gone, for they were strolling through the churchyard when Miriel stopped with a shudder. The funeral was too recent. Drunken gravestones, their inscriptions worn to rivers in the soft local stone, leant around them. But she had stopped at a very tall and broad headstone.

"Look," she said uncertainly, "Roy, you could have had an ancestor here."

"Well, could be, certainly ends with 'Back,' and it certainly has an R as second letter, and the length looks right. Can't make out the forename, can you?"

"No, I don't think I can. And what a long inscription."

"From the few words I can make out, it was one of those paragons of all the virtues. Local bigwig, I expect. They used to make them out to be saints, on their tombstones, in those days; whereas they probably fathered half the brats in the parish really, and twisted their tenants. I must have a look at the parish register some time, just in case he really had the same name. Still, it's not absolutely unique as a name."

"What is all this about the Snevley Fields?" said the big man at the bar.

Roydon turned half round from his half-pint. Miriel was upstairs. The big man, who looked like a landowner or a business man, was talking to a squat little fellow who might be a farmer or a lawyer.

"What do you want to know about the Snevley Fields?"

"Something queer is going on there—what is it?"

"Something decidedly queer is certainly going on there," said the squat man, who, like the big man, had a whisky in front of him. Roydon cocked his World-Day-educated ear. "It seems that all Morris's cattle have disappeared there. So has Midgley's dog. Midgley was walking the Carruthers side and his dog went after rabbits. That was a week ago and no one has seen the dog since."

"But it's perfectly open country, no badger-holes or foxholes either."

"Exactly. And no cow-holes! . . . Midgley's a bit scared to go in himself. As for Morris, he thinks the place is bewitched. Talks about fairies and I don't know what. Won't stir near there. A bit superstitious, old Morris is."

"Was it in daylight?"

"We don't know about Morris's cattle. But Midgley's dog went early one afternoon."

"Any clues?"

"No! Only thing is, the Snevley Fields seem to have been rehedged by someone. The old hawthorn's given way to hazel, Morris says. He looked through binoculars. Says it goes beyond the brook, too."

"Snevley's is let, isn't it?"

"Yes—to someone from Scrutton. But they haven't been there for weeks."

"You talking about them Snevley Fields?" put in a long man in an overcoat, drinking stout, on the far side.

"Yes, and Harry says it goes on beyond the brook."

"Too true; and another thing," said the long man; "you know that brook runs straight down a fair way between them two hedges? Someone digged it that way long since." The other two nodded assent. So did three other listeners. "Well now it don't. It runs all squiggly-squaggly. And them hedges—they've gone!"

There was a heavy silence. "I know another man as lost a dog thereabouts," called a dark man in a corner.

Silence. Heads turned. "'Twere Ted. His bitch were round Parker's Knoll, a week come Friday 'twere. *She* were chasing rabbits, too. Ted says he had his eye on her, and she just vanished."

"How d'you mean, vanished?" put in the big man.

"Vanished in full view, right in the middle of the next field. Here, Fred, turn up the aero-what'sit. That crossness is seeping in again—I can feel me hackles rising."

"'Tis the whisky in you, Bill," called the squat man amid general laughter, but the landlord picked up an aerosol hand-sprayer and pumped the cordial-tranquilizer over the room.

"Well, as I were saying. She vanished in full view. One moment she were there, going hell for leather in the middle of a field. Next moment—she weren't there. Never came back no more."

"That's a hell of a lot of land that is. From Snevley's to Parker's Knoll."

"And from Goff's Brook to t'other side of Snevley, I shouldn't wonder," came from a small man who had not yet spoken.

Roydon, who was used to interviewing, or failing to interview, rural types, held his peace, but after a moment or two found occasion to ask the barman the name of the long man and the squat man, and still later buttonholed the landlord and got from him their addresses (they turned out to be the village grocer and the local garage man) and the approximate location of Goff's Brook, Snevley's, and Parker's Knoll. He represented himself as an amateur landscape painter with some ideas about later fishing.

Next morning, with a strong instinctive drive prevalent and a cordial temperament abroad, Roydon took Miriel out on foot looking for the mystery area. The forecast was fairly optimistic and he thought it would be good for her to tramp around with him while he tried to work up what promised to be something of a news story. In two hours they were in sight of the farmhouse known as Snevley's. Beyond it down a slight slope were the Snevley Fields, a set of meadows already powdered with buttercups. The pair paused. "Let's work round this field and up to that copse. We might get a better view of that break in the hedges they were talking about."

When they reached a field-corner next the copse, where a distinct drop in the emotional temperature could be felt, Roydon took some photographs. The chilliness was becoming palpable hostility, and his wife was unprotected by drugs. "You stick it out here, Miriel. I'll walk uphill and see what can be seen from that tree." Roydon strode off. A brusquely suspicious mood dominated the summit. Reaching the tree at the top he turned. Miriel was not to be seen.

Roydon, shouting her name at the top of his voice, glared round an arc of countryside. Away down a narrow meadow between two hedges he thought he saw a flickering speck running, running very hard. An instant later it was swallowed up, in the line of the nearer hedge. Perhaps it was a rook in the air between. Moving cloud-shadows confused the view. After a minute of calling Roydon ran back down the long slope and at length arrived, gasping and dizzy, his knees aching, at the spot where he had left her. There were some snapped twigs and after staring around he thought he could see the imprint of her shoes in the earth not far off, pointing homeward. But beyond this on all sides tall wiry grasses swallowed up everything. The feeling of hostility grew, mingled with acute fear. The wind hissed among the twigs and grasses. "Bitch, bitch!" Roydon found himself muttering. He forced himself to swallow a pill, but found minutes later that it must have been a slow-acting one he had chosen. Hoarse with shouting and cursing, he began to stumble back the way they had come, convinced that she had started home. As he approached Snevley's a squall of rage and grief burst upon him. Sobbing and swearing, tears coursing down his cheeks, he ran round the yard and burst in through the open doorway. No one was at home. He rushed through the rooms without finding anyone or any trace, tried all the cupboards, and finally ran out again, and on to the village. At last, in a state of maudlin warmth now that the pill had taken effect in more cordial surroundings, he stumbled into the inn. Miriel was not in their room. No one had seen her. Someone brought him to the police-station, in whose tranquillized air he told his story.

"That settles it," said the sergeant; "I'm ringing HQ. These disappearances are beyond us."

Roydon found himself at the receiving end of the inter-viewing on that evening's World-Day. Ken had shot up from London by jet to see him personally. By next day the C.I.D. and half the newshawks of the west of the country were in the district. No one dare enter the "For-bidden Zone" and a cordon was to be thrown up by the army. During the week a helicopter and a set of tracker-dogs on the end of microphoned long lines were brought up.

The tracker-dogs found nothing, but two disappeared, their lines neatly cut. The helicopter only discovered fields empty of all but birds; but two locals (Midgley and the squat man) who were persuaded to go up in it, averred that (so far as they could tell since they had never flown before) the country had changed quite a lot. The area was closed off now with rolls of barbed wire, military posts established round it, and a desultory watch was kept up, with an occasional searchlight at night. "I'd sooner run straight acrost a bleedin' minefield 'n gow in theer," Roydon heard one soldier say to another.

"Reckon it *is* a minefield—only the other sort. I reckon it's holes in it, bloody great pits, all camouflaged up," said the other.

Roydon flew up to London. He meant to resign. The city seemed to him meaningless, like an undubbed film in a foreign language. Its noise and bustle seemed to be all on the other side of an invisible barrier.

"Look here, Royo," said Vic, taking him aside near the studio; "a team of investigators is going up there; why not join them as a reporter? Panset'll recommend you, he says."

"Who are they?"

"Scientists of some sort. You know they got some anom-

alies with their lidar probe when Ken was there—or
perhaps you don't? Some of them think there's something
odd about the spacetime geometry of the region. That's
the line they're working on now."

May was adopted by her aunt and uncle. Roydon was
attached to the group of scientists, shut up the house, and
returned to that accursed green countryside to which he
was now bound, as with the thongs of a rack, by ties of
fear, hatred, memory and love. He came gradually to
follow, in a hazy way, the investigators' reasoning and the
drift of their experiments with masers and charged particles. So it was that six months later Roydon himself,
carrying out a prepared "interview" of the group's spokes-
man on TV, had given the public its first picture of what
was happening.

"A set of anachronistic cells or domains has come into
being on the landscape, covering a wide area. Each cell
has reverted to an earlier point in time—we are not at
present sure exactly what point—and its neighbor cells
have similarly reverted, but apparently with no discernible
pattern. We have a patch-work quilt of time-levels."

"How far back are these time-levels from ours?"

"We don't know. Some may be only a few seconds or
even microseconds. Others may be a few weeks, years,
even centuries. Some are certainly many years back. The
change in visible landmarks fits that, according to early
tithe-maps."

"But if we can see the country how is it we can't see the
persons and animals that have disappeared?"

"We think they have moved out of the area, but in the
time of the cell in which they found themselves."

"Does the first cell you meet fix your time-level,
then?"

"We don't know. It may—or it may not."

One day Roydon, allowed past the army posts as one of
the team, slipped quietly away towards the spot where he
had last seen his wife. He was certain now that she had
run off further into the area and believed he might have
caught a glimpse of her running and not of some bird

flying. But the landscape was confusing, was difficult to identify. Where he thought to have found the field-corner below the hill there seemed to be a long stone dike with stone steps jutting out of it, and a fence to one side. He climbed over the dike, keeping bent low in case he was spotted from outside. He was determined to follow Miriel and search, if need be for years, in this past world. The atmosphere was serene, with a slight intellectual drive in it. He combed the copse, returned, walked along the fence, slithered down some rocks which he never remembered seeing before, ran into a richly cordial atmosphere, skirted a round dewpond, and past a gnarled old thorn came face to face with a stinking old man in tatters, who touched his forehead and sank on one knee.

"Where do you come from?"

Roydon had to repeat this three times before the man answered: "Scrootton, ant plaze thee, Serr."

"Have you ever see a young woman in strange dress in these parts?"

"?"

"Have—you—seen—a young—woman—near here—ever—wearing—strange—dress?"

Roydon had to repeat this once more, then: "Noo, Serr, hant nivver seen noo witch, Serr!" and the creature took to his heels. As Roydon stared after him he vanished in mid-stride. Much shaken, Roydon walked slowly onward, stumbled over some gravel, was pushing through some lush undergrowth, and found himself on a sheep track among tussocks of grass. A grotesque sight met his eyes a few yards further on down the track. A thin man in a sort of sacking hood, ragged hose like ill-fitting tights, and bare feet, was perched on a short ladder leaning crazily in towards the track. The ladder was leaning on nothing, and indeed its poles ended at their tops in a curious vertical chopped cut, which kept changing its pattern, yet this ladder stood still and only rocked slightly with the man's movements. It was some time before Roydon realized that the changing texture at the tops of the poles coincided with their growing slightly shorter or longer as they rocked. The man kept descending and coming up again with bundles of what looked to Roydon (who had seen a museum of antiquities) like thatching straw, and thrusting them above the ladder where, together with his hands, they disappeared. His handless arms, each obscenely terminated by a fluctuating blue-white and crimson cross-section, would ply about for a time, then the hands would reappear, but not the bundles. A great heap of these bundles lay on the ground. The place was thick with flies and gnats. The ladder-man was humming an endless, eery, plaintive chant. Behind him was the rim of a forest clearing. Two lean dogs like lurchers, but with longish pointed ears, were slinking about near it. The trees of the forest seemed to be chopped short at about ten feet up. The ladder-man and his dogs were all totally oblivious of Roydon's shouting and gesticulating. Something, however, held Roydon back from passing under or beyond the ladder. Perhaps it was that only ten feet on the far side of the man the forest-clearing swung in abruptly to march right up to the sheep-track. This part of the beheaded forest, moreover, was frost-laden, from the boughs to the ground, and devoid of undergrowth, and a light snow shower was scudding down from nowhere. Through this wintry woodscape, lit by a ruddy glow from the east, a pack of huge savage hounds presently broke, baying fiercely, and plunged obliquely towards the still oblivious ladder-man and his dogs. Instead of overwhelming them the pack vanished one by one in the still air of the clearing, and the silence returned piecemeal hound by hound.

A last hound, a straggler, was still bounding up, when the man called out, as if to someone well beyond Roydon's shoulder: "Pest taak they, Will, maak hust, 'tis aal boot nohn!" He paused, apparently listening, then broke into a snort of laughter and resumed his whistling and humming.

An obscure trumpeting, mingled with cries, broke out deep in the frosty wood; crackling branches and rhythmical thuds intervened.

Seized with a kind of panic, Roydon turned down the
track thrust through a dark thicket, and found himself
without warning in the middle of a curious wide tunnel or
cave apparently made of blackish glass, and dimly lit from
nowhere in particular. There was a marked cheerfulness
and a strong organizing drive in the air. Coming out into
the daylight he saw a wide flat level strip, like the track of
a gigantic snail a hundred yards across, made of the same
material, stretching out from his feet. On its edges a
number of glassy boxes and tubes, on spring legs or
spikes, were standing, some winking and clicking busily.
The strip looked rather as if it had been sprayed on.

"What kind of a past era is this?" he thought. Beyond
the strip were banks of rich shrubs powdered with exotic
butterflies. The growl of a helicopter came from the west,
and Roydon took cover beneath a shrub, disturbing the
butterflies somewhat. When the helicopter appeared it had
an unfamiliar look, and most of it was formed of greenish
and blackish glassy material. After it had gone Roydon
walked on above the shrubs. Then he took cover beneath
the shrub, disturbing the butterflies, hearing the machine.
When it had gone he began to walk on. Then he took
cover under the butterfly-laden shrub, keeping the helicopter under observation. When it had departed he
walked on, shaking his head uncertainly. There was something he could not quite remember. A *déjà vu* sensa-
tion. Odd. He recalled the tunnel and the strip. What an
odd strip! What kind of past age could this be? And what
peculiar gadgets these are down its edges. Why do they
click and blink like that? . . . He found himself walking
about the shrubs, feeling unaccountably odd and dazed.
Then he saw Parker's Knoll or what should have been
Parker's Knoll, miles ahead. It was topped by a device
like a glass water tower. The entire landscape between
seemed to be dotted with tallish block buildings of greenish opaque glass, with banks of shrubs between. Men,
women and children, in closely clinging clothing with a
dull whitish lustre, were moving about. The sound of their
voices came to him. The sky was pullulating with aircraft

like a swarm of insects, and droned and screamed with
them, but the voices could be heard quite clearly nevertheless. Only the strip and its neighborhood seemed deserted. Then he saw a sort of Parker's Knoll, but decorated
with a glassy tower, and the people in their clinging
clothes, and the aircraft overhead. He shook his head to
clear it, and saw Parker's Knoll, topped with a tower, and
the population, and the crowded skies, and heard the
noises. Roydon sat down (and in between the first bending
of his knees and being seated, had a visionary flash of
millions upon millions of—what? of the same event,
which he instantly forgot). He sat down, and tried to
collect his thoughts. Could it be that he was somewhere in
the future, not the past? Could the helicopter have come
out of the world of that future? The machine came back
and for the second time (was it the second time?) Roydon
took cover, but he was astonished to hear a loud-hailer of
sorts address him:

"We can detect you under that growth. Who are you?
Can we help you? . . . Who are you? Are you Roydon
Greenback? Please come out from under. Please come out
from under. We would like to help you." There was
something peculiarly vulgar and sprawling about the accents of the speaker, and his vowels were difficult to recognize.

Roydon clambered out and waved. After a moment he
called out, "Yes, I am Roydon Greenback. Who are you?
Where am I?"

The helicopter descended some way and a rope ladder
was lowered. "Please climb in."

"I am looking for my wife."

"We don't know where she is, but perhaps we can help
you. Will you come with us first?"

Silently, Roydon climbed up the ladder, which was at
once extraordinarily smooth and very easy to hold on to.
As he went up there was a sort of blink, and looking
down by the helicopter hatch, he was astonished to see
that the landscape was once more deserted and green,
indeed rather lush, except that the glassy strip and a few

of the shrub-banks up to a little past where he had sat down, were still there below him. A big gloved hand hauled him in.

"Roydon Greenback. Well. You are something of a legend to us, the man who entered the poikilochronistic jungle to search for the woman he loved. Well, well. As luck would have it, you got into a domain that started at plus-sixty-one years and has been running a cog-slipper static ever since. So you leveled up with our time. You are sixty-one years behind us in source. We shall take you to our world of sixty-one years ahead."

The voice was no longer sprawling, but the same slip-shod quality seemed to slur its vowels, and what with this and the unfamiliar vocabulary, Roydon could hardly comprehend two words in three. He looked at its owner, a tall, red headed man of middle age with shaggy locks and a long beard. His clothes, like those of his companions, seemed to consist of a translucent skin-diving suit with pockets, and without mask or oxygen, and, encasing the hands and upper arms, long translucent gloves. There were half a dozen persons in the cabin, two of them women.

"I am Paul Sattern, chronismologist in chief. This is Fenn Vaughan, chronismologist-maturator; Mary Scarrick, entomologist; Richard Metcalfe, chronistic metrologist; Elizabeth Raine, air chemist; Morris Ekwall, transitional diathesiologist; Zen Haddock, botanist, who also takes soil samples for the podologists; and at the controls, Peter Datch."

The correct response to an introduction seemed to be a nod. It appeared that Morris Ekwall was concerned, in some esoteric way, with the violent local changes in mood-weather that accompanied the area's time-shifts, while Richard Metcalfe spent most of his time dumping gadgets on the terrain and reading their messages on instruments in the helicopter. What Vaughan and Sattern actually did Roydon never discovered, but the others were concerned with the insects, plants, soil and atmosphere itself. At intervals one or more of them would go down the ladder and come up again rather swiftly.

"Teams of chronismologists," Sattern told Roydon, "are engaged in mapping the poikilochronism and its changes; the domains are constantly altering."

"How do you mean? Do they change their time-level?"

"Usually a domain divides into several quite independent domains, especially if it's a big one; or a whole set of bounds and domains is replaced by new unrelated ones, in one part of the poik. There's not always much visible sign—you have to instrumentate to discern."

"And Richard here," said Vaughan, "is trying just now to catch them at it. He thinks they don't just go click, they go whoosh—eh Richard?" and he sang, softly:

> *"Micro, nano, pico, femto,*
> *   it's all the same to metro Met.;*
> *No matter what he pegs down there,*
> *   he hasn't snapped them switching yet."*

Richard looked pained.

"Are we free of it now?" asked Roydon.

"Free?" said Sattern. "You mean, beyond the poik? No. It's much bigger than in your day. It's growing about three hectares a year now. Swallowed many square kilometres of our normal-density regions in the last ten years —but slowly. We had to reallocate the population. Devil of a lot of economic and social problems. Lost some strays, too—like you."

Sattern broke off and gave a terse account of their discovery of Roydon into a microphone.

Roydon, looking over the side some minutes later, saw the hated green, already peppered with odd glassy lumps and bumps, cease abruptly. Beyond was a tangle of curved highways crawling with moving specks. Helicopters seemed now to jostle them on all sides, and above them a dense crowd of swift jetcraft littered the sky. Soon an endless forest of multistoried buildings, glassy in texture, gawky oblongs, jetting into the air, thrust all round them and in every direction. Here and there great banks of flowers or butterfly-powdered shrubs glowed at the buildings' feet, but much of the ground was a close-cropped gray-green herbage. The helicopter dropped on to a squat cube of a building, and Roydon was escorted down into the Chronismatic Centre.

Here he found a small quiet crowd gathered, all clothed like the helicopter party. One wall of the huge room converted itself silently into a colored vision screen, and for the next hour he was subjected to a merciless interview from the reporters in that screen, with their unfamiliar flat accents and phraseology. After that a series of interchanges took place between the helicopter party, some of the crowd, and the screen reporters, who seemed to be in London, with occasional shunts to New York, Moscow, and Peiping. The exchanges were largely lost on Roydon, whose nerves seemed to be dancing a jig all over his body. A girl with darkish red hair and green eyes, whom he took for Sattern's secretary, led him off for a meal and a sleeping potion.

He woke on a couch and the purgatory began again. Housed in the building, occasionally treated to visitape recordings of his interview, interviewed anew by scientists and reporters, invited to appear in feature programmes, put through tests of blood-pressure, skin-potential, electro-encelphalogram, blood-fluid makeup, olfactronic signature and many others, he collapsed at the end of a week and was kept under deep narcosis for ten days.

He came to to find the red-haired girl, whose name was Sal, contemplating him. "Someone is asking to see you," she said. "Prepare yourself for a shock." She looked serious.

"Who is it? Are they here?"

"No of course not. On the screen. It's someone from your family. Think now—who could be alive after sixty-one years?"

"It's not—it's not May?"

"It's your daughter. She was called May. Now remem-

ber, she has lived all her life in ordinary time. How old
was she when you last saw her?"

Even so, Roydon could not believe for a long time that
the rather bowed, though well-preserved, old lady in gray
slacks and tunic could be his own daughter. He was
unspeakably embarrassed when after a minute of awkward speech a slow tear or two rolled down the face on
the screen. "You are just like your photo," she whispered
brokenly, then broke down completely and sobbed. "You
never came back—you never came back!"

Gradually he pieced out her history. Brought up for the
rest of her growing years with her uncle's children she had
adjusted to the situation but had always mourned her parents, especially Roydon. An unhappy marriage at twenty
had lasted four years. Another at thirty with an older man
had terminated with his death seven years before. Her two
children—she held up their stereo-photographs—were
grown up. She brought out stereo-photographs of five
grandchildren. Four minutes' link-up with her son and
three with her daughter followed. She herself was living in
the section of normal-density Britain still known as Aber-
deen, where her husband's folk were. Roydon offered to
go and see her but it seemed that no ordinary person
traveled much today. "Surface and even air travel are too
crowded, and stratocruising is only for long distance," said
Sal, who had come back in after half an hour. May
assured him she was content with the screen, and they
agreed he should contact her once a week.

Sal, it began to appear, was a liaison officer for the
Centre with other institutions. But she took Roydon under
her particular care and few minutes of a day went by
without her turning up with provender, conversation or
means of entertainment. She got him to fix himself up
with one of the translucent suits by means of some sort of
long-distance measurement recorder. She explained many
ways and words that he could not understand. Her green
eyes fixing his, she would speak slowly in her husky voice.
She kept a sharp eye on his reaction to the mood-weather
if he were outside, and produced the antidote.

"The mood-climate's not what it was," Sattern complained to Sal and Roydon one day, looking in from a conference with the chiefs of other helicopter-parties. "Spring used to be hopeful, summer serene, autumn regretful, winter gloomy. Now, it's all mixed up. You never know what to expect."

"You're getting more vulnerable in your old age, Paul," said Sal, grinning.

"Something in what you say, actually. The inocs are wearing off. I must get some boosters."

"How do you make out here with mood-weather?" asked Roydon.

"It doesn't worry us much," said Sal. "We inoculate during childhood; only the most violent moodstorms touch us. Your age hadn't got inocs for that; we'll have to cross-dope you pretty carefully for outside. But the endocrine typometer gave us enough data on you to give you a reasonable safeguard."

A week or two later Sal told Roydon that Paul Sattern's team would like him to accompany them on trips, hoping he could set them right on some points about the past. He was given unlimited credit for purchase, and the official position of "historical adviser." Chronismologists were in great demand, as the poikilochronism was regarded as a public danger, and were highly paid, partly because of the risks they ran. "QUALIFIED CHRONISMOLOGIST," Roydon read on an old-fashioned plastic news-sheet's advertisement page: "Vacancies for chronismologists. Higher Sc. degrees essential. Starting credit equivalent £5,000 to £6,000 p.a. rising by £500 p.a. Minimal service one year."

"Two other poiks have been detected," Sal told him, "one in Bonnium and one in Ceylon."

"Yes," said Paul; "and we think there are some in Central Africa and one in Antarctica, only Antarctica is rather sparsely populated, and news from much of Central Africa is nil—mood-climate closed chunks of it down. The whole world, including the oceans, might become one vast poik in a few millennia or even centuries, unless we can find out enough about these chronismatic processes to know how to stabilize or reverse them. It's a race against Time, in two senses."

"I had no idea how things were," said Roydon weakly.

"Well, we have enough to do in our own little corner of ordinary time and space. Do you feel like coming with us tomorrow?"

I must see, Roydon thought, if I can't get a better clue to where she went. That rook—was it a rook? Can I trace the place? Will they take me there? Miriel's dark hair and oval face swam up at him suddenly and he groped his way out of the room, muttering something. Paul Sattern looked after him and, turning to Sal with a bitter smile, shook his head ever so slightly. The girl flushed and, biting her lip, picked up a nest of tapes and walked out of the other door. She encountered Richard, the gadget-man, past the doorway. Richard, who had his eyes on her face, turned pale and said nothing, but came on into the room.

"Well?" said Paul.

"Those linking atto-second counters—will they be ready?" uttered Richard harshly, as though the technical sentence was code for something else.

"Of course. You can peg them in a new line from LV3 to PN8 tomorrow. But I think the femto-counters may show something yet."

"Too slow," said Richard and began a brisk discussion, but his manner was distrait and he jumped when Sal came back in. Roydon, recovering next door, heard much of the discussion, but it might as well have been the conversation of rooks or starlings. Fenn Vaughan strolled in and past the trio, singing:

> *"Where the femto-seconds pass*
> *Richard sits upon—"*

Paul kicked his shin. Fenn walked on whistling. The group broke up in silence.

"What are all those things?" said Roydon. The craft was slowly cruising over the greenery.

"Those are future buildings," explained Sal, who had pressed Paul to take her along to keep an eye on Roydon. "We don't know whether they're some kind of plascrete or something new. The three-metre top bound stopped them existing above that at first, but they're growing up now a centimetre a week by infection, and pushing up the top bound. One day they'll be complete. That's why they look like ruins. Dick says the time is plus-ninety-four years in that patch below. But of course it's mostly the same with present and past buildings—if they're new domains, the buildings can't grow above the top bound at first. Look at all that lot to the west; they're all sorts of dates, mostly present to past, but they grew up when there wasn't any building there so they are still incomplete."

"But surely the whole world from one of these domains must look very queer—masses of foundations and nothing else?"

"No, no, if you went down there you'd see complete buildings, probably a normal-density district, all around you; only the domain part itself would have these shells. Someone coming on to the domain from the world of that date would probably think it was a patch where demolition work had been going on. One reason why we don't often see people near those shells."

"What's that odd brown patch down there?"

"Oh, that's just the other way. It's minus-three-hundred-odd years, Dick says. Most of the domains are minus a century or more round here—aren't they, Paul? —which is why they're still un-built up."

"How big are the domains?"

"Anything from a metre to a couple of kilometres across, and any shape. Dick says they may even start by growing quickly from a mere point, and changing time-level as they grow. That's where his atto-second lines may pick up something."

Roydon's eyes devoured the hated green. The craft sank and Richard went down the ladder with his first gadget. They proceeded methodically across country like a mathematically-minded crane-fly ovipositing on a lawn.

"Why, that—that looks very like the village! Is it part of the—the poik?"

"Yes, been inside it for dozens of years. A lot of it is minus-twenty-five-years now."

"Is that why it's got all those odd buildings among it?"

"Yes."

"Look, there are some people! How is it they don't know they're isolated?"

"Don't you realize?" cried Paul. "The 'open' domains can be entered. They're mostly on the poik margins. But most of the inner domains, once entered, can only be left geographically. You can see men and animals crossing them and vanishing. Watch that nineteenth-century laborer on that ploughland. There—he's gone! But he doesn't know that. He's in a complete nineteenth-century world. Once you're down in a patch of, say, minus-twenty-five years like the village, you've dropped through a hole twenty-five years deep, and have to walk about on that level forevermore. That's the risk we all run if we happen to cross a domain-bound without knowing it. We can't get back. That's what your wife must have done. *You* were lucky, what with the cog-slipper."

Roydon shuddered—but not from fear—and choked.

"And of course, there's not much sign of a bound in an agricultural area like that when it's mostly minus a century or so; it had been broadly the same for generations."

"How is it you can see all those domains from the air?"

"The top bound at roughly three metres, that Sal was talking about. It rises to three metres above the tops of 'old' buildings too. All domains are 'open' at the top bound, more or less, and you can see them from above. Sound travels both ways there, too. Down below you can only see or hear neighboring domains from an 'open' one. Some 'open' ones harden up into 'closed' ones, by the way."

"Don't the villagers and so on see the helicopter?"

"Yes, but they must have helicopters at minus-twenty-five-years, so they probably just think we're another. If

another came by they'd see us go through each other in a
ghost-collision that neither lot of us would know anything
about—above the three-metre bound."

"What about the people in the place you picked me up
from?"

"That was approx-zero. It showed how the area would
have been today if there hadn't been a poik at all. The
population was real there to themselves, but unreal in our
poik-ridden world. Ghosts, if you like."

"Can I go down by the village?"

"Village? No. It's tricky with people about. Let Richard peg his ninth counter down behind that big barn, on
his own."

At the eleventh descent: "Why that's the hill I ran
down!" shouted Roydon.

"Is that the Spot on the east?" asked Paul.

"I think so."

"Well, that's where Richard pegs his next counter."

"Can I go down then?"

"Yes, but don't do anything rash. Tell us what you
think and we'll take action."

Roydon followed Richard down the ladder when they
came over the place. "Wait, Royo, I'm coming too," called
Sal and clambered down third. Richard said nothing, but
his face was set as he peered at the ground before fixing
into it on its long prong his gadget for recording millionths
of millionths of millionths of a second.

"Can't make it out—the dike's rubble, the fence is all
rotted away; brambles and nettles everywhere too, and all
those docks," muttered Roydon. He turned, his eyes searching along what he hoped was the line taken by that
hurrying speck so long ago. Richard straightened his back
and stared at him, but said nothing. The fool thinks,
Richard said to himself, because we snatched him from a
cog-slipper, that all domain-time is frozen for ever, doesn't
realize most of it's moved sixty-one years on, is going
onward all the time, let alone what's shunted or
rebounded.

Sal, who, a little way off, was anxiously watching

Roydon, happened to glance at Richard and read his expression in a flash of intuition. "Roy!" she shrieked. At that moment an unexpected and violent gust of instinctive drive invaded the hollow. At the cry, which sounded to him like his wife's voice, Roydon's pale face turned white. He rushed off along the old hedge-line. The hedge seemed to him to swing round and to flicker beside him—was She running along its far side?

Sal, racing at an angle to cut him off, had reached twenty strides when she vanished. Two seconds later and some way off, Roydon vanished too. "Richard, you fool, come up!" roared Paul from the helicopter. "That patch is a maze of little domains. Come up! We can winch you down where she vanished." But when Richard, white and babbling, was lowered down on the spot, he saw five paces onward the brink of a deep quarry. Below, men in tiny white shorts working ultrasonic excavators, far in the future, were gaping at the broken body.

Roydon's flickering hedge was the edge of a furze thicket. Roydon was running on dry heath. It was very hot. The flickering was the bobbing of twenty-seven crouching heads. A dozen bone-tipped wooden spears flashed towards him, aimed at his hamstrings. Three struck him high in the calves, one went in above a knee. He fell. The skin-clad figures, quacking and barking, loped toward him.

"Leave Richard. We must get that madman!" shouted Fenn Vaughan in Paul's ear. "I've pin-pointed his vanishing. I think I saw something strike him just before."

"All right. Swing her round, Peter. Let Fenn con."

In ten seconds the craft was over the point of Roydon's disappearance, a patch of heath. Half a naked, shaggy thigh could be seen, and a queer coughing uproar rose from the ground. Paul and Fenn, stun-guns at the ready, slipped down the ladder.

The tribe was tying Roydon up with leather thongs. He looked dazed. With blood-curdling howls Fenn and Paul rushed on them. A flash of lightning and a simultaneous crack of thunder completed the tribe's panic, and in a

torrential rain-squall they scattered over the heather. Paul
and Fenn carried Roydon a few paces back inside the
domain bounds where the helicopter could again be seen
ghostily through the diminishing downpour, and slashed
his bonds loose, looking anxiously about them. From the
helicopter's wall the echo of a blackbird's call could be
heard ten feet away, somewhere in the nineteenth century.
Paul clamped emergency dressings on the wounds. Roydon
staggered to his feet. "Must find her," he said thickly.

"We've had one death on your account—we don't want
three. Up the ladder, you fool, before the tribe comes
back." The sun was glinting on the wet heath.

At that moment an even fainter echo from the helicopter's base reached the group on the ground. "Miriel,
Miriel," it seemed to say. The men and women in the
craft, speechless, were gesturing wildly to one side. "Up
the ladder to the red mark—they'll trawl you over,"
shouted Paul. All three clambered post-haste above the
red three-metre mark.

"We'll drop you quietly and try to pick up Richard,"
said Peter's voice at last. The helicopter drifted some
metres north, its loaded ladder swaying dangerously. An
old gentleman clad in a somber jacket, a deal of lace at
the neck, and breeches, was kneeling on the ground by a
little plot of smooth grass. He did not look up even when
the three dropped beside him, and seemed not to hear the
noise of the machine which now vanished southward. A
green May morning burgeoned all around him. "Miriel,
Miriel!" he was crying.

At last he looked up at the group around him. He
seemed not quite right in the head: at any rate he gave
little sign of surprise. "Here is a lock of her hair cut off
when she came to us, here is a lock of white hair when she
was taken, here is her ring, her wedding ring. She be-
sought I would bury them near to the place where she
came to us, for her body is in Mafford churchyard and her
soul with her Maker, but her heart, I fear, is here, though
she cherished our people for sixty years. Who are you,

sirs, are you of the company of the blessed angels, are you come to take me to Heaven to be with her?"

"She was my wife," said Roydon quietly.

"Ah, sir, but she was an old old woman when she departed this life on Friday last. How can that be?"

"Never mind: it is true. I should like to see her grave, though I know where it lies: I have seen it long since. Did she live here all her life after she came to you?"

"Yes, sir, she was, as you might say, the mother of our little flock. Mourned and lamented by one and all, sir, by young and old, by man and woman, and a noble stone they will put up, sir, at the head of the grave. Matthew is carving it but 'twill not be ready for a day or two, I fear. She was the mother of our village, though her heart, I fear, was elsewhere, and that gave her a sadness, a kind of resignation all her days. Resigned to God's will she was, and indeed she loved our people dearly. Miriel has cherished and succoured our village, but she will not come among us again." And the old man, smiling sadly, nodded off among the meadow flowers.

Roydon picked up the ring and slipped it on the little finger of his left hand. His spear wounds were yelling at him, but in his heart a vast dark gray calm was spreading.

THE RIME OF THE ANCIENT SF AUTHOR, OR CONVENTIONS AND RECOLLECTIONS

J. R. PIERCE

Dr. Pierce, executive director of the Research and Communications Sciences Division of the Bell Telephone Laboratories, has published such works as Quantum Electronics *and* Electronics and Waves. *His other personality is that of J. J. Coupling, author of much-anthologized SF stories. In this latter role he has had ample opportunity to observe the other science fiction authors and, with his physicist's eye, he can apparently see right through to their component atoms. That he should present these observations in this delightfully witty poem is an unexpected pleasure for us all.*

See them cavort in little herds,   How he sees them
Stamping feet and twinkling words,   In their purity
Cropping imagination's plane,
Far from envy, far from gain.
Oh vision rare, beyond compare,
Fair writers stripping fair souls bare—
And how I wish that I was there.

Some write straight technology,   Some peculiar habits
And others write philosophy,   and how he loves them
Stale subjects, charming only here,
Or after cans and cans of beer.
Oh cans of beer, apartments drear
And points unclear of friends most dear,
How, how I wish you all were here.

Fettered by convention's gyves   Some stray
With editors if not with wives,   but many return
Seduced away by slicks and sex,
How can SF survive its checks?
Oh, riches pall, commitments gall;
What fat cats want cannot be all,
And back into their ways they fall.

Writing tripe for gold's a sin,   His horror at those
A venial, heart-whole giving in;   who lust after the
A whoring after foreign gods   mainstream
Makes SF writers boring clods.
Oh lovers pure, I can't endure
The tawdry mainstream's tinsel lure;
The bait is bright, the wages sure.

THE ANNEX

John D. MacDonald

John D. MacDonald is a volcano—though as far as critics are concerned, he might be erupting, invisibly, far out to sea. There is a journal, The JDM Bibliophile *devoted to the appreciation of his works, while these same works sell in the hundreds of thousands of copies. Perhaps he does not need the critics. Yet I do wish they would notice that he is one of the best American authors writing today. It has been over ten years since he last wrote a SF short story, so "The Annex" is more than doubly welcome. You will read it with pleasure. Perhaps the literary establishment would also read it if I told them that it has very definite Kafkaesque overtones.*

Well—it has.

During the last hour of the night, the charge nurse looked in at the critical in Room 11, intensive-care section, coronary. She scowled and made an ugly, displeased mouth and hastened to replace the dislodged I.V. needle in the vein inside the elbow of the right arm, immobilized by the straps, the board and the side rail of the bed. She checked the glucose drip, made a small adjustment of the flow valve, checked oxygen supply, listened to the ragged labor of the pulse and went off and found the pretty little special drinking coffee in the treatment room and joking with the red headed intern.

After chewing her out with a cold expertise that welled tears into the blue eyes, she herded her back to her night watch over the patient.

"I wasn't gone three minutes, honest," she said.

"An hour before dawn they get restless," the charge nurse said. "As if they had someplace to go, some appointment to keep."

When the first gray light of the morning made the shape of the window visible, he dressed quickly and went out. He guessed that they would not be expecting him to leave that room so soon after arriving.

There were shadows of night still remaining in the empty streets, so that even though he knew his way and walked swiftly, the city seemed strange to him. They were changing it so quickly these past few years. The eye becomes accustomed to the shape and bulk of structures, giving them only a marginal attention; yet when, so abruptly, they were gone, one had the feeling of having made a wrong turn somewhere. Then even the unchanged things began to look half strange.

He turned a dark corner and saw the hotel lights in the distance. A taxi came swiftly to the cross-town corner, made a wrenching, shuddering turn and sped up the empty avenue, and he caught a silhouette glimpse of the sailboat hats of nuns in the dark interior, two or three of them.

He had not been in the hotel for years. He saw at once that it was quite changed. That certain quaintness of the lobby that once set off the high style of the moneyed people and the women of the theatre was now merely a shabbiness. He realized that he could have guessed it, because were it not changed, they would not be mixed up in this sort of thing. And his shabby assignment in an unknown room would have occurred in some other place, perhaps even in another city at another time.

There was no one behind the desk. He felt in his pocket for the identification he would have to present and felt fear and irritation when he did not find it at once. Then, among coins, he fingered the shape of it and took it out and held it in his clasped hand. As he wondered whether to tap the desk bell, he saw movement out of the side of his eye and turned and saw a man walking toward him out of the lobby shadows.

"Mr. Davis?" the small man said; and as he came into the light, his face was elusively familiar. He searched memory and finally recalled the image of the same face, a bellhop uniform in dull red and gray, big brass circle of the master key ring looped around the scrawny neck. And the name came back.

"Do you remember me, Leo? From before?"

"Sure," the man said. He leaned against the desk and yawned. Davis knew the man did not remember him at all.

"You're the manager now?"

"So they keep telling me."

"Come up in the world, eh?"

"I guess so." He yawned again. "You got that thing?"

He felt unaccountably shy about revealing what they had given him. He said, "I keep telling them that they should use ordinary things. But they get fanciful. It just makes everything harder to explain when things go wrong. What kind of a sentimental nut would have a gold miniature of his own dog tag made? A grown man is supposed to get over being in a war."

"Look, I have to see it." Leo's tone was patient and bored, and Davis knew the man had no interest in what he thought and very little interest in why he had come here.

He held his hand out and the little wafer gleamed on his open palm. Leo took it, glanced at it and put it in his own pocket.

"They didn't tell me you'd keep it."

"The room you want is four-two-four-two."

"Are you supposed to keep it? Did they make that clear?"

"Forty-two forty-two. Four thousand, two hundred and forty-two, Mr. Davis. OK?"

"All right. I'll assume you're supposed to keep it, Leo. It's their problem, not mine. But you're supposed to turn over the key, I know *that*."

"I can't, buddy, because the only keys here are the keys to the main house here. You should know that and they should know that. Right? What we're talking about is the annex. Which is being torn down."

"Then there isn't anybody in it?"

"Did I say that mister? Did anybody say that?"

"There's no reason to get ugly about it, Leo."

"Who's ugly? Listen, they got old foops in there living there since the year one, and lease agreements and all that stuff, so about the only thing they can do is work around them until they get sick of all the noise and mess and get out. There aren't many left now. I think maybe your party is the only one left on that floor, but I don't keep close track. I've got enough to do here without worrying about over there."

"So what do I do about a key? Am I supposed to go knock on the door, for God's sake?"

"Mrs. Dorn is over there. She's got a master key to the whole annex."

"Does she know about me?"

"Why should she? Just con her a little, Mr. Davis. Play it by ear. OK?"

"I don't have much choice, I guess."

"Has anybody lately? Come this way."

Leo led the way back through the lobby and through a huge empty kitchen, where night lights picked up the gleam and shape of stainless steel racks and tables. He pulled a door open and turned on a weak bulb at the head of a narrow flight of stairs.

"The regular way over there has been boarded up, so

what you do is just follow the way a red pipe runs along the ceiling there, and when you come to stairs finally, go on up and you'll find her around someplace."

Three steps down, he turned to say his thanks in some massively sarcastic way; but as he turned, the door was slammed. There were distant lights in the vast reaches of the basement, just enough for him to make out the red pipe suspended by straps from the low ceiling overhead. There was a sweaty dampness in the basement. In some far corner, a laboring machine was making a slow and heavy chuffing sound. It made a vibration he could feel through the soles of his shoes as he walked. He noticed that the red pipe overhead was of some kind of plastic material, sufficiently flexible so that there was a perceptible expansion and contraction as the machine made its thick and rhythmic sound.

He estimated that he had walked more than a city block before he came to the stairs, where the red pipe disappeared into a wall. These were unexpectedly wide and elegant stairs, marble streaked with gray and green, ascending in a gentle curve. At the top of the stairs, he pushed a dark door open and found himself in an enormous lobby. It had the silence of a museum. Dropcloths covered the shapes of furniture. Plaster dust was gritty on the floor. Some huge beams had fallen and were propped at an angle, as in pictures of bombings.

"Mrs. Dorn!" he called. "Mrs. Dorn!" The sound did not seem to carry. It died at once into the silence.

Then he heard a click-tock of high heels and he could not tell where the sound was coming from. "Yes?" she said. "You, there! Up here!" Her voice was musical; the tone, impatient. He looked up and saw her standing at the broad ornate railing of a mezzanine floor, looking down at him, in silhouette against a window beyond her. "Yes? What do you want?"

"Can I speak to you a minute?"

"I'm very busy. Well . . . come on up."

She turned away. He looked around and saw the stairs and went up. There was a library and writing room at the top of the stairs. Several doors opened from the room. He tried them, one by one, and found they opened onto corridors. Then, close behind him, she chuckled and, as he turned, startled, she said, "It's really very confusing. I used to get hopelessly lost when I first came here."

She looked like someone he had known, somewhere, perhaps a long time ago. She had a soft and pretty face, dark wings of careless hair, and she looked at him in a familiar and mocking way of old secrets shared. She wore a shift of some tweedy gray substance over a young, sturdy body with a vital heft of hip and weight of breast.

"I wonder, Mrs. Dorn, if you could. . . ."

"Just a moment, please. I missed this room somehow, and the crews will be arriving any minute, and it would be just my rotten luck if they started here, wouldn't it?" She began to walk slowly around the room, pausing from time to time, pausing to hold at arm's length a piece of soft yellow chalk in the measuring gesture of the artist. She nodded to herself from time to time and then would mark with the chalk a piece of paneling, or a chair, or the frame of an old painting.

At last she sighed and turned toward him with a smile of enduring patience.

"Done, I guess. As well as I can do it, anyway. They don't really give a damn about saving anything. You have to watch them like hawks. They'll pretend they didn't see the mark and they'll smash stuff to powder and then look so *terribly* innocent. They hate old things, I guess. And hate the loveliest old things worst of all. They just want to come in and biff, bang, crunch and truck it away and get it over with and go on to the next job. My, how they resent me, and resent having to save things and handle them so gently and take them to our warehouse. You wouldn't believe it."

The marks she made each time was a D with a cross drawn through it, like a cancellation.

"What did you want?" she asked.

"They told me that you're the one to see. You can lend me the master key."

"Really? And exactly what room do you want to get into? And why?"

"Four-two-four . . . oh, Forty-two forty. It will take only a . . . very few minutes."

"On the forty-second floor. Now isn't that quaint! Isn't that the living end!"

"What's so funny, Mrs. Dorn? I don't think anything is particularly funny."

"I couldn't possibly explain it to you. I'll have to show you."

"You could let me take the key, couldn't you?"

"My dear man, so much has been torn down and thrown away and smashed, you could wander around up there for weeks trying to find a way to the right floor and the right wing. Even if I believed you, I'd have to go with you in any case."

She led the way back down and through the silence of the lobby and to a back corridor, and into a bird-cage elevator no more than five feet square. She reached and clanged the door shut, turned a worn brass handle and they began to creak slowly upward. He stared up through the ceiling of woven metal strips and saw the sway of the moving cables and, far overhead, a pale square of gray sky.

The animation and mocking amusement had gone out of her. She leaned sagging, looking downward, finger tips on the brass lever, and he sensed that he had no part in what she was thinking. He could look at her with that feeling of invasion one has in watching someone sleep. There was a small mole below the corner of her mouth, on the pale concavity below the soft weight of her underlip. Her lashes were long and dark. He saw the lift and fall of her slow breathing and was aware of a warmth and scent of her breath. There were two deep pockets in the gray shift. The master key would have to be in one or the other. So it could be done. There was always a way.

Suddenly he had the feeling he was being trapped in

some curious way, was being led from his assignment into a plan devised for some other reason, a plan wherein his role was minor; and looking at the panel above her resting hand, he saw what had probably given him subtle warning. There were brass buttons for the floors, pressed so many hundred thousand times the incised digits were almost worn away; yet when the gray light struck them properly, he could make out the topmost numeral of the vertical row—21.

"So that's it," he said. "That's what's funny." He made his mouth stretch wide in the knowing grin. The girl looked at him, startled and puzzled. "There's no forty-second floor," he said.

Frowning, she turned and looked at the row of buttons and then back at him. "You're serious? Don't you know about the annex at all? You know how the transients are. Top floor. Top floor. It's all they can think about. But the people who stay have to have private lives, don't they? Not all cluttered up with salesmen and people coming to town for the theatre and all that. You've never been in the business, have you? All the city hotels are just the same, you know. The elevators for the transients go only so high, just to such and such a number, and the quiet floors, where people live, are above that, always, and they have their private ways to get up to them."

She was so very patient that he felt ashamed of accusing her and felt irritated with himself for not having guessed, long ago, what she told him. There had always been enough clues. There were always people going through the hotel lobbies, looking neither to the right nor to the left, walking by the regular elevators to some special place and service awaiting them.

But when the elevator stopped and they got out, she reached back into it, pressed the lowest button, yanked her arm out quickly and slammed the latticework door. It began to creak downward, with a clicking of pulleys and rasp of cables. She looked up at him and wrinkled her nose in mischief and mockery, saying, "Don't look so worried. There'll be other ways down." He remembered that she had not told him the joke, and he was once again annoyed at her.

These were broad corridors, pale gray, with composition floors, lighted by misted glass panels set into the ceiling. He tried to walk beside her, but she kept quickening her pace, and he realized she wanted him to walk behind her, a person guided rather than a companion. Many times they reached an intersection where the corridors stretched for vast distances, and sometimes she would pause to orient herself and then turn confidently right or left.

He noticed that all the numbers had been taken off the doors. He could see the raw holes where they had been screwed through gray paint into the plywood.

She was fifteen feet ahead of him, the dark hair bouncing at the nape of her neck to her swift, buoyant stride. The coarse gray fabric pulled in alternating diagonal tensions against her rear, and somehow he knew that were she quite still and quite bare, were he to place his hands so that his finger tips were hooked around the shelf of hip socket, feeling the warm, smooth slide of membrane over bone, holding her from the rear, his hands placed as a player holds a basketball for the long set shot, then through some delicious coincidence of design, the pads of his thumbs would fit precisely into the two deep dimples spaced below her spine. He shook himself out of the erotic musing, remembering how often they had told him that assignments were mishandled too often for exactly this reason.

At the end of a corridor, she pulled a heavy fire door open and turned to give him a bawdy wink, to run her tonguetip across her lips, as though she had read his mind and his weakness; and he determined not to look at her as she climbed the stairs ahead of him, and looked instead at the steel treads set into the concrete. He lost track of the number of flights they climbed. It winded him; and when he helped her push another fire door open, he tried to conceal his laboring lungs and to seem as fresh as she.

These corridors were a pale yellow, like weak winter

sunlight, and at last they came to a small elevator standing open. The flourescence inside was harsh and there was a sharp minty odor, as though it had recently been scrubbed with some cheap, strong antiseptic. It accelerated upward with silent velocity that hollowed his belly and made his knees bend slightly. It opened automatically on a narrower, dingy, old-fashioned corridor. She reached into the elevator as before; and when the door hissed shut and she turned to speak, he said, "I know. There'll be other ways down."

"That isn't what I was going to say."

"I'm sorry. What were you going to say?"

"I can't say it now. You spoiled it."

Again he followed her. These corridors were set at odd angles. The room doors were shiny dark with old coats of varnish. The room numbers were not removed and they were of tarnished brass, fluted and curly and ornate. All the rooms were in the 4000 series, but they were not in any reasonable order, 4100 and something across from or next door to 4800 and something.

She stopped very abruptly; and as he came up upon her, he heard what she had heard—the gritty sound of latch and bolt—and then, twenty feet ahead of them, an old couple, dressed for winter, came out of one of the rooms, complaining at each other, fussing, asking if he or she had forgotten this or that, dropping small packages and picking them up.

Just before the old couple turned and noticed them, Mrs. Dorn hooked her arm around his waist and forced him into a slow walk. He put his arm, interlocked, around her, and she reached up with her free hand, placed it against his cheek, chuckled in a furry way, turned her mouth up to the awkward kiss while walking, so that as they passed the couple, he heard tsk's and clucks of their disapproval. "Darling, darling," she murmured. "Dave, darling."

Behind them he heard the old man's voice, without making out the words. There was a harsh resonance to it and then it cracked into a high quaver and then went deep again.

He smiled inside himself, thinking it sounded exactly like Ricky trying to manage his fourteen-year-old voice as it alternately squeaked and rumbled. The finger tips of the arm that was around her waist touched the top of the pocket on the left side of the gray shift, and with sneaky and daring inspiration, he slid his hand down into the pocket, bending his knees inconspicuously to lower himself just enough, the palm of his hand against round, warm thigh under fabric, and with his finger tips he touched the cylinder of yellow chalk and then the thin edge of metal. With the metal held against the nail of his index finger by the pad of his middle finger, he drew it out of the deep pocket and worked it into the palm of his hand.

She stopped and turned and leaned against the corridor wall and, with her hands resting lightly on his shoulders, looked up at him, still mocking him, saying, "You're just not very bright, Dave, darling."

The old people were gone, around a distant corner of the old hallway. Suddenly, he realized that she had cleverly kept them from seeing his face, so that they would be unable to identify him later. And with a sense of disbelief, he realized she had called him by his name.

"You could have told me how much you knew about this," he said.

"It's better for you to guess, dear. Look at what you took."

He opened his palm and saw the miniature gold tag. Name, rank, serial number, blood type O, meaning zero, meaning blood type nothing. The shock was enormous. He was suddenly afraid he might cry like a child and shame himself in front of her. "How did you ... How could Leo have. . . ."

"Leo? Don't be silly. I had it all along. There were always two, you know. Don't you remember that, even? No, keep it, dear. If I have to have it back, you can always give it to me. Without any fuss. Promise?"

"Sure, but if you could just tell me. . . ."

"I can show you, Dave. Come along."

She paused at the next turning and bit her lip and, standing beside her, he saw that the floor itself dipped down in a gentle curve and lifted again at another place in the distance, where it turned again. It was swaying slightly, the whole corridor, like the bridges primitive peoples wove across deep swift rivers. She told him to walk carefully and stay close to the corridor wall. She motioned to him to stop and they were, he saw, on either side of a double door. It was room 4242. If she knew the rest of it, she would know the right number. It had been so placed that half of it was on each door, so that each was labelled 42. Even though she knew, he did not want her to watch what had to be done, watch the task assigned him; but before he could ask her to go away, to give him the key and go away, go back and wait for him around the corner, out of sight, she put a bright red key in the lock and the double doors opened inward.

Inward, but outward. They opened onto the nothing of a dizzy height, making a vent for a cold wind that came husking down the hallway behind him and pushed him a long clumsy stride to stand on the very brink. Far, far, far below, the bug shapes of city cars and trucks moved very slowly, as when seen from an aircraft. He teetered, toes over the edge, and slowly fought back the sickness and the terror, knowing he could not let her see that he suddenly realized how cynically and savagely they had tricked him. He adjusted himself to the slight sway of the corridor and rode it easily, smiling and casual for her benefit, aware of how narrowly she was watching him.

Then came a deep and powerful thud, more vibration than sound. It came welling up from below and it danced the swaying corridor, nearly toppling him out. It came again and again and again. He learned to ride the new motion. The girl whimpered. He looked far down, almost directly down, and said, "It's nothing. Your friends have come to work. They've got some kind of a derrick thing down there and they're swinging one of those big cannon balls against the foundation."

He stepped back with care and reached and took her hand. Her hand was cold and hesitant. He led her past the open and windy space and back to where, once again, the structure was solid underfoot, trembling almost imperceptibly to each subsonic thud. She pulled her hand free and, after walking slowly, looking at the room numbers, chose one, and opened the door, motioning him to come in. The room was in semidarkness, gray light outlining the window. She closed the door and he heard her sigh.

Reaction made him feel weak and sick. He saw the shape of the bed and moved to it and sat on the edge of it. She came to him and pushed at his shoulder and he lay back, grateful that she understood. He swung his legs on to the bed and she went to the foot and unlaced his shoes and took them off.

"We'd better not make very much noise," she whispered.

"Of course."

"Do you understand about the old people?"

"I know there's something I'm supposed to understand."

"That's enough for now."

She disappeared in the shadows and then he saw her again in silhouette in front of the gray of the window. He heard her sigh and he saw her, with slow and weary motion, tug the shift off over her head, toss it aside, pat her rumpled hair back into order, then bend and slip her shoes off. She stood near the corner of the window, half turned, standing quite still in silhouette, hips in relaxed and wary tilt, and he remembered one of the girls in that Degas print standing off at the side, standing in exactly the same position.

He knew she would turn and come to him but would not understand about what weakness had done to him. He did not want to confess that kind of weakness to her.

He said, "Even when they do very tricky things, that

doesn't mean the rules are changed. We have to follow the rules, just as if everything were happening to someone else, to some people they want to keep, instead of to us. You did it their way, and you know there isn't really any other way down from here. This is all we have left."

"So if I knew all along?" she asked prompting him.

"If you knew how it was going to be, then you had to know you were a part of it, too."

Not turning, still standing at the gray of the window, she said sadly, softly, "See? You keep understanding more and more of it. Sleep for a little while, darling. Then you'll know the rest of it."

At a few minutes past six, Dr. Samuel Barringer opened the door of Room 11 in the intensive-care section. In the shadows of the room, he saw the young nurse standing in silhouette by the gray of the window, looking out, standing there with a look of wistful grace.

At the sound of the latch as he closed the door, she spun with a guilty start, greeted him in her gentle and formal morning voice and handed him the clip-board with the patient's chart and the notation she had made since his visit four hours earlier. He held it under the low light for a moment, handed it back to her, then reached through the orifice in the transparent side of the oxygen tent to gently place the pads of his first two fingers against the arterial throb in the slack throat. He stood in a half bow, his eyes closed, listening and measuring through his finger tips. He was a big blond bear of a man, simultaneously clumsy and deft, as bears can be.

The nurse stood, awaiting instructions. He told her he would be back in a few minutes, and he walked to the far end of the corridor, to the waiting-room beyond the nurses' station. Sylvia sat alone there, at the end of the couch by the lamp table, staring out the big window. The hospital tower was higher than the buildings to the west of it, and she could see the wide, slow river in the morning haze. Daylight muted the yellow glow of the lamp beside her.

She turned and saw him and suddenly her dark eyes looked enormous and her face was more pale. "Sam? Is—"

"They didn't call me back. I just came in and checked him, and I have a couple of others to check, and it's standard procedure, Sylvie. No perceptible change."

He walked past her to the big window and shoved his fists into his hip pockets and looked out at the new day.

After a little while, she said, "He's been trying to take it easier since that little coronary. He really has. But you know how Dave is. He said he was going to weed his practice down to about eight very rich and nervous old ladies with minor ailments. Sam?"

He turned and looked at her, at the lean, mature vitality of her face. "What, honey?"

"What's the prognosis, Sam?"

He shrugged his bear shoulders. "Too early to tell." He looked out the window and saw a freighter being nudged into the channel by the tugs. He wished he were on it and that everybody on board was sworn never to tell Dr. Barringer where they were going or how long they'd be gone.

"Sam, please! That was a big one. Oh, God, I know that was a big one! Remember me, Sam? Eighteen years we three have known one another. I'm a nurse . . . was a nurse. Remember? You don't have to pat me on the head, Sam."

It was easy to remember the Sylvie Dorn of 18 years ago, that chunky, flirtatious, lively girl, now a whip-slender matron, dark hair with the first touches of gray. Thirty-eight? Mother of Ricky, Susan, Timmy—godmother to his own pair of demons. And Dave is—was—is forty-two.

"Sam?" she said again.

He turned from the window and went lumbering to the couch, thinking of all the times you make this decision and then decide how to wrap words around it to match the person you tell. But this one was close to the past and all the years, close to the heart.

He sat beside her and took her hands, and swallowed a rising thickness in his throat, blinked, swallowed again and said in a pebbly voice, "I'm sorry, Sylvie. Dave hasn't got enough heart muscle left to run a toy train. And there's not one damned thing we can do about it or for it."

She pulled her hands free and lunged against him, and he held her in his big arms and patted her as she strained at the first great hard spasmodic sob and got past it and in about two or three minutes pulled herself back to a control and a forlorn stability he knew she would be able to maintain.

She dabbed her eyes and blew her nose and said, "Today sometime?"

"Probably."

"Tell them you've given permission for me to stay in there with him, will you?"

"Of course. I'll be in every once in a while."

"And thank your dear gal for taking over our tribe, Sam. Sam? Do you think he'll know I'm . . . I'm there with him?"

First, he thought, you throw the stone and then you throw the lump of sugar. No point in telling her that death had occurred, that Dave, as Dave, was long gone and that the contemporary miracles of medical science were keeping some waning meat alive, in the laboratory sense of the word.

"From everything we can learn and everything we can guess, Sylvie, I feel certain that he'll be aware of you being there, holding his hand."

When the first gray light of the morning made the shape of the window visible, he dressed quickly and went out. He guessed that they would not be expecting him to leave that room so soon after arriving.

There were shadows of night still remaining in the empty streets, so that even though he knew his way and walked swiftly, the city seemed strange to him.

SEGREGATIONIST

Isaac Asimov

It is not that the tireless Asimov has been away from writing, it is just that he has not been writing much science fiction. During the past calendar year he had a round dozen books published, ranging from a collection of detection stories, Asimov's Mysteries, *to the first of two rather thick volumes enthusiastically entitled* Asimov's Guide to the Bible. *Rumor has it that he will tackle Shakespeare next, in the same grand fashion, and Baconians are already going into hiding. But, happily, between hefty shakes at the pillars that support our civilization, he did think about science fiction. And wrote "Segregationist." A compact, strong, and enjoyable story.*

The surgeon looked up without expression. "Is he ready?"

"Ready is a relative term," said the med-eng. *"We're* ready. He's restless."

"They always are. . . . Well, it's a serious operation."

"Serious or not, he should be thankful. He's been chosen for it over an enormous number of possibles and frankly, I don't think . . ."

"Don't say it," said the surgeon. "The decision is not ours to make."

"We accept it. But do we have to agree?"

"Yes," said the surgeon, crisply. "We agree. Completely and wholeheartedly. The operation is entirely too intricate to approach with mental reservations. This man has proven his worth in a number of ways, and his profile is suitable for the Board of Mortality."

"All right," said the med-eng.

The surgeon said, "I'll see him right in here, I think. It is small enough and personal enough to be comforting."

"It won't help. He's nervous, and he's made up his mind."

"Has he indeed?"

"Yes. He wants metal; they always do."

The surgeon's face did not change expression. He stared at his hands. "Sometimes one can talk them out of it."

"Why bother?" said the med-eng, indifferently. "If he wants metal, let it be metal."

"You don't care?"

"Why should I?" The med-eng said it almost brutally. "Either way it's a medical engineering problem and I'm a medical engineer. Either way, I can handle it. Why should I go beyond that?"

The surgeon said stolidly, "To me, it is a matter of the fitness of things."

"Fitness! You can't use that as an argument. What does the patient care about the fitness of things?"

"I care."

"You care in a minority. The trend is against you. You have no chance."

"I have to try." The surgeon waved the med-eng into silence with a quick wave of his hand—no impatience to it, merely quickness. He had already informed the nurse and he had already been signalled concerning her approach. He pressed a small button and the double-door pulled swiftly apart. The patient moved inward in his motor-chair, the nurse stepping briskly along beside him.

"You may go, nurse," said the surgeon, "but wait outside. I will be calling you." He nodded to the med-eng, who left with the nurse, and the door closed behind them.

The man in the chair looked over his shoulder and watched them go. His neck was scrawny and there were fine wrinkles about his eyes. He was freshly shaven and the fingers of his hands, as they gripped the arms of the chair tightly, showed manicured nails. He was a high-priority patient and he was being taken care of . . . But there was a look of settled peevishness on his face.

He said, "Will we be starting today?"

The surgeon nodded. "This afternoon, Senator."

"I understand it will take weeks."

"Not for the operation itself, Senator. But there are a number of subsidiary points to be taken care of. There are some circulatory renovations that must be carried through, and hormonal adjustments. These are tricky things."

"Are they dangerous?" Then, as though feeling the need for re-establishing a friendly relationship, but patently against his will, he added, ". . . doctor?"

The surgeon paid no attention to the nuances of expression. He said, flatly, "Everything is dangerous. We take our time in order that it be less dangerous. It is the time required, the skill of many individuals united, the equipment, that makes such operations available to so few . . ."

"I know that," said the patient, restlessly. "I refuse to feel guilty about that. Or are you implying improper pressure?"

"Not at all, Senator. The decisions of the Board have never been questioned. I mention the difficulty and intricacy of the operation merely to explain my desire to have it conducted in the best fashion possible."

"Well, do so, then. That is my desire, also."

"Then I must ask you to make a decision. It is possible to supply you with either of two types of cyber-hearts, metal or . . ."

"Plastic!" said the patient, irritably. "Isn't that the alternative you were going to offer, doctor? Cheap plastic. I don't want that. I've made my choice. I want the metal."

"But . . ."

"See here. I've been told the choice rests with me. Isn't that so?"

The surgeon nodded. "Where two alternate procedures are of equal value from a medical standpoint, the choice rests with the patient. In actual practice, the choice. rests with the patient even when the alternate procedures are *not* of equal value, as in this case."

The patient's eyes narrowed. "Are you trying to tell me the plastic heart is superior?"

"It depends on the patient. In my opinion, in your individual case, it is. And we prefer not to use the term, plastic. It is a fibrous cyber-heart."

"It's plastic as far as I am concerned."

"Senator," said the surgeon, infinitely patient, "the material is not plastic in the ordinary sense of the word. It is a polymeric material true, but one that is far more complex than ordinary plastic. It is a complex protein-like fibre designed to imitate, as closely as possible, the natural structure of the human heart you now have within your chest."

"Exactly, and the human heart I now have within my chest is worn out although I am not yet sixty years old. I don't want another one like it, thank you. I want something better."

"We all want something better for you, Senator. The fibrous cyber-heart will be better. It has a potential life of centuries. It is absolutely non-allergenic . . ."

"Isn't that so for the metallic heart, too?"

"Yes, it is," said the surgeon. "The metallic cyber is of titanium alloy that . . ."

"And it doesn't wear out? And it is stronger than plastic? Or fibre or whatever you want to call it?"

"The metal is physically stronger, yes, but mechanical strength is not a point at issue. Its mechanical strength does you no particular good since the heart is well protected. Anything capable of reaching the heart will kill you for other reasons even if the heart stands up under manhandling."

The patient shrugged. "If I ever break a rib, I'll have that replaced by titanium, also. Replacing bones is easy. Anyone can have that done anytime. I'll be as metallic as I want to be, doctor."

"That is your right, if you so choose. However, it is only fair to tell you that although no metallic cyber-heart has ever broken down, mechanically, a number have broken down electronically."

"What does that mean?"

"It means that every cyber-heart contains a pacemaker as part of its structure. In the case of the metallic variety, this is an electronic device that keeps the cyber in rhythm. It means an entire battery of miniaturized equipment must be included to alter the heart's rhythm to suit an individual's emotional and physical state. Occasionally something goes wrong there and people have died before that wrong could be corrected."

"I never heard of such a thing."

"I assure you it happens."

"Are you telling me it happens often?"

"Not at all. It happens very rarely."

"Well, then, I'll take my chance. What about the plastic heart? Doesn't that contain a pacemaker?"

"Of course it does, Senator. But the chemical structure of a fibrous cyber-heart is quite close to that of human tissue. It can respond to the ionic and hormonal controls of the body itself. The total complex that need be inserted is far simpler than in the case of the metal cyber."

"But doesn't the plastic heart ever pop out of hormonal control?"

"None has ever yet done so."

"Because you haven't been working with them long enough. Isn't that so?"

The surgeon hesitated. "It is true that the fibrous cybers have not been used nearly as long as the metallic."

"There you are. What is it anyway, doctor? Are you afraid I'm making myself into a robot . . . into a Metallo, as they call them since citizenship went through?'

"There is nothing wrong with a Metallo as a Metallo. As you say, they are citizens. But you're *not* a Metallo. You're a human being. Why not stay a human being?"

"Because I want the best and that's a metallic heart. You see to that."

The surgeon nodded. "Very well. You will be asked to sign the necessary permissions and you will then be fitted with a metal heart."

"And you'll be the surgeon in charge? They tell me you're the best."

"I will do what I can to make the changeover an easy one." The door opened and the chair moved the patient out to the nurse.

The med-eng came in, looking over his shoulder at the receding patient until the doors had closed again. He turned to the surgeon. "Well, I can't tell what happened just by looking at you. What was his decision?"

The surgeon bent over his desk, punching out the final items for his records. "What you predicted. He insists on the metallic cyber-heart."

"After all, they are better."

"Not significantly. They've been around longer; no more than that. It's this mania that's been plaguing humanity ever since Metallos have become citizens. Men have this odd desire to make Metallos out of themselves. They yearn for the physical strength and endurance one associates with them."

"It isn't one-sided, doc. You don't work with Metallos but I do; so I know. The last two who came in for repairs have asked for fibrous elements."

"Did they get them?"

"In one case, it was just a matter of supplying tendons; it didn't make much difference there, metal or fibre. The other wanted a blood system or its equivalent. I told him I couldn't; not without a complete rebuilding of the structure of his body in fibrous material. . . . I suppose it will come to that some day. Metallos that aren't really Metallos at all, but a kind of flesh and blood."

"You don't mind that thought?"

"Why not? And metallized human beings, too. We have two varieties of intelligence on Earth now and why bother with two. Let them approach each other and eventually we won't be able to tell the difference. Why should we want to? We'd have the best of both worlds; the advantages of man combined with those of robot."

"You'd get a hybrid," said the surgeon, with something that approached fierceness. "You'd get something that is not both, but neither. Isn't it logical to suppose an individual would be too proud of his structure and identity to want to dilute it with something alien? Would he *want* mongrelization?"

"That's segregationist talk."

"Then let it be that." The surgeon said with calm emphasis, "I believe in being what one is. I wouldn't change a bit of my own structure for any reason. If some of it absolutely required replacement, I would have that replacement as close to the original in nature as could possibly be managed. I am *myself*; well pleased to be myself; and would not be anything else." He had finished now and had to prepare for the operation. He placed his strong hands into the heating oven and let them reach the dull red-hot glow that would sterilize them completely. For all his impassioned words, his voice had never risen, and on his burnished metal face there was (as always) no no sign of expression.

FINAL WAR

K. M. O'DONNELL

". . . Although most of the comments I've received to date on this novelette have noted its parallels to Catch-22, *I respectfully decline the question; I think that Heller and I both approached some source-material to render it in individual ways which might only indicate that we could have a drink together comfortably (we live a block from one another here in NYC; I guess it might be about time). "Final War" is about neither war nor death; it is about the polarization of existences re-enacted on several levels over and again and if that makes no sense, I suppose human life makes no sense either. The longer I write— correction, the longer I unsuccessfully resist not writing— the more I think that humanity is either a slight, almost inconsequential aberration in the universe or that life itself is but a blank metaphor for something More Important. If these insights seem contradictory, I am not noted for my consistency. I thank Ed Ferman for seeing exactly what I was trying to do, and I owe him a great debt."*

Barry N. Malzberg
(K. M. O'Donnell)

" 'Twas a mad stratagem,
To shoe a troop of horse with felt . . ."

Lear, Act III

Hastings had never liked the new Captain.

The new Captain went through the mine field like a dancer, looking around from time to time to see if anyone behind was looking at his trembling rear end. If he found that anyone was, he immediately dropped to the end of the formation, began to scream threats, told the company that the mine field would go up on them. This was perfectly ridiculous because the company had been through the mine field hundreds of times and knew that all of the mines had been defused by the rain and the bugs. The mine field was the safest thing going. It was what lay *around* the mine field that was dangerous. Hastings could have told the new Captain all of this if he had asked.

The new Captain, however, was stubborn. He told everyone that, before he heard a thing, he wanted to become acclimated.

Background: Hasting's company was quartered, with their enemy, on an enormous estate. Their grounds began in a disheveled forest and passed across the mine field to a series of rocks or dismally piled and multicolored stones which formed into the grim and blasted abutments two miles away. Or, it began in a set of rocks or abutments and, passing through a scarred mine field, ended in an exhausted forest two miles back. It all depended upon whether they were attacking or defending; it all depended upon the day of the week. On Thursdays, Saturdays and Tuesdays, the company moved east to capture the forest; on Fridays, Sundays and Wednesdays, they lost the battles to defend it. Mondays, everyone was too tired to fight. The Captain stayed in his tent and sent out messages to headquarters; asked what new course of action to take. Headquarters advised him to continue as previously.

The forest was the right place to be. In the first place,

the trees gave privacy, and in the second, it was cool. It was possible to play a decent game of poker, get a night's sleep. Perhaps because of the poker, the enemy fought madly for the forest and defended it like lunatics. So did Hastings' company. Being there, even if only on Thursdays, Saturdays and Tuesdays, made the war worthwhile. The enemy must have felt the same way, but they, of course, had the odd day of the week. Still, even Hastings was willing to stay organized on that basis. Monday was a lousy day to get up, anyway.

But, it was the new Captain who wanted to screw things up. Two weeks after he came to the company, he announced that he had partially familiarized himself with the terrain and on this basis, he now wanted to remind the company not to cease fighting once they had captured the forest. He advised them that the purpose of the war went beyond the forest; it involved a limited victory on ideological issues, and he gave the company a month to straighten out and learn the new procedure. Also, he refused to believe his First Sergeant when the First Sergeant told him about the mine field but sent out men at night in dark clothing to check the area; he claimed that mines had a reputation for exploding twenty years later. The First Sergeant pointed out that it was not twenty years later, but the Captain said this made no difference; it could happen anytime at all. Not even the First Sergeant knew what to do with him. And, in addition to all of these things, it was rumored that the Captain talked in private to his officers of a *total* victory policy, was saying things to the effect that the war could only be successful if taken outside of the estate. When Hastings had grasped the full implication of all of this, he tried to imagine for a while that the Captain was merely stupid but, eventually the simple truth of the situation came quite clear; the new Captain was crazy. The madness was not hateful: Hastings knew himself to be quite mad. The issue was how the Captain's lunacy bore on Hastings' problem: now, Hastings decided, the Captain would *never* approve his request for convalescent leave.

This request was already several months old. Hastings had handed it to the new Captain the day that the new Captain had come into the company. Since the Captain had many things on his mind at this time—he told Hastings that he would have to become acclimated to the new situation—Hastings could understand matters being delayed for a short while. But still, nothing had been done, and it was after the election; furthermore, Hastings was getting worse instead of better. Every time that Hastings looked up the Captain to discuss this with him, the Captain fled. He had told the First Sergeant that he wanted Hastings to know that he felt he was acting irresponsibly and out of the network of the problem. This news, when it was delivered, gave Hastings little comfort. *I am not acting irresponsibly,* he told the First Sergeant who listened without apparent interest, *as a matter of fact, I'm acting in quite a mature fashion. I'm trying to get some leave for the good of the company.* The First Sergeant had said that he guessed he didn't understand it either and he had been through four wars, not counting eight limited actions. He said that it was something which Hastings would have to work out for his own satisfaction.

Very few things, however, gave Hastings that much satisfaction, anymore. He was good and fed up with the war for one thing and, for another, he had gotten bored with the estate even if the company hadn't: once you had seen the forest, you had seen all of it that was worthwhile. Unquestionably, the cliffs, the abutments and the mine field were terrible. It might have been a manageable thing if they could have reached some kind of understanding with the enemy, a peaceful allotment of benefits, but it was obvious that headquarters would have none of this and besides, the enemy probably had a headquarters, too. Some of the men in the company might have lived limited existences; this might be perfectly all right with *them,* but Hastings liked to think of himself as a man whose horizons were, perhaps, a little wider than those of the others. *He* knew the situation was ridiculous. Every week, to remind him, reinforcements would come from somewhere in the South and tell Hastings that they had never seen anything like it. Hastings told them that this was because there had never *been* anything like it; not ever. Since the reinforcements had heard that Hastings had been there longer than anyone, they shut up then and left him alone. Hastings did not find that this improved his mood, appreciably. If anything, it convinced him that his worst suspicions were, after all, completely justified.

On election day, the company had a particularly bad experience. The president of their country was being threatened by an opposition which had no use for his preparedness policy; as a defensive measure, therefore, he had no choice on the day before election, other than to order every military installation in the vicinity of the company's war to send out at least one bomber and more likely two to show determination. Hastings' company knew nothing whatever of this; they woke on the morning of the election cheerful because it was their turn to take the forest. Furthermore, the tents of the enemy seen in the distance were already being struck, a good sign that the enemy would not contest things too vigorously. The men of the company put on their combat gear singing, goosing one another, challenging for poker games that night; it looked as if it were going to be a magnificent day. All indications were that the enemy would yield like gentlemen. Some of the company began to play tag, leaping through the abutments, comparing them to the forest that would soon be theirs.

Then, from all conceivable directions, airplanes came; they wandered, moaning, a few hundred feet above the surface of the cliffs and apparently waited. When all of them were quite sure that no others were coming (there would have been no room for them anyway), they began to methodically drop bombs on the company. Naturally, the pilots and crews of the airplanes were terribly excited and, as a result, they misplaced their fire quite badly, missing direct hits on the company more often than not.

After a while, there was so much smoke around the vicinity of the cliffs that the pilots were unable to see at all, and they drifted over and peevishly sent excess bombs on the mine field. Hastings, lying on his back, guessed that the First Sergeant had been proved right because, just as everyone had been telling the Captain, the mine field did not go up. It took the bombs quite nicely, as a matter of fact, not heaving a bit. When every plane had released its bomb (some had to actually go over to the forest and drop one on the enemy; there was no other space left), they flew off in a dazzle of satisfaction, leaving the largest part of the company choking with laughter. Those that were not choking were unable to because they were dead. The point seemed to be that here it was the company's day in the forest, and now their own or some other force had come in and had screwed everything up. In the distance, the enemy could be seen holding cautious formation and then, with no hesitation whatsoever, they put themselves into lines and marched briskly away from the forest, taking the long route back to the cliffs. The new Captain got up on an abutment and made a speech; he said that this had been the first step in a whole series leading to mass realignment. The company applauded thinly, wondering if there was any chance that he might have a stroke. Then everybody packed up and went over to the forest; all of them, of course, except those who were dead. Hastings stayed with a work detail and labelled all of them so that headquarters, if they ever sent anyone up, would know who in the company had failed to take the proper precautions and was therefore to be permanently removed from the master roster list and placed in the inactive files, never to be bothered by formations again.

It was the election day disaster that caused certain men in the company to begin behaving in a very bizarre fashion. News received through the First Sergeant that headquarters believed that the president had won re-election had no effect upon the decision of these men to take up indefinite residence in the forest; they told anyone who asked them that the whole thing was a futile proposition and the company was always going to come back there, anyway. They refused to make formations and had friends answer for them; they covered their tents with mud and pitched them in the shadow of trees; they washed their garments in the rain and, furthermore, they told everyone in the company that they were fools not to join them. One morning, lining up in the cliffs, the First Sergeant noticed for the first time that five men were gone. He became furious and said he would not stand for it; he told the company that he had been through four wars, not including eight limited actions, and there was simply no basis ever, to performances of this sort. The First Sergeant said that he was going personally to lead the company back to the forest to shoot those five men. They were all prepared to go, looking forward to the objective really, when a misguided enemy pilot flew uncertainly over the forest and, perhaps in retaliation, dropped thirty-seven bombs on it, blowing every tree to the ground, leaving the earth quite green and shuddering and completely decimating his own troops. They were unable to fight for a week because the enemy had to ship reinforcements, and when they finally got back to the forest, they could find, of course, no trace of their five men at all; only a few belt buckles.

It was right then that Hastings decided that the matter of his convalescent leave had come to a head. He had had the idea and he knew that it was covered in regulations: *he was entitled to it.* Army manuals noted the existence of something called convalescent leave: if it wasn't for situations such as these, well then, for what was it? *They had to deal with it.* One morning, he carefully re-drafted his original request with a borrowed pencil on the back of an old letter from his fiancée and brought it again into the First Sergeant. Hastings reminded the First Sergeant that he had originally put this request in months ago. The First Sergeant, groaning, said that the Captain could not possibly look at it because he was still getting acclimated to the situation. But, the First Sergeant added, he had been talking to the Captain on and off and he had some prom-

ising news: the Captain had been saying that he would
probably be completely familiarized by Christmas. It was
only a matter of taking time to get hold of a situation.
Hastings said was that a fact and, mumbling promises to
himself, left the headquarters tent; he told the Corporal
with whom he slept that he hoped to be out of this, sooner
or later. Most of the company were still gathering for
hours around the belt buckles, looking solemnly, telling
each other that it was a damned shame what the Army did
to people. Hastings, looking it over again, decided that he
had written a strong appeal: How *could* it be ignored?

Gentlemen (Hastings had written), listen: I am applying
for convalescent leave as I have already done because I
have been in vigorous combat and, while adding little or
nothing to the company effort, have driven myself to the
ridges of neurasthenia. What fighting skills I do possess and
what morale I have acquired through recommended reading materials have fallen to a very low point because of the
discouragement involved in the present situation. We are
capturing and capturing again one forest and some wasted
hills. The forest is bearable; the hills are not, but in the
exhaustion of this repeated effort, both have levelled to a
kind of hideous sameness; *now there is no difference.*
Indeed, everything has become the same, as is common
now in cases of great tension occurring under stress situations to certain limited individuals. Recently, I have had
cold sweats, nausea, some vomiting and various nervous
reactions including migraine of relative severity that has
cut my diminishing effectiveness even further. Most of the
time, I can barely lift a rifle . . . and for all of these
reasons, I am repeating my ignored request of three
months' duration that I be given convalescent leave for a
period of several weeks to months for the purposes of
renewed vision. Ideally, I would like to go back home, see
my civilian friends, share my experiences with them, but if
it is found that I cannot be sent there due to problems
with transportation allotments and the like, I would settle
for being sent alone to the nearest town where there are

women and where it is possible to sleep. I would even be willing, if the nights were quiet, to go to a place without women; as a matter of fact, this might be the best action at this time. I am certainly in no condition for relationships, not even those of the fragmentary kind necessitated by copulation. Hoping that this request meets with your attention and approval; hoping that you will see it not as the frenzied expression of a collapsed man but only as the cool and reasoned action of the professional soldier under stress, I remain yours truly, Hastings, 114786210. *P.S.* I wish to note that my condition is serious; how serious only a qualified professional judgement could determine. If this request is not met with your prompt attention, therefore, or not, at least sent to a competent psychiatrist for an opinion, it is impossible for me to predict what the scope of my reactions will be: *I can no longer control my behavior.* I have been brought up all my life to believe that institutions are the final repository of all the good sense left in this indecent world; at this point in my life it would assume the proportion of a major disaster if I were to learn that the Army, one of our most respected and ancient institutions, were not to be trusted. *P.P.S.* Please note that the mines here are *already defused;* inform the Captain that they need not worry him.

On the other hand, the *first* request had been good, too. The day that the *old* Captain's reassignment to headquarters came through, all of the men in the company had come to his tent to stand around him, giving him notes and wishes of good will. Hastings had given him his request in a sealed envelope, and the Captain had taken it for another farewell message and placed it carefully in his knapsack; he told Hastings and the others that he was moved by their display of affection and he hoped that any of them who came into his territory later in the war would drop in and say hello; he would like to find out personally how everything was going. After all of this was over, the old Captain had crawled into his tent, saying, over his shoulder, that the company had given him an experience that he simply would never forget. The company smiled at the Captain's closed tent and wandered off to play poker. (They had been in the forest that day.)

Hastings thought that he would join them and then decided that this would not do; he would have to force the issue, and so he crawled, quite respectfully, into the Captain's tent and, finding him wrapped in an embryonic ball on his bunk, told him that he had a few things to explain. Hastings told the Captain that he had submitted a request for convalescent leave and not a good will message. At this, the Captain's legs kicked from the ball he had made of himself, and he told Hastings that he felt that he had very little consideration. Hastings said that this might all well be true, but he *was* a sick man and he then outlined the substance of his request. The Captain wrapped himself up intently and thought about it, said that he could court-martial Hastings. He added cheerfully that, since he was not legally in command of the company now, Hastings could be placed in the stockade for divulging confidential material to an outsider. Hastings kneeled then and asked the Captain what the proper thing would be to do, and the Captain said that he hadn't the faintest idea. He suggested that Hastings recall his request and, as a concession, court-martial proceedings would be dropped. He said that the appeal itself was unexceptionable; the new Captain, if one ever came, surely would approve it.

Hastings took his envelope and left the Captain, went back to his tent singing an Army song and fixed up his pegs neatly, but by the time he had all of them firmly in the ground, he found himself stricken with a terrible intimation. He went back to see the Captain, learned that he was in the officers' latrine, and waited outside there until the Captain came out. Hastings asked the Captain if headquarters or the new Captain might think that his request was a joke. The Captain said that he could not speak professionally but from what he had gathered from summation, he saw nothing funny in it at all; it seemed quite serious, quite to the point. Hastings said that the Captain might feel that way but, after all, he had been heading up the war, maybe at headquarters, they did not glimpse the urgencies. The Captain said that headquarters was filled with understanding people: they were people who had approved his own request for transfer, and they could be counted upon to comprehend the necessary. Hastings said a few unfortunate words about possible prejudice against enlisted men, and the Captain's face became bright green; he said that he suddenly realized that he had not finished his own business in the latrine. Hastings could not follow him in there, of course, but he waited two hours until the Captain came out and tried to pursue the matter. But the Captain, walking away hurriedly, said that he did not know what Hastings was talking about: he did not even know what this request was, had never heard of it in fact; and then he said that, upon consideration, he realized that he did not know Hastings either; surely, he had never seen him before. The Captain ordered Hastings to return to his proper company, wherever that might be. Hastings explained that theirs was the only company within two hundred miles, and the Captain said that Hastings was obviously an AWOL with energy. Then, he ran briskly away.

Hastings gathered that there would be very little point in following and instead went back to his tent. His tent mate was sleeping inside, and Hastings methodically demolished the tent, wrapped it around the Corporal, picked all of this up, groaning, and threw it into a tree. The Corporal hit with a dull noise. When he came out rubbing himself, he said that he was shocked at this; he did not know that Hastings was the type. Hastings shrugged and said that some men changed personality under stress. He wandered away, not breathing very hard, and bought a pencil from someone, took some toilet paper from the latrine and began a very serious letter to his fiancée. He had just brought matters through the Captain's second flight when the sun set violently, and he had to put everything away. He slept quite badly in the mine field that night (he did not feel like returning to his tent; not quite yet) and in the morning, found that his letter had been somehow stolen. Hastings had a good reputation as a letter writer, and men in the company were always stealing his correspondence, trying to get useful phrases. Hastings did not care about this particularly, except that lately he had begun to feel that he had only a limited number of things to say and they were diminishing rapidly. This theft, then, intensified his gloom, and he almost decided to seek another interview with the Captain but then he said: *The hell with it. We'll give the new man a chance. That is the least we can do.* Looking sadly at the enemy tents, Hastings again decided that he was in a highly abnormal situation.

Headquarters (wrote Hastings some time later on the back of a letter from an old acquaintance), I am forced to take this most serious and irregular action because of the prejudicial conduct of the recently installed Commanding Officer concerning my re-request for convalescent status. As you may or may not know, I originally placed this request several months ago and rewrote it last week because of the failure of the Commanding Officer to pay any heed, whatsoever. This Commanding Officer has subjected me to an exposure of terrifying inadequacy without precedent in a Captain of this Army and has imperilled my entire image of your institution. He has never confronted me concerning either request but has relayed statements through the First Sergeant (who is a war veteran with great sympathy for my position) that I am behaving irresponsibly. Headquarters, I ask you, is it irresponsible of me to request a convalescent leave? I have been fighting this war for a considerable period of time now, exposing myself over and over again to the same dreary set of experiences while around me the company ebbs and flows and the reinforcements creep in darkly. The reinforcements tell me again and again that they do not think that there is any sense to this engagement, and I am compelled to agree with them. This entire action has acquired the aspect of nightmare, I am sorry to say, and although I am not an unstable man, I have found myself becoming, not neurasthenic as previously noted, but truly psychotic. This is terrible ritual, gentlemen, terrible sacrifice, really deadly convolution of the soul. Also, they are stealing my correspondence. I have not been able actually to mail a letter for months even to tell my fiancée that I have terminated our engagement. Gentlemen, I *like* my fiancée and what is more important, after two years of distance, I now wish to make an arrangement to spare her of me. What more significant proof can I provide of insanity? Hoping that you will give this request the most serious consideration and hoping that you will review the folder of the Commanding Officer here very thoroughly indeed, I am sending this letter out by and through devious and covert means. Yours truly, Hastings, serial number posted.

When he was finished, Hastings took the letter to the officers' section and gave it to the First Sergeant, who was cleaning some bits of litter from the top of his desk. He gazed dully at the First Sergeant and asked if it could be submitted through special channels, around the Captain. The First Sergeant gave him a look of wonderment and said that the letter could not possibly pass: it was not written in code as all direct communications to headquarters were compelled to be. Furthermore, the First Sergeant said, he had received exciting news from headquarters: there were plans to start a newspaper which would be distributed by airline to the company; this newspaper would tell them how they were progressing in their battle. The First Sergeant said that headquarters considered it a major breakthrough in morale policy. And, in addition to all of this the First Sergeant whispered, there was one other piece of news which had come through from headquarters which he was not authorized to disclose but which the Captain would make the subject of an address to the troops on this day. The First Sergeant said that this would probably be a revelation even to Hastings, a real surprise from headquarters. Hastings, still thinking about the newspaper, asked if it would contain anything except statistics, and the First Sergeant said there would probably be some editorials written by military experts. Hastings said that he wanted to awaken the Captain. The First Sergeant said that this was impossible because the Captain was already awake; he was drafting his speech, and he was too excited to deal with Hastings now. The First Sergeant added that he agreed that this was a shame. Hastings said that he was at the end of his rope. The Sergeant said that things were getting better: he recommended that Hastings learn headquarters code if he was serious about the message and then re-submit it, and he handed him a book. Hastings saw that the book was really a folder containing sheets of typewriter paper, and he asked the First Sergeant what this was. The First Sergeant explained that this was a copy of his short novel detailing his experiences as a veteran of four wars and eight limited actions. Hastings asked what the hell this had to do with learning code or with sending his message, and the First Sergeant said that he was astonished; he said that Hastings was the only man in the company so far to be offered his novel, and he added that everything in it contained the final answer, if it was only studied. The First Sergeant then said that the convalescent leave business was Hastings' problem, anyway; he had never cracked the code completely himself, and he doubted if it were possible to solve it.

When he came back to his tent, still carrying the First Sergeant's novel in one hand, Hastings decided that he had reached a moment of major crisis. There were obviously no points of reference to this life; he was definitely on his own. All of the company were getting up one by one, discussing the push to the cliffs which they were going to make later in the day. Some of the reinforcements insisted that to achieve the cliffs would be to attain a major objective, but older members of the company gently explained that the battle was probably endless. When they heard this, the reinforcements sat tearfully and had to be persuaded to strike their tents. The First Sergeant came out after a while and called a formation, saying that the Captain was going to address them. When they heard this, the company, even Hastings, became very excited because

the Captain had never talked to any of them before; he
had always been at the end of the marches, saying that he
had to be acclimatized. Now, apparently, he had completed his assessment of the situation, and everybody was
very anxious to find out what he had learned. Also they
were curious, some of them, about his rear end and
figured that at one time or another they would probably
be able to get a glimpse of it now. Standing in the ranks,
Hastings fondled the First Sergeant's novel and his letter
and made a decision: he would present both of them to the
Captain just as soon as he had finished talking. He would
wait until the end of the Captain's speech that was, only if
the speech was very interesting: if the Captain had nothing
to say or only detailed how he intended to further famil-
iarize himself, he would go up to him in the middle and
simply hand him the letter. At least, he would have the
man's attention. This would be a new element in the
situation, right away.

Preceded by the First Sergeant, the Captain came from
his tent and, walking carefully, came in front of the
company. No one could see his buttocks because all of
them were facing in the same direction. The Captain stood
there, nodding, for several minutes, making some notes in
pen on fresh paper, beaming at the motion. Hastings found
this frightening. He had never before noticed how small
the Captain's face was; at this distance it was seen to be
covered with a hideous stubble superimposed over the
features of a very young boy. In spite of all this evidence,
he had not been convinced, apparently, because he wore a
wedding ring. The Captain backed carefully against a tree
and leaned against it, smiling at the company. "Some of
you," he said, "have brought it to the attention of my
First Sergeant that you are unhappy.

"More than unhappiness. I know that you are vitally
concerned. You're concerned because you see no point in
what you're doing. You're concerned because you can't
see how what you are doing affects anything or anybody
else. You're worried about this. This is serious. It is a real
problem.

"It's a legitimate matter of concern, all right. When a group of men such as yourself cannot feel dignity in the work they do, cannot feel that what they do is important to a much larger number of people, they break down. They become nervous. They begin to function in a cold sweat, and sometimes they do not function at all. I have noticed this about one or two of you. But even those I do not condemn. In fact, I have all kinds of sympathy for men in this predicament; it is not pleasant. I know what it can be like. But now and for all of you, this part of your life is over."

The company cheered thinly. Hastings folded his letter and put it away.

"The situation, in fact," said the Captain, "is now entirely changed; more than you would have ever thought possible. *General war has been declared.* The enemy, who have become increasingly provocative in recent weeks, bombed one of our ports of installation last week, reducing it to a pulp. How about that? As a result of this action, the president of the country has declared that a general and total state of war now exists between the countries of the enemy and ourselves. At this moment, troops all over the globe are actively pouring in and out of our military installations; their weapons at the ready!

"Now, what does this mean? I'll tell you what it means. Gentlemen, you are the first. But, you are only the beginning. What you have gone through will be absorbed, will be a spearhead. And when we go out today, we go into these fields with the entire Army, with the country behind us. You are some lucky bunch of fellows. I congratulate all of you, and I congratulate you individually."

After the Captain had finished, he stood against the tree, apparently waiting for the company to disperse, so that he could return to his tent without anyone having seen his rear end. Hastings, weeping, drifted behind him, stood in a clearing, destroyed his letter. The trunk covered the Captain's behind from that angle, too. *I do feel better, already*, Hastings told himself, *I feel better already.* But when the Captain finally gave a cautious look in all directions and started backing slowly from the tree, Hastings took his bayonet and threw it at him, cleaving the left buttock of the Captain, bringing forth a bright scream.

"I still feel lousy," Hastings said.

The Captain had never liked Hastings. Hastings walked in the middle of formations, telling everyone as they went over the mine fields that they were absolutely harmless, a fraud. No one would have taken *any* precautions going over the mine field, if it had not been for the Captain running behind them. Some of the men picked up stones and threw them at each other; some men said the war would never end. When things got utterly out of hand, the Captain would have to shout at the troops, at distances of hundreds of yards he found himself bellowing and, even then, the company would not listen. All of this traced back to Hastings. He was destroying the morale of the company. The Captain suspected that, beneath all of this, Hastings was trying to sink the progress of the limited war.

In addition to saying that the mine field was just as safe as a playground, this Hastings was a letter writer. He wrote letters to everyone; now he had written a request to headquarters (which was peculiar enough already; the messages coming from headquarters now were enough to confuse anyone, let alone a Captain just trying to get acclimated), giving his situation and asking for convalescent leave; he cited obscure regulations. The Captain knew, of course, that if he forwarded this material to headquarters, two or three field grade officers would come out in a jeep, capture Hastings and place him in a hospital for mental cases, and the Captain wanted to spare Hastings this. He was governed, then, by common if causeless, feelings of mercy but nevertheless, there was Hastings, insisting that his form go through. The Captain did not know what to do with him. In the first place, he had only been with this company for six weeks and he was having all he could do to get acclimated to the situation; in the second place, he badly missed his wife and the cottage they had had in officers' quarters on a small post in the Southern tier. Furthermore, the Captain found himself wondering at odd moments in the night whether the war effort would truly be successful. There seemed to be some very peculiar elements about it. The bombing was so highly irregular, and some of the pilots did not seem to be very interested; they dropped bombs on their own side and also flew out of pattern. In addition, some of the men in the company had become attached to a certain part of the terrain; they were maintaining now that the entire purpose of the war was to secure and live permanently within it. The Captan did not know what to do about this. Also, Hastings waited outside of his tent often, trying to find out what he was doing with the leave request, and the Captain found that his free rights of access and exit were being severely limited, above and beyond the Army code.

The Captain had nothing against the war. It was all working out the way the preparation courses had taught. Certainly, it had its strange facets: the enemy also seemed to be attached to the forest part of the map and fought bitterly for the retention of certain cherished trees, but things like this were normal in stress situations anyway; after a while, all conflicts, all abstractions came down, in a group of limited men, to restricted areas. The Captain had been trained to see things in this fashion, and he had also been given a good deal of instruction in the intricacies of troop morale. So, he understood the war; he understood it very well. There was no doubt about that. *However,* the Academy had neglected to prepare him for Hastings. There was no one like Hastings at the Academy, even in a clean-up capacity. The Captain had taken to writing his young wife long letters on stationery he had borrowed from his First Sergeant (a war veteran of four major conflicts and eight limited actions), telling her all about the situation, adding that it was very odd and strained but that he hoped to have matters cleaned up by the end of the year, that is, if he was ever unleashed. Other than this, he did not write her about the war at all but instead wrote at length about certain recollections he had of their court-ship, entirely new insights. In the relaxation of the war, he found that he was able to gather astonishing perceptions into the very quality of his life, and he told his wife the reasons for his action at given times, asked her if she understood. *We will get to the bottom of this,* he often reminded her, *if only you will co-operate.* His wife's letters in return were sometimes argumentative, sometimes disturbed; she told him that he was wasting his energy in the forgotten wastes, and that all of his strength was now needed to become acclimated to a new situation. When he read these letters, the Captain found that, unreasonably, he wanted to cry, but his bunk was too near to that of his First Sergeant, and he was ashamed. None of the officers wanted to be caught crying by the First Sergeant, a combat veteran.

Meanwhile, the Captain found that his communications with headquarters were being blocked for days at a time, and also that his messages, when they did come, were increasingly peculiar. Sometimes, the Captain succumbed briefly to the feeling that headquarters did not truly understand the situation, but he put such thoughts away quickly. Thinking them or putting them away; it made no difference, he was almost always depressed. *Continue on as you have done, worry not,* headquarters would tell him three days later in response to a routine inquiry. Or, *we are preparing new strategy here and ask you to hold line while formulating.* Such things were highly disturbing; there was simply no doubt about it.

One morning near Christmas, the Captain went through a near-disaster, a partial catastrophe. The First Sergeant came into his tent and told him that Hastings was thinking of submitting a letter to headquarters directly on the subject of his convalescent leave. The Captain said that he could not believe that even Hastings would be crazy enough to do something like that, and the First Sergeant said that this might well be true but, nevertheless,

Hastings had brought in some kind of a letter that morning, and asked to have it forwarded. The Captain asked the First Sergeant if he could see the letter, and the First Sergeant said that he had told Hastings to go away with it but that Hastings had promised to come back later. The Captain put on some old fatigues and went out into the forest in real grief; he looked at Hastings' tent, which was of a peculiar, greyish shade, and he sighed. Hastings was sitting outside the tent on his knees with his back to the Captain, scribbling something in the dirt with a stick. The Captain decided that he was ill; he did not want to have anything whatever to do with Hastings. Instead, he went back to his tent intending to sleep some more, but when he got there, the First Sergeant was waiting for him with astonishing news. He told the Captain that somehow a message *had* gotten through on Hastings because some Corporal was up from headquarters saying he had orders to put Hastings away in the asylum. When the Captain heard this, he felt himself possessed by absolute fury, and he told the First Sergeant that he was running this company and he refused to take treatment like this from anyone. The First Sergeant said that he absolutely agreed with the Captain and he would go out to deal with the Corporal, but the Captain said that, for once, *he* was going to handle the situation the way it should be. He told the First Sergeant to leave him alone, and then he went over to a clearing where the Corporal sat in a jeep and told him that Hastings had been killed a few hours ago in an abortive attack and was being buried. The Corporal said that that was a rotten shame because everyone in headquarters had heard the story and was really anxious to find out what kind of lunatic this Hastings was. The Captain said that he could tell him stories but he would not and ordered the Corporal to return to his unit. After the Corporal had explained that he was in an administrative capacity and therefore not at all vulnerable to the Captain's orders, he got in the jeep and said that he would go gack to his unit and report what had happened. He asked the Captain if Hastings had had any special characteristics which should be noted in a condolence letter. The Captain said that Hastings had always been kind of an individualist and forceful in his own way; also he was highly motivated, if somewhat unrealistic. The Corporal said that this would be useful and he drove away. For almost an hour, the Captain found himself unable to move from the spot, but after a while, he was able to remember the motions of walking, and he stumbled back to his tent and began a long letter to his wife. *I gave an order today in a very difficult capacity,* he began it, but he decided that this was no good and instead started, *I have become fully acclimated to the situation here at last and feel that I am at the beginning of my best possibilities: do you remember how ambitious I used to be?* After he wrote this, he found that he had absolutely nothing else to write and, thinking of his wife's breasts, put the paper away and went for a long walk. Much later, he decided that what had happened had been for the good; it was only a question now of killing Hastings, and then he could begin to take control.

The First Sergeant had nothing to do with things, anymore. He slept a twisted sleep, crawling with strange shapes, and in the morning, the First Sergeant awakened him, saying that headquarters had just sent in a communique declaring that a total-win policy was now in effect; war had been declared. When the Captain heard this, he became quite excited and began to feel better about many things; he asked the First Sergeant if he thought that it meant that the company was now unleashed, and the First Sergeant said that he was positive that that was what had happened. The Captain said that this would definitely take care of Hastings; they could work him out of the way very easily now, and he added that he had studied the morale problem of troops: now he was going to be able to put it into effect. Troops, he said, were willing to get involved in anything, but if they felt they were being used to no good purpose, they tended to get childish and stubborn. The Captain felt so good about this that he invited the First Sergeant to forget things and look at one of his wife's recent letters, but the First Sergeant said that he felt he knew the Captain's wife already and, besides, he had to make preparation for the war; he had real responsibilities. The First Sergeant explained that this would be his fifth war, but since each one was like a new beginning, he felt as if he had never been in combat before and he wanted to make some notes. The Captain said that this was fine, and then, right on the instant, he decided to make a speech to the company. He requisitioned two sheets of bond paper from the First Sergeant and sat down to draft it, but he found himself so filled with happy thoughts of Hastings impending assassination that he was unable to keep still, and so he decided to speak extemporaneously. He knew that he could deal with the company in the right way. When he was quite sure that he was in the proper mood to make the speech, he ordered the First Sergeant to call a formation, and when the First Sergeant came back to tell him that all of the men were assembled, he walked out slowly behind the First Sergeant, knowing how good a picture he was making. He stood near a tree for shelter, and smiled at all of the men, especially Hastings, but Hastings, looking at something in his hands, did not see the smile and that, the Captain decided, was Hastings' loss. It was one more indication, this way of thinking, of how well he had finally become acclimated. Everything, after all, was only a matter of time.

"You men," the Captain said, "are plenty upset because you see no purpose in this whole operation. In fact, it seems absolutely purposeless to you, a conclusion with which I am in utter sympathy. It is no fun when emptiness replaces meaning; when despair replaces motive. I know all about this; I have shared it with you over and over.

"Today, we mount another attack and many wonder; what is the point? it's all the same; it always was. We've been back and forth so many times, what the hell's the difference, now?

"In line with this, I want to tell you something now, something that will, I am convinced, change the entire picture in your minds and hearts. *Something is different;*

things have changed. We are now in a state of war with the enemy. Our ports of installation were bombed last night; in return, our president has declared that we are now in a position of total war. How about that?

"Before we have finished our mission now, ten thousand, a million men will have shared our losses, our glories, our commitments, our hopes. And yet, because these began with us, essentially we are the creators of the war.

"Are we fortunate? I do not know. Such is our responsibility. Such is our honor."

After the Captain had finished, he stood near the tree for a long while, marvelling at his speech. There was no question but that it had gotten right through to the middle of the situation; it left no room for any doubt of any kind. Surely he had, just as he had promised, become fully acclimated and now, *now* there was no stopping him at all. And it took care of that Hastings; it took care of him but good. The next step for Hastings was darkness. Therefore, the Captain was enormously surprised when he saw Hastings, grinning hysterically, come toward him, a bayonet shining in his hand. It just showed you, if you didn't know it well already, that there was just no predicting anything with enlisted men. Before the Captain could move, Hastings raised his arm and threw the instrument at the Captain.

"What are you doing?" the Captain screamed. "I'm your Commanding Officer in the midst of a war!"

"I still say I'm not crazy!" Hastings screamed.

"We're in the middle of a war!" the Captain said, dying. But Hastings, apparently quite mad now, would not listen.

The First Sergeant had never liked Hastings or the Captain. Both of them were crazy; there was no doubt about it. Hastings, a Private, told everyone in the company that the mine fields were a sham, quite safe, really, and the Captain insisted that they were ready to fire. When the company walked over the mine fields, Hastings cursed to the troops that they were a bunch of cowards, and the Captain, his stupid ass waving, fell to the end of the formation and screamed at them to keep going. The two of them were wrecking the company, making the entire situation (which had had such potential, such really nice things in it) impossible. The war *was* peculiar, there was no question about this, but there were ways to get around it and get a job done. But the two of them, Hastings and the Captain, were lousing things up. The First Sergeant found himself so furious with their business that after a while he could not even keep his communiques straight: all the headquarters messages were getting screwed up in the decode because he was too upset to do it right and no one would leave him alone. There was no sense to most of the messages; they all seemed to say the same thing anyway, and the First Sergeant knew that headquarters were a pack of morons; he had decided this three days after he had taken over his job and began getting their idiotic messages. Meanwhile, the new Captain would not leave him alone; all that he wanted to talk about was Hastings. It was Hastings, the Captain said loudly to the First Sergeant, who was fouling everything up. He asked the First Sergeant if there might be any procedures to get Hastings to keep quiet, because everything that had gone wrong was all his fault. Over and over again, the Captain asked the First Sergeant to figure out a way to get rid of Hastings *without* giving him convalescent leave. All of this was bad enough for the First Sergeant but then, on top of all of this, there was Hastings himself hanging around all the time, trying to find out things about the Captain, asking if the men had yet initialled his request. All in all, it was just ridiculous, what they were doing to him. When the First Sergeant decided to do what he did, he had every excuse in the world for it. They were a pack of lunatics. They were out of control. They deserved no mercy.

One morning, for instance, around Thanksgiving, the Captain woke the First Sergeant to say that he had figured out the entire situation: Hastings was insane. He was investing, said the Captain, terrible dependency in an effort to become a child again and his functioning was entirely unsound. The Captain asked the First Sergeant if he felt that this was reasonable and whether or not he thought that Hastings belonged in some kind of institution. The First Sergeant, who had been up very late trying to organize some confusing communiques from headquarters in relation to the Thanksgiving supper, said that he was not sure but that he would think some about it, and if the Captain wanted him to, he would even check into Army regulations. He added that Hastings might have combat fatigue, something that he had seen in a lot of men through the course of four wars and eight limited actions; some men were simply weaker than others. The point here was that the First Sergeant was trying to be as decent to both the Captain and Hastings as any man could be, but there were limits. Later that day, Hastings found him sitting behind a tree and told him that he had figured out the whole thing: the Captain was obviously mad. He suggested that the First Sergeant help him prepare a report to headquarters listing all of the peculiar actions of the Captain and asked for some clean paper to do this. Hastings added that he though that most of the Captain's problem could be traced back to his shame over his rear end. The rear end made the Captain look feminine, said Hastings, and the Captain was reacting to this in a very normal, if unfortunate, fashion. The First Sergeant said that he didn't know enough about modern psychiatry to give an opinion on that one way or the other. Hastings asked the First Sergeant to simply *consider* it, and the First Sergeant said that he would do that. After a while, Hastings left, saying that the First Sergeant had hurt him.

In all of this, then, it could be seen that the First Sergeant had acted entirely correctly, in entire justice. He was in a difficult position but he was doing the best he could. No claims could be made against him that he was not doing his job. But, in spite of all the times the First Sergeant repeated this to himself, he found that, finally, he was getting good and fed up with the whole thing. There were, he decided, natural limits to all circumstances and

Hastings, headquarters, the Captain and the war were passing theirs; after a point simply no part of it was his responsibility, any more.

This, the First Sergeant told the officers who knew enough to listen, was his fourth war and eighth limited action, not counting various other difficulties he had encountered during his many years in the Army. Actually, this was not entirely true, but the First Sergeant had taken to feeling that it was, which was almost better. The truth of the situation, which the First Sergeant kept to himself except for occasional letters to his wife was that he had worked in a division motor pool for fifteen years before he had been reassigned to the company, and that reassignment had been something of a fluke, hinging on the fact that the company had, before the days of the limited war, been established as a conveyance unit, and the First Sergeant had absent-mindedly been assigned as a mechanic. That things had worked out this way was probably the fault of headquarters; at least, the First Sergeant did not question them on *that* score.

Early in the career of the First Sergeant, he had accidentally shot a General while in rifle training. The General, fortunately had only lost an ear which, he had laughingly told the First Sergeant at the court-martial, he could spare because he never heard that much that was worth hearing, anyway. The General, however, claimed that the First Sergeant had had no right to shoot at him when he was in the process of troop-inspection, even if the shots had only been fired from excitement, as was the claim of the First Sergeant's defence. The General said that he felt the best rehabilitative action for the First Sergeant, under all the principles of modern social action, would be to be shot himself, although not in the ear. When the First Sergeant heard this, he stood up in court and said that for the first time in his life, he was ashamed that he had chosen to enlist in the Army.

When the head of the court, a Major, heard this, he asked the First Sergeant to stay calm and state, just off the record, what he wanted to do with his life. When the First

Sergeant said that all he wanted to do was to make an honorable career and a First Sergeancy (at this time he had been considerably less, a Private in fact), the Major advised the General that the First Sergeant would probably have to be treated differently from the run of the mine soldier, and the General said that he found the First Sergeant's testimony very moving. It was agreed to fine the First Sergeant one month's salary every month for the next five years and send him to automobile training in the Far North. The General said that he could think of some places right off the top of his head where the First Sergeant might do well, but he reminded him that he would have to remember to cut down very sharply now on all of his expenses as he would be living on somewhat of a limited budget.

The First Sergeant learned to live frugally (even now, he was still forgetting to pick up his pay when headquarters delivered it; he was always astonished) and repaired vehicles for fourteen years, but inwardly, he was furious. Because of his duties in the motor pool he lost out on several wars and limited actions, and also, his wife (whom he married before he enlisted) was ashamed that he had not been killed, as had the husbands of many of her friends. As a result of this, he and his wife eventually had an informal separation, and the First Sergeant (who *was* by then a First Sergeant) took to telling people just being sent into the motor pool that he personally found this work a great relief after fighting one war and three limited actions. They seemed to believe him, which was fine, but the First Sergeant still had the feeling that he was being deprived of the largest segment of his possibilities. He moved into a barracks with a platoon of younger troops and taught them all the war songs he knew.

In September of his next to last year in the Army, the First Sergeant fell into enormous luck. He often felt that it had all worked out something like a combat movie. A jeep for whose repair he had been responsible exploded while parked in front of a whorehouse, severely injuring a Lieutenant Colonel and his aide-de-camp who were waiting, they later testified, for the area to be invaded by civilian police. They had received advance warning and had decided to be on the premises for the protection of enlisted men. As a result of the investigation which followed, the aide-de-camp was reduced to the rank of Corporal and sent to give hygienic lectures to troops in the far lines of combat. The Lieutenant Colonel was promoted to Colonel, and the First Sergeant was sent to the stockade for six weeks. When he was released, he was given back all of his stripes and told by a civilian board of review that he was going to be sent into troop transport. The head of the board said that this would extend his experience considerably, and told him that he would be on the site of, although not actually engaged in, a limited action war. Standing in front of the six men, his hastily re-sewn stripes trembling, the First Sergeant had been unable to comprehend his stunning fortune. It seemed entirely out of control. Later, getting instructions from an officer, he found that he would take over the duties of a conveyance First Sergeant in an important action being conducted secretly on a distant coast. As soon as he could talk, the First Sergeant asked if he could have three days convalescent leave, and the officer said that regulations would cover this, he was entitled to it because of the contributions he had made.

The First Sergeant borrowed a jeep and drove several hundred miles from post to a dark town in which his separated wife worked as a waitress. He found her sitting alone in the balcony of a movie house, watching a combat film and crying absently. At first, she wanted nothing at all to do with him, but after he told her what had happened to him, she touched him softly and said that she could not believe it had worked out. They went to a hotel together, because her landlady did not believe in her boarders being with other people, and talked for a long time; and for the first time, the First Sergeant said that he was frightened at what was happening as well as grateful. He had been away for so long that he did not know if he could trust himself. His wife said that finally, after fifteen years, she felt proud, and she told him that she knew he would do well. Later on he remembered that. But he never remembered answering her that only distress can make a man.

They went to bed together and it was almost good; they almost held together until the very end, but then everything began to come to pieces. The First Sergeant said that he would probably not be able to write her letters because he was going to an area of high security, and she said that this was perfectly all right with her as long as the allotment checks were not interrupted. When he heard this, the Sergeant began to shake with an old pain and he told her that the jeep had blown up because he had deliberately failed to replace a bad fuel connection. She told him that if this were so, he deserved anything that happened to him. He told her that nothing he had ever done had been his fault, and she said that he disgusted her.

After that, both of them got dressed, feeling terrible, and the First Sergeant drove the jeep at a grotesque speed toward the post. In the middle of the trip he found that he could not drive for a while, and he got out and vomited, the empty road raising dust in his eyes, the lights of occasional cars pinning him helplessly against dry foliage.

When the First Sergeant came to the company, they were just at the true beginning of the limited war, and he was able to get hold of matters almost immediately. The first thing that he learned was that his predecessor had been given a transfer for reasons of emotional incompetence and had been sent back to the country as the head of a motor pool. The second thing he found out was that his job was completely non-combatant, involving him only in the communications detail. When the First Sergeant discovered that his duties involved only decoding, assortment and relay of communiques from division headquarters to the company and back again, he felt, at first, a feeling of enormous betrayal, almost as if he had been in the Army all his life to discover that there was absolutely no reason for it at all. The Captain of this company communicated with headquarters from one hundred to one hundred and fifty times a day; he tried to keep himself posted on everything including the latest procedure for morale-retention. Other officers also had messages, and in the meanwhile, enlisted personnel were constantly handing him money, begging him to send back a hello to relatives through headquarters. The First Sergeant found this repulsive but the worst of it was to trudge at the rear of formations while in combat, loaded with ten to fifteen pieces of radio equipment and carrying enormous stacks of paper which he was expected to hand to the officers at any time that they felt in need of writing. In addition, his pockets were stuffed with headquarters communiques which the Captain extracted from time to time. It was a humiliating situation; it was the worst thing that had ever happened to him. When they were not in battle, the First Sergeant was choked with cross-communiques; it became impossible for him to conceive of a life lacking them: he sweated, breathed and slept surrounded by sheets of paper. He took to writing his wife short letters, telling her, in substance that everything she had said was absolutely right. In what free time he had, he requisitioned a stopwatch and tried to figure out his discharge date in terms of minutes, seconds, and fifths of seconds.

Then, at the beginning of the first summer, the First Sergeant had his second and final stroke of luck, and it looked for a long while as if everything had worked out for the best after all. He stopped writing letters to his wife almost immediately after the Captain was called back to headquarters and a new, a younger Captain was assigned to the command. This new Captain was not at all interested in communications; he told the First Sergeant the first day he was in that before he got involved in a flow of messages, he had first to become acclimated to the situation. That was perfectly all right with the First Sergeant; immediately he saw the change working through in other things; it was magical. Messages from headquarters seemed to diminish; there were days when they could be numbered in the tens, and the First Sergeant found that he had more time to himself; he started to write a short novel about his combat experiences in four wars and eight limited actions. Also, his role in combat had shifted drastically. Perhaps because of the new Captain's familiarization policy, he was permitted to carry a rifle with him, and now and then, he even took a cautious shot, being careful to point the instrument in the air, so that there would be no danger of hitting anyone on his own side. Once, quite accidentally, he hit one of the enemy's trees (they were attacking the forest that day) and destroyed a shrub; it was one of the most truly important moments of his life. Meanwhile, the new Captain said that he would contact headquarters eight times a day and that would be that.

The First Sergeant moved into one of the most wholly satisfactory periods of his life. His wife's letters stopped abruptly after she said she had been promoted to the position of hostess, and he quietly cut his allotment to her by three dollars a month; no one seemed to know the difference. He went to bed early and found that he slept the night through, but often he was up at four o'clock because starting each new day was such a pleasure. Then, just as the First Sergeant had come to the amazed conviction that he was not by any means an accursed man, Hastings came acutely to his consciousness.

Hastings, who was some kind of Private, had put in for convalescent leave months before, during the bad time of the First Sergeant's life, but the old Captain had handled the situation very well. Now, the new Captain said that he had to be acclimated to the situation, and so it was the First Sergeant's responsibility to deal with Hastings, to tell him that the Captain could not be distracted at this time. For a while, Hastings listened to this quietly and went, but suddenly, for no apparent reason, he submitted *another* request for leave. From that moment, the difficult peace of the First Sergeant was at an end. Hastings insisted that this message had to reach the Captain, and the First

Sergeant told him that it would be forwarded, but the Captain refused to take it because he said that he was in an adjustment stage. So, the First Sergeant kept the request in his desk, but then Hastings began coming into the tent every day to ask what action the Captain had finally taken. The First Sergeant knew right away that Hastings was crazy because he had a wild look in his eyes, and he also said that the Captain was a coward for not facing him. In addition to that, Hastings began to look up the First Sergeant at odd times of the day to say that the Captain was functioning in a very unusual way; something would have to be done. When the First Sergeant finally decided that he had had enough of this, he went to the Captain and told him what was going on and asked him if he would, at least, look at this crazy Hastings' request, but the Captain said that it would take him at least several months to be acculturated to the degree where he would be able to occupy a judgmental role; in the meantime, he could not be disturbed by strange requests. Then, the Captain leaned over his desk and said that, just between them, he felt that Hastings was crazy: he was not functioning like an adult in a situation made for men. When he heard this, the First Sergeant laughed wildly and relayed this message to Hastings, hoping that it would satisfy him and that now the man would finally leave him alone, but Hastings said that all of this just proved his point: the Captain was insane. Hastings asked the First Sergeant if he would help him to get the Captain put away. *All* of this was going on then; the Captain saying one thing and Hastings another, both of them insane; and in addition to this, the limited war was still going on; it was going on as if it would never stop which, of course, it would not. The First Sergeant would have written his wife again if he had not completely forgotten her address and previously thrown away all of her letters.

Hastings and the Captain were on top of him all the time now, and neither of them had the faintest idea of what they were doing. Only a man who had been through four wars and eight limited actions would comprehend how serious the war effort was. Three days a week the company had a *forest* to capture; three days a week they had the cliffs to worry about, and on Mondays they had all of the responsibility of reconnoitering and planning *strategy*, and all of this devolved on the First Sergeant; nevertheless, neither of them would leave him alone. The First Sergeant had more duties than any man could handle: he supervised the officers' tents and kept up the morale of the troops; he advised the officers of the lessons of his experience, and he had to help some of the men over difficult personal problems; no one, not even a combat veteran such as himself, could handle it. He slept poorly now, threw up most of his meals, found his eyesight wavering so that he could not handle his rifle in combat, and he decided that he was, at last, falling apart under the strain. If he had not had all of his obligations, he would have given up then. They were that ungrateful, the whole lot of them. Hastings, the Captain; the Captain, Hastings: they were both lunatics, and on top of that, there was the matter of the tents and the communications. One night, the First Sergeant had his penultimate inspiration. In an agony of wild cunning, he decided that there was only one way to handle things. And what was better, he knew that he was right. No one could have approached his level of functioning.

He got up at three o'clock in the morning and crept through the forest to the communications tent and carefully, methodically, lovingly, he tore down the equipment, so that it could not possibly transmit, and then he furiously reconstructed it so that it looked perfect again. Then, he sat up until reveille, scribbling out headquarters communiques, and he marked *DELIVERED* in ink on all of the company's messages to headquarters. After breakfast, he gave these messages to the Captain, and the Captain took them and said that they were typical headquarters crap; they were the same as ever. The Captain said then that sometimes, just occasionally, you understand, he thought

that Hastings might have a point, after all. The First
Sergeant permitted himself to realize that he had stumbled
on to an extremely large concept; it was unique. Nothing
that day bothered him at all.

The next morning, he got up early again and crept
through the cliffs to the communications tent and wrote
out three headquarters messages advising the Captain to
put his First Sergeant on the point. When the Captain
read these, he looked astonished and said that this had
been his idea entirely; the First Sergeant led the column
that day, firing his rifle gleefully at small birds overhead.
He succumbed to a feeling of enormous power and, to test
it, wrote out no messages at all for the next two days,
meanwhile keeping the company's messages in a *DELIV-
ERED* status. The Captain said that this was a pleasure,
the bastards should only shut up all the time like this. On
the third day, the First Sergeant wrote out a message ordering that company casualties be made heavier to prove
interest in the war effort; two men were surreptitiously shot
that day in combat by the Junior-Grade Lieutenants. By
then, the First Sergeant had already decided that, without
question, he had surpassed any of the efforts of western
civilization throughout five hundred generations of modern
thought.

Headquarters seemed to take no notice. Their supply
trucks came as always; enlisted men looked around and
cursed with the troops and then went back. They did not
even ask to see the First Sergeant because he had let it be
known that he was too busy to be bothered. The First
Sergeant got into schedule, taking naps in the afternoon so
that he could refer daily stacks of headquarters messages
in the early morning. One morning, he found that he felt
so exceptionally well that he repaired the equipment,
transmitted Hastings' request for convalescent leave without a tremor, affixed the Captain's code counter-signature,
and then destroyed the radio for good. It seemed the least
that he could do in return for his good luck.

This proved to be the First Sergeant's last error. A day
later, a Corporal came from headquarters to see the

Captain, and later the Captain came looking for the First Sergeant, his white face stricken with confusion. He asked who the hell had allowed that Hastings to sneak into the tent and thus get hold of the equipment? The First Sergeant said that he did not know anything about it, but it was perfectly plausible that this could happen; he had other duties and he had to leave the radio, sometime or other. The Captain said that this was fine because headquarters had now ordered Hastings' recall and had arranged for him to be put in a hospital. The Corporal had come up to say something about a psychiatric discharge. The First Sergeant said that he would handle this, and he started to go to the Corporal to say that Hastings had just died, but the Captain followed and said that this was not necessary because he himself had had Hastings' future decided; he would take care of things now. The Captain said that Hastings was not going to get out of any damned company of his any way at all; he would make things so hot for that lunatic now that it would not be funny for anyone at all. The Captain said that *he* was in control of the situation and there was no doubt about that whatsoever. The Sergeant left the Captain's presence and went outside to cry for half an hour, but when he came back, he found the space empty, and he knew exactly what he was going to do. He stayed away from the Captain until nightfall and, as soon as it was safe, dictated a total war communique. In the morning, breathing heavily, he delivered it to the Captain. The Captain read it over twice and drooled. He said that this was the best thing that had ever happened to anyone in the entire unfortunate history of the Army. He said that he would go out immediately and make a speech to his troops. The First Sergeant said that he guessed that this would be all right with him; if he inspired them, it could count for some thing in combat.

The First Sergeant did not even try to listen to the mad Captain's idiotic speech. He only stood behind and waited for it to finish. When Hastings came over after it was done and cut the Captain's rear end harmlessly with a bayonet, the First Sergeant laughed like hell. But, later, when he went to the broken equipment, wondering if he could ever set it up again, he was not so sure that it was funny. He wondered if he might not have done, instead, the most terrible thing of his entire life. Much later and under different circumstances, he recollected that he had not.

2001: A SPACE ODYSSEY—

Directed and produced by *Stanley Kubrick*
Screenplay by *Stanley Kubrick*
and *Arthur C. Clarke*
The cast includes:
Keir Dullea . . . . Bowman
Gary Lockwood . . . . Poole
Douglas Rain . . . . Hal 9000

SOME SELECTED REVIEWS

This volume attempts to include the best science fiction of the year. The biggest SF event of the past twelve months has certainly been the motion picture that afficionados refer to as "Twenty-oh-one." In addition to making a great deal of money for all concerned, this film seems to have provided a constantly renewing source of speculation and comment. When people discover that I am associated with the world of science fiction a great many of them— from children to college professors—all ask the same question. What did it mean? I now give them the answer. Or rather four answers. All of them quite positive. All of them different. Here del Ray speaks for Galaxy, Delany *and Emshwiller for* Fantasy and Science Fiction (*one for fantasy and one for science?*), *while the good Doctor Stover devoted all of his* Amazing *science column to a*

125

*point by point analysis of every detail. Here are the facts.
Now you know.*
   I think . . .

Reviewed by LESTER DEL REY

Nobody slept at the New York press preview of *2001,*
but only because the raucous and silly noise from the
sound track screamed painfully into our ears. Space was a
tumult of din and the hero breathed in his spacesuit like a
monstrous locomotive at 60 gasps a minute. It was the
only evidence of excitement in the place. Almost half of
the audience had left by intermission, and most of us who
stayed did so from curiosity and to complete our reviews.

The pictorial part was superb. The color photography
was generally excellent, and the special effects and technical tricks were the best ever done. Even the acting was
unusually good. With all that, Stanley Kubrick and Arthur
C. Clarke should have given us the superlative movie
promised by a barrage of publicity. If they had put
Clarke's *Earthlight* on the screen with equal genius, it
would have been a great science-fiction movie. Unfortunately, they didn't. Instead they gave us dullness and
confusion.

The whole affair dragged. Every trick had to be
stretched interminably and then repeated over and over
again. Nothing was explained or given coherent flow, but
everything was run on to boredom. Further cutting might
help; surely it couldn't hurt.

The story staggers through four vaguely related episodes. First we get the theme of man's humanoid ancestors
being given intelligence by an alien slab only to become
murderers. Next we go to the moon to find future men
have dug up the same slab—excellent background but no
drama—and no reason for it being there. Then we take a
trip to Jupiter because—as we learn eventually—men
think the slab came from there.

This episode has a conflict between men and an articu-
late computer. It might have been good, except for the lack

of rationality. No motivation is provided for the computer's going mad, and the hero acts like a fool. He knows the computer can't be trusted, and we've seen that the computer can at least operate a rescue craft to bring back his dead friend. But he goes out himself, leaving his companions in hibernation to be killed by the computer.

Finally, we get an endless run of obvious and empty symbols on the screen, followed by our hero in a strange room. Apparently he's undergone intergalactic transfer and now grows old and dies in the room, followed by a metaphysical symbol at the end. The alien contact we've been promised is no more than a brief shot of the slab again.

If possible wait to see it for the effects until you can buy the soft cover book. Book and movie don't entirely agree, but maybe the book will provide some relief to the confusion of the movie.

The real message, of course, is one Kubrick has used before: intelligence is perhaps evil and certainly useless. The humanoid reaction and pointless madness of the computer show this. Men can only be saved by some vague and unshown mystic experience by aliens.

This isn't a normal science-fiction movie at all, you see. It's the first of the New Wave-Thing movies, with the usual empty symbolism. The New Thing advocates were exulting over it as a mind-blowing experience. It takes very little to blow some minds. But for the rest of us, it's a disaster.

It will probably be a box-office disaster, too, and thus set major science-fiction movie making back another ten years.

It's a great pity.

Reviewed by SAMUEL R. DELANY

Once past the titles, you see landscapes: muted earth colors, yellows, lots of rock, little vegetation. The feeling is horizontal stasis. Almost every line is as long as the horizon itself. The point of view is immobile.

In the penultimate sequence, you are propelled with fantastic energy through landscapes full of verticals: crags, mesas, canyons, waves and precipices, as rich and violent as the opening ones are serene. Some of the scenes are solarized, some are developed with color replacement techniques that increase the visual violence.

The journey between the two is an odyssey that takes a million or so years. We watch proto-humans begin it with a brilliant sequence in which men/apes learn to distinguish the subjective from the objective, and so invent tools, first used to gain food, then as weapons against their own kind. At its end a starchild, man-become-something-more-than-man, moves through space inside a translucent amnion, regarding the planet earth. The journey has unexpected twists, goes in many odd directions, is ultimately circular; and great steps of it are bridged in the space between two frames of film.

Kubrick concentrates perhaps two-thirds of his vision on one "moment" of the journey: the incidents up to and including the nine month expedition of the space ship *Discovery* to Jupiter. The ship is seeking, unbeknownst to the two conscious humans on the crew, still another of the possibly-sentient slabs that have stood as guide posts since the beginning of the journey. In this section of film, the images are highly mechanized. People talk to one another, make speeches, listen to orders (and in the un-cut version, one set of orders is run twice verbatim to great ironic effect), and only moments later do we realize that the information content is nil. Machines on the vast cinerama screen, showing jeweled Lunar and trans-Lunar nights, dance, offer themselves to one another, supplicate and entreat each other: in one scene, mechanical hands bear a corpse before an implacable, sperm-shaped space ship whose computer-brain has possibly gone ". . . half crazy over the love of you . . ." Throughout this center section of the movie, Kubrick carefully creates a gravity-less universe; as the film progresses, concepts like *up* and *down* disintegrate under the cinerama medium, until at last a human standing with his head pointing straight at the audience has the same visual weight as another standing "upright" in the same frames. In the un-cut version we were given a long and lyric sequence of Gary Lockwood walking, running, jogging about the walls of a great, circular room. The original length of the scene gave the audience time to make the very difficult translation of their own physical movements into this new space. Now the scene is considerably truncated, and in the viscera (or more accurately, in the dark coils of the middle ear) where the film grabs, the hold is a little looser.

But even with the excised twenty minutes (cut by Kubrick himself after the first blunderings began to come through from critics completely at a loss over what to do with a film so blatantly unconcerned with the nineteenth century problems of human mistakes grown from the passions—rather than the intellect, the spirit, or defects in other sensibilities) the bones are still very much intact.

The problems in interpreting the film do not lie in the visual glut of the closing half hour. With all its complex and exquisite imagery, I think everyone will agree it is a visualization of rebirth. The problem throws us back to the ship *Discovery*: what sort of man is being reborn?

Two men and a computer are the three conscious entities that make the voyage. By the time the ship is in Jupiter space, the computer has killed one of the conscious men (and all three of the ones in hibernation), and the survivor has lobotomized the computer. But all three are presented as dehumanized products of a bureaucratic culture where people congratulate one another on how well they can use jargon to avoid saying anything.

When Keir Dullea undergoes transmogrification, is he a hero who is being rewarded for avenging his companion? Is he the murderer who destroyed the only "mind" on the expedition that understood the real purpose of the journey? Or is he a purely mechanical person acting soley under the dictates of the situation, and who bears no moral weight one way or the other? These are the interpretive decisions the audience has to make before it can decide whether it agrees or disagrees with what Kubrick is saying. Whether one agrees or not, the argument is austere and staggering. The pacing (at least in the original) was elegant and stately, and set the viewer up magnificently for the final explosion of light, sound, and imagistic juxtaposition.

The amazing white on white on white scenes in the Orbiting Hilton (cf. the unpainted apartment in Godard's technicolor, cinemascope film *Contempt*) is an incredible visual dare that works. There are myriad little gems like this for the buff. For the rest of us there is an amazing amount of visual excitement. It is not the excitement of fast-cutting. In cinerama, three hours of that and you'd be ready for dramamine and cornea transplants. It is simply that the images and objects are presented with superb visual intelligence: they are exciting to look at, and they are exciting to think about after you have looked at them.

Reviewed by ED EMSHWILLER

When Ed Ferman phoned and asked if I'd write a short review of Stanley Kubrick's movie *2001: A Space Odyssey*, I gladly agreed. I had one strong reservation, however. I've maintained ever since I got involved in making films myself that I hated all critics and reviewers, and here I was, agreeing to join the "enemy" ranks. All my complaints about how inadequate and myopic all such reviews are seem to have come home. Now I have the problem of trying, in a few words, to say something about another man's film, something I'm hesitant to do even with my own work.

So, after all the hemming and hawing, let me say I liked the movie. I recommend it to people who are interested in cinema, to those who are interested in expanding the variety of their experiences, and to those who are interested in science fiction. But, to all those who go to the movies for ritualistic involvement in a standard adventure story, beware. The film does have one strongly dramatic sequence which is quite effective, but that drama and its resolution is not the basis of the film, merely an episode, and if you are going to savour the picture, you must enjoy other aspects as well. For example, what I would call the second sequence in the picture is a beautifully choreo-graphed passage with just a space ship, a space station, the earth, and the stars. There is no "action" except the docking of the ship to the station. The pace is unhurried, as is true of much of the picture, yet this sequence, with its sweeping, turning movements, makes great kinesthetic use of the big screen in an almost abstract sense, a joy of pure movement. At the same time the viewer is introduced to some of the many exceptionally good "science fiction" sets and special effects. Somehow I was prepared not to like most of the "hardware" but found that most was very good indeed. I expected everything to be too smooth. Happily there are some nice, knobby spaceships. Obvious-ly, a tremendous amount of care and concern for detail went into the making of this film.

But it's in the very area of detail where the picture falls short of its potential for me. There don't seem to be any wrinkles or grease spots on either the people or the ma-chines. I mean this mostly in a figurative sense. I realize the film is stylized, but the manner of conveying "human" touches, even when ironic, seems studied and unreal. I've just spent the past six months making an impressionistic film of Project Apollo and have encountered a lot of bureaucrats and spaceman types. Some I liked and some I didn't, but in all cases they were somehow more textured than their counterparts in *2001*.

I should say here that there are virtually no films I see that don't have areas that bother me. This one is no exception. I guess it's my inclination to say, even of good films, "that's nice but I would do it another way," which would be a different film, of course.

An especially interesting aspect of the film for me in that respect is the handling of the final sequences. At one point early in making the film, Kubrick asked me if I would assist in designing the part. I read the script he and

Arthur Clarke had written. The problem obviously was to create an overwhelming alien world experience. For various reasons I did not become involved in the project, but I was intensely curious to know how he would solve the problem. As it turned out he did it beautifully, with apparent economy of means and with great visceral impact. In this sequence his use of semi-abstractions and image modification (solarization, color replacement, etc.) brings to the big screen techniques which once seemed the province of the avante-garde or experimentalists. (Which prompts me to say that it is encouraging to see the range of cinematic vocabulary being used in commercial movies and television today. True, it's still a relatively small segment of the total output that really uses so-called advanced techniques, but it's there and growing rapidly. So is its audience. The net result is that there are more types of films to choose from. The various value systems available are increasing, and this is a healthy thing, I think. Of course, it also means that the cutting edge of the avant-garde is being pushed by an ever-growing sophistication and has to keep moving in new directions to stay in the game.)

So, anyway, let me get on with my response to *2001*. I like the fact that Kubrick chose "The Sentinel" by Arthur Clarke to base his science fiction movie on. The result is a good science fiction picture without the usual overemphasis on bug-eyed monsters (however much fun they can be sometimes). I like the sense of scale and journey he got. It is the "biggest" science fiction film yet in theme, execution and actual dimensions, at least as far as I can remember. (I'd like to see again some of the old pictures I only dimly recall, like *Things To Come*.) I liked it when he implied, disliked it when he explained, which, happily, wasn't often. I liked the way the styles varied for the different episodes, giving the overall structure a variety in character and mood. I was at times unhappy with the dialogue. The picture is strongest in its non-verbal sense (a type of filmmaking that appeals to me) even though its concept is based on a story. I thought his use of sound was good, very effective at times: massed voices in rising crescendo at the sight of the mysterious slabs, lonely breathing in empty space. I liked the open-ended ambiguities of the ending. The film had, for me, a satisfying amount of what Sam Moskowitz calls a "sense of wonder," and a feeling which some good science fiction has for the sensual and mysterious regions surrounding our feeling about machines, time and space. All in all it was a fine experience.

Apeman, Superman—or
2001's *Answer to the World Riddle*

Reviewed by LEON E. STOVER

Nobody who can identify the opening and closing bars of music in *2001* need puzzle long over the film's meaning.

At the start the eye of the camera looks down from barren hills, under the rising sun at dawn, into a still valley below. As the sun mounts, the eye advances into the valley. Zarathustra is come forth out of his cave; hailing the sun—"Thou great star!"—he descends from the hills once more to invest himself in humanity and go at man's progress again. Zarathustra's cosmic mission is given out in the great blast of trumpets which pronounces the World Riddle theme (C-G-C) from *Thus Spake Zarathustra*, by Richard Strauss.

Richard Strauss wrote of this music that it was his homage to the philosophical genius of Nietzsche:

I meant to convey by means of music an idea of the human race from its origins, through the various phases of its development, religious and scientific, up to Nietzsche's idea of the Superman.

Down there in that awesome valley human destiny is on the starting line with the apemen, members of the genus *Australopithecus*, discovered for anthropology in South and East Africa. The savannahland in the opening scenes is authenitc East African landscape, which today is exactly as it was when the apemen roamed there during Lower Pleistocene times. The apemen are shown to be peaceful and vegetarian. They spend all day eating and chewing plant foods.

But one morning a great, black monolith appears in the midst of their usual feeding place. The sheer perfection and improbability of this artifact arouses in the dim chambers of one apeman's preadamite brain some sense of form, and he reaches out to touch—fearfully at first, then with great yearning—the smooth surfaces and smart edges of this magnificently artificial thing. He is inspired to artifice himself. He discovers the principle of the lever, an extension of his arm, in a long bone picked out of a crumbled tapir skeleton. He bashes this club around experimentally in the pile of old bones from which he lifted it out, in a slow motion sequence of his great hairy arm lifting up and crashing down, causing debris to flower outward in floating arcs, intercut with visions of a falling tapir.

This insightful apeman leads his kind to hunting and meat eating. Meat eating takes less time than plant eating, and with it comes the leisure for tool making which in turn leads, eventually, to science and advanced technology. This first triumph of artifice, the hunting club, is underlined by the C-G-C World Riddle theme, climaxing in full orchestra and organ. The weapon is tossed to the air in a fit of religious exaltation the while the apemen dance around the monolith, and . . .

. . . In a wipe that takes care of 3 million years of evolutionary history, the bone in its toss is replaced by a spaceship in flight. The camera comes upon a great wheel-shaped orbital station that turns slowly and majestically to the tune of the Blue Danube, which waltzes for man's easy, technological virtuosity. The audience, accordingly, is treated to a long appreciation of the docking manoeuvers, in 3/4 time, of a shuttle craft come up from Earth. Its single passenger is an American scientist on a secret mission to the crater Clavius on the moon, where mystery awaits.

The space platform is fitted out with Hilton, Pan Am and Bell Telephone services. The audience always ohs and ahs to see these familiar insignia in the world of the future, which goes to confirm what anthropologists have learned from disaster studies, that people really love their culture. It is part of them. People are thrown into a state of shock when floods, tornadoes or other destructive events remove large chunks of their familiar material environment.

The scientist from Earth continues the last leg of his journey in a low flying moon bus, the while its occupants eat ham and cheese sandwiches. The juxtaposition of the eternally banal picnic lunch with the fantastic lunar landscape zipping by below serves to re-emphasize the confident virtuosity of space technology. But this confidence is shattered by the mystery at Clavius: the monolith again, this time excavated out of lunar soil. While the suited party examines it, a stinging, ringing beam of shrill sound penetrates their helmets. The camera looks up from the very base of the monolith to the sun in a wide angle shot duplicating the one that brought the apemen sequence to a close with the bone club soaring high.

The wipe from the screaming monolith to a ship headed for deep space covers just a decade or so. The energy emitted from the monolith fled toward Jupiter, the ship's destination. A crew of five (three in hibernation) and a talking, thinking I.B.M. 9000 series computer, occupy an enormous, sperm-shaped craft: man seeding the cosmos.

During the outward voyage the two men acting as caretakers on the ship are shown to display flatter personalities than the spirited computer, HAL, which is plugged into everything and runs everything. Man's technology has advanced so far that it is overwhelming. Technology, basically, is an artificial means of extending human organs.

Clothes are an extension of the skin, a computer is an extension of the brain, a wheeled vehicle is an extension of the legs, a telephone is an extension of the ear and mouth, and so on. The more such extensions are elaborated by man, the more they seem to take on a life of their own and threaten to take over. A simple example of extensions getting out of hand is the urban congestion and air pollution created by use of the automobile in great numbers. Another is big organization, made possible by electronic extensions of the speech functions, which makes for suffocating dehumanization in the "organization man." To paraphrase Hamlet, "How like a cog is man!" The two men aboard ship are exactly that. HAL runs the ship and they act like low grade robots, passively eating coloured paste for food that comes out of a machine, passively watching TV broadcasts from Earth, passively receiving birthday greetings from home.

Hal symbolizes that point of no return in the development of technology when man's extensions finally take over. They possess the more life the more man is devitalized by them. It will be suicide for man to continue in his love for his material culture. Dependence on an advanced state of technology makes it impossible to revert to a primitive state of technology. And it is too late to solve the problem with a "technological fix."

HAL reports an imminent malfunction in the directional antenna of the ship. One of the men, Astronaut Frank Poole, leaves the ship in a space pod in order to replace the unit. The old unit is brought back, tested, and found to be without defect. The two men worry about HAL's lapse of judgment. HAL insists the unit will fail on schedule. So Poole replaces the unit by way of testing HAL. But HAL tested is HAL irritated. When Poole steps out of the space pod to reinstall the unit, HAL works one of the pod's mechanical arms—a runaway extension of the human arm—to snip off his oxygen line. Poole's partner, Mission Commander David Bowman, goes after the body in another space pod and returns to the ship. But HAL won't obey the command to open the port. The only way into the ship now is through the emergency air lock, providing the entrant is fully suited. Bowman, in his haste to rescue Poole, forgot to bring his helmet into the pod.

Meanwhile, HAL has turned off the life-support systems for the three men in hibernation. The blinking lights which register their deaths say, LIFE PROCESSES TERMINATED, a fitting obituary for technomorphic man.

But at bottom, Bowman is a real hero. He triumphs over the technomorphism that turns men into dull machines. He manipulates the pod's waldo arm to open the airlock on the ship, then aligns the pod's hatch with it. Bowman calculates that if he blows the hatch bolts, the air exploding outward from the pod will blast him into the evacuated airlock; perhaps he can survive half a minute in hard, cold vacuum. In a realistic sequence of human daring and bravery, Bowman is exploded into the ship with a silent frenzy that does not pick up sound until the lock is closed and air pressure is restored.

Bowman's next move is to lobotomize HAL, who pleads sorry for the four murders in a parody of a guilty human trying to get off the hook: "I admit I've made some pretty bad decisions lately." The humor of this line conceals an affirmation of HAL's autonomy. Removal of his higher control centers is a significant act forecasting things to come. It looks forward to the time when man shall be able to cut himself loose from his extensions altogether. The solution to a runaway technology is not mastery over it but abandonment of it. The liabilities of human dependence on material means are to be left behind in the conquest of some higher form of existence.

The monolith appears outside the cabin windows at this juncture to indicate the direction of that conquest. Bowman follows it in his space pod, but the monolith vanishes in a purple glow. Straining his eyes on the spot he suddenly is led down a rushing corridor of computer-generated effects that represent his translation through a fourth dimensional experience.

During this sensational ride, Bowman is given a godlike vision of whole galaxies in full form, turning wheels of hot gasses and their embedded star clusters. Through this cosmic whirlpool shoots a symbolic representation of the parent ship: a fiery, sperm-shaped comet thing that drives across the screen and into a pulsing, luminous gas cloud. A delicate point of theology is raised here. In that novel of theological science-fiction, *Perelandra* (1944), C. S. Lewis argues that man is evil; space travel will only spread the blight. He is out to rebut the idea that

> humanity, having now sufficiently corrupted the planet where it arose, must at all costs contrive to seed itself over a larger area: that the vast astronomic distances which are God's quarantine regulations, must somehow be overcome.

The viewpoint of *2001,* however, is that man's seeding of the cosmos is a positive good. For the men who will go out to quicken the universe with the human presence will be supermen, lifted beyond the evil they did on Earth as captives of their technology. Man's extensions always carried a built in margin of wickedness, beginning with the apeman's weapon of the hunt that could be used also as a weapon of war. But the supermen will be fully emancipated from material extensions as from the material body that is extended by technology. The universe will be made full with the essential goodness of a disembodied humanity.

The transition for Bowman takes place in a hotel suite, mocked up beyond Jupiter by the kind of super beings he and the rest of mankind are destined to join. There Bowman ages rapidly and takes to bed, living out the childhood of man to the end. When the end comes, the great monolith stands before his bed, that recurrent symbol of the great yearning that prompted the apemen millions of years ago to reach for tool making and that now prompts Bowman to reach out for something beyond artifice. He struggles upward from his sheets, unrecognizable in his stupendous oldness, yet reaching painfully for that ineluctable goal waiting beyond the mysterious form standing before him. He reaches forward to touch it, reaching for rebirth . . .

Cut to a view of planet Earth as seen from outer space. The camera moves aside from the great green disc in the sky to include another luminous body nearby. It is an enormous transparent globe that contains an alert, watchful embryo of cosmic proportions, looking down on Earth with the eyes of Bowman, as he prepares to liberate all humanity from the disabilities of material existence and promote it to the status he has attained to. This giant embryonic figure is a symbolic show, for the sake of something to visualize on the screen, of Bowman's leadership in attaining to a state of pure, incorporeal intellect.

Such a destiny is predicted not alone by science fiction writers. It is to be found also in *The Phenomenon of Man* (1959) by the late Pierre Teilhard de Chardin, the Catholic father and anthropologist, who explains that the gathering force of mind that has come to envelope the surface of the planet Earth out of prehuman beginnings must eventuate in a projection into space as a purely spiritual component that will converge ultimately at the Omega point in one single intellectual entity, the very stuff of God. But once all the consciousness of the universe has accumulated and merged in the Omega point, God will get lonely in his completeness, and the process of creation must begin again by way of arousing conscious creatures to reach out once more for closure in one collective identity.

2001 comes to an end on a great trumpeting blast of the World Riddle theme, C-G-C, the shimmering globe of Bowman's pure mind stuff staring the audience in the face. Soon the whole population of Earth will join him. But the story of man is not complete with the evolution from apeman to superman. When the curtain closes, the superman is still one step away from evolving into God.

But even then the story is not finished. For the universe is cyclical. God will come down from the hills again. Thus spake Zarathustra:

Lo! I am weary of my wisdom. I need hands reaching

out for it. For that end I must descend to the depth, as thou dost at even, when sinking behind the sea thou givest light to the lower regions, thou resplendent star! Zarathustra will once more become a man.

Now that the theologians tell us that God is dead, it appears that the burden of theology is upon SF.

THE SERPENT OF KUNDALINI

BRIAN W. ALDISS

Is it possible that time is sickening on the tree? Brian Aldiss believes that, "Straight narrative depends on chronology; when chronology is awry, you don't seem to need straight narrative." In his two most recent novels, Cryptozoic! *and* Report on Probability A, *he examines this concept, and is now venturing still further with the series of Charteris/acid-head stories of a future where psychedelic drugs have been used in warfare. The stories are not to everyone's taste, because they sometimes require a certain effort at understanding on the part of the reader. But, as "The Serpent of Kundalini" proves, it is an effort well worth making.*

After his long drive across Europe, from south to north, Charteris was tired. On the ferry going across to England, he slept.

When he woke, the ship had already moored in Dover harbor and was absolutely deserted except for him. Even the sailors had gone ashore. White cliffs loomed over the boat. The quays and the sea were empty. The entire desolation was the more bare because it was covered in flawless early spring sunshine.

Just inside one of the customs sheds on the quay stood a man in a blue sweater with his arms folded. Charteris saw the man just as he was descending the gangplank, and paused with his hand on the rail. The man would hardly have been noticeable; after all, he was perhaps thirty yards away; but, by a curious trick of acoustics played by the empty shed and the great slope of cliff, the man's every sound was carried to Charteris and magnified.

He halted between ship and land, hearing the rasp of the waiting man's wrists as he re-folded his arms, hearing the tidal flow of his breath in his lungs, hearing the infinitesimal movement of his feet in his boots, hearing his watch tick through the loaded seconds of the day.

Very slowly, Charteris descended to the quay and began to walk toward the distant barriers, still water lying pallidly on his left, marching over great yellow-painted arrows and letters meaningless to him which reduced him to a cipher in a diagram. His course would take him close to the waiting man.

The new vision of the universe which Charteris had been granted in France was with him still. He knew that all other human beings were symbols. This waiting man symbol could be death. He had come to England to find other things.

"This deadness that I feel will pass," he said aloud. The waiting man breathed by way of reply: a cunning and lying answer, thought Charteris. There was danger. A flock of seagulls, white with black heads that swiveled like ball-bearings, sailed down from the clifftop, scudding in front of Charteris, and landed on the sea. They sank like stones. A cloud slid over the sun and the water was immediately the brown nearest black.

He reached the barrier. As he swung it wide and passed through, the noises of the waiting man died. To stand here was the ambition of years. Charteris knelt to kiss the ground; as his knees buckled, he glanced back and saw, crumpling over one of the yellow arrows, his own body.

He jerked upright and went on. He recalled what Gurdjieff had said: attachment to things keeps alive a thousand useless I's in a man; these I's must die so that the big I can be born. The dead images were peeling from him. Soon he himself would be born.

He was trembling. Nobody wants to change.

The town was large and grand. The windows and the paintwork, Charteris thought, were very English. The spaces formed by the buildings were also alien to him. He believed that architecture was a kinetic thing essentially: and that photography had killed that true spirit because people had grown used to studying buildings on pages rather than by walking through them and round them and seeing them in relationship to other urban objects. In the same way, the true human spirit had been killed. It could only be seen in and by movement.

Conscious of the drama of the moment, he paused, clutching his chest, whispering to himself, *Zbogam!* For the thought was revelation. A philosophy of movement. ... Sciences like photography must be used to a different purpose, and motion must be an expression of stillness.

In his mind, flaring vision: a stony continental city in the grey prodigal European tradition, of wide avenues and little crooked alleys—a German city perhaps, perhaps Geneva, perhaps Brussels. And he was arriving in a motor cavalcade, leading them, talking an incomprehensible language, letting them worship him. And a sullen English chick parting her white thighs.

Then it was gone.

Simultaneously, all the people in the Dover street began to move. Till now, they had been stationary, frozen, one-dimensional. Now, motion gave them life and they went about their various business.

As he walked through them, he saw how miscellaneous they were. He had imagined the English as essentially a fair northern race with the dark-haired among them as startling contrast. But these were people less sharp than that, their features blunted by long inter-marriage, many stunted with blurred gestures, and many Jews and dark people among them. Their dress also presented a more tremendous and ragged variety than he had encountered in other countries, even his own Montenegro.

Although these people were doing nothing out of the ordinary, Charteris knew that the insane breath of war had blown here too. Psychochemical bombs had splashed down from England's gray clouds; and the liquid eyes that turned toward him had a frightening glimpse of madness. He thought he could still hear the breathing of the waiting man; but as he listened to it more closely, he realized that the people near him were whispering his name—and more than that.

"Charteris! Colin Charteris—funny name for a Jug!"

"Charteris is pretending that he swam the Channel to get here."

"What's Charteris doing here? I thought he was going to Scotland!"

"Did you see Charteris kiss the ground, cheeky devil!"

"Why didn't you stay in France, Charteris—didn't you know it's neutral?"

A woman took her small girl by the hand and led her hurriedly into a butcher's shop, saying, "Come away, darling, Charteris raped a girl in France!" The butcher leant across the counter with a huge crimson leg in his hands and brought it down savagely on the little girl's— Charteris looked round hastily and saw that the butcher was merely hanging a red boloney sausage on a hook. His eyes were betraying him. His hearing was probably not to be trusted either.

Anxious to get away from the whispering, whether real or imaginary, he hurried up a shopping street that climbed uphill. Three young girls walked before him in very short skirts. By slowing his pace, he could study their legs, all of which were extremely shapely. The girl on the outside of the pavement, in particular, had beautiful limbs. He admired the ankles, the calves, the dimpling popliteal hinges, the thighs, following the logic of them in imagination up to the sensuously jolting buttocks. Motion, again, he thought: without that elan vital, they would be no more

interesting than the butcher's meat. An overpowering urge
to exhibit himself to the girls rose within him. He could
fight it only by turning aside into a shop; it was another
butcher's shop; he himself hung naked and stiff on a
hook, white, and pink-trottered. He looked directly and
saw it was a pig's carcass.

But as he left the shop, he saw another of his discarded
I's was peeling off and crumpling over the counter, life-
less.

He hurried on to the top of the hill. The girls had gone.
Like a moth, the state of the world fluttered in his left ear,
and he wept for it. The West had delivered itself to the
butchers.

A view of the sea offered itself at the top of the hill.
Breathing as hard as the waiting man, Charteris grasped
some railings and looked over the cliff at the sea. One of
those hateful phantom voices down in the town had suggested he was going to Scotland; he saw now that he was
indeed about to do that; at least, he would head north. He
hoped his new-found mental state would enable him to see
the future with increasing clarity; but, when he made the
effort, as if, it might be, his eyesight misted over at any
attempt to read small print, the endeavor seemed
bafflingly self-defeating: the small print of the future bled
and ran—indeed, all he could distinguish was a notice
reading something like LOVE BURROW which would not
resolve into GLASGOW, some sort of plant with crimson
blooms and . . . a road accident?—until, trying to grapple
with the muddled images, he finally even lost the *direction*
in which his mind was trying, myopically and illiterately,
to peer.

Clinging to the railings, he tried to sort out his random
images. LOVE BURROW was no doubt some sort of Freudi-
an nonsense; he dismissed the crimson Christmas blooms;
his anxiety clustered round the accident—all he could see
was a great perspective of crashing and clanging cars,
aligned down the beaches of triple-carriageways like a

tournament. The images could be past or future. Or merely fears. Always the thought of crashing.

But he had left his car on the ship. What was ahead was unknown, even to him with the budding powers—powers so far away from what the sane accepted that he realized in a breathless moment like a ducking that he must yield to madness—and the sea was gray. Clutching the railings, Charteris felt the ground rock slightly. The deck. The deck rocked. The sea narrowed like a Chinese eye. The ship bumped the quay.

He stood at the rail, trying to adjust, as the passengers left the ship and the cars were driven away from the underdeck. He looked up at the cliffs; gulls swooped down from them: and floated on the oily sea. He listened and heard only his own breathing, the rasp of his own body in his clothes. In or out of trance, he stood: and the quay emptied of people.

"Is the red car yours, sir?"

"You are Mr. Charteris, sir?"

Slowly he turned toward the English voice. He extended a hand and touched the fabric of the man's tunic. Nodding without speaking, he made his way slowly below deck. Slowly, he walked down the echoing belly-perspective of the car deck to where his Banshee stood. He climbed in, searched in his pocket for the ignition key, slowly realized it was already in the ignition, started up, and drove slowly over the ramp on to English concrete.

He looked across to the customs shed. A man stood there half in shadow, in a blue sweater, arms folded. He beckoned. Charteris drove forward and found it was a customs man. A small rain began to fall as the man looked laconically through Charteris' grip.

"This is England, but my dream was more true," he said.

"That's as maybe," said the man, in surly fashion. "We had a war here, you know, sir, not like you lot in France. You'd expect a bit of dislocation, sort of, wouldn't you?"

"Dislocation, my God, yes!"

"Well, then. . . ."

He drove away, enormously slow, and the slimy yellow arrows licked their way under his bonnet. TENEZ LA GAUCHE. LINKS FAHREN. DRIVE ON THE LEFT. WATNEY'S BEER. The enormous gate swung open and he felt only love. He waved at the man who opened the gate; the man stared back suspiciously. England!

The great white lumpish buildings along the front seemed to hesitate. He turned and looked back in fear at the ship—where—what was he? In the wet road, crumpled over one of the arrows, lay one of his I's, just as in the vision, discarded.

Only now did he clearly recall the details of the vision.

To what extent was a vision an illusion, to what extent a clearer sort of truth?

He recollected the England of his imagination, culled from dozens of Saint books. A sleazy place of cockneys, nurse-maids, policemen, slums, misty wharves, large houses full of the vulnerable jewelry of beautiful women. That place was not this. Well, like the guy said, there had been a war, a dislocation. He looked at these people in these streets. The few women who were about moved fast and furtive, poorly and shabbily dressed, keeping close to walls. The men did not move. A curse of alternate inertia had been visited upon the English sexes. Men stood wait-ing and smoking in little groups, unspeaking; women scur-ried lonely. In their eyes, he saw the animal glints of madness. Their pupils flashed toward him like animal headlights, feral with guanin, the women's green, the men's red like wolf-hounds or a new animal.

A little fear clung to Charteris.

"I'll drive up to Scotland," he said. Bombardment of images. He was confusing his destiny: he would never get there. Something happened to him . . . would happen. Had happened—and he was here and now was but a past image of himself, perhaps a dead image, perhaps one of the cast-off I's that Gurdjieff said must be discarded before a man could awaken to true consciousness.

He came to the junction where, in his vision, he had

turned and walked up the steep shopping street. With
determination, Charteris wrenched the wheel and accelerated up the hill. Under sudden prompting, he glanced over
his shoulder. A red Banshee with himself driving had split
away and was taking the other turning. Did that way lead
to Scotland or to . . . Love Burrow? His other I caught his
gaze just momentarily, pupils flashing blank guanin red,
teeth bright in a wolf snarl.

That's one I I'm happy to lose. . . .

As he climbed up the hill, he looked for three girls in
miniskirts, for a butcher's shop. But the people were the
shabby post-catastrophe crowd, and most of the shops
were shuttered: all infinitely sadder than the vision, however frightening it had been. Had he been frightened? He
knew he embraced the new strangeness. Materialism had a
silver psychedelic bullet through its heart; the incalculable
took vampire-flight.

Already, he felt a cooler knowledge of himself. Down
in the south of Italy, that was where this new phase of life
had festered for him, in the rehabilitation camp for thousands of Slav victims of the war. There he had been
forced to wander in the mazed caverns of their derange-
ments: and had learnt there in a hidden part of himself
that sanity had many alternatives.

Now, unbecaverned, he could see that his forte was
action directed by philosophy. He was not the introspec-
tive; on the other hand, he was not the simple doer. He
was rarely conscious of himself, yet rarely unfeeling for
others. As a good (lapsed) Communist, he had little time
for soul-searching; yet he had always spared a moment for
inquiring into his own motives. Psychoanalysis was ana-
thema to him—yet he could detect the many forms that
self-gratification took.

And where did these thoughts lead? Something impelled
him: perhaps only the demon chemicals; but he needed to
know where he was going. It would help if he could
examine one of his cast-off I's. As he reached the top of
the hill, he saw that he still stood gripping the railings and
staring out to sea. He stopped the car.

As he walked toward the figure, monstrous things wheeled in the firmament, sank like stones.

His hearing became preternaturally acute. Although his own footsteps sounded distant, very near at hand was the tidal flow of his breathing, the tick of his watch, the stealthy rustle of his body inside its clothing. Like the man said, there had been a war, a dislocation.

As his hand came up to touch the shoulder of the Gurdjieffian I, it was arrested in mid-air; for his glance caught the sight of something moving on the sea. For a moment, he mistook it for some sort of a new machine or animal, until it resolved itself under his startled focus into a ship, a car ferry, moving close in to the harbor. On the promenade deck, he saw himself standing remote and still.

The figure before him turned.

It had broken teeth set in an indefinite mouth, and dark brown pupils of eyes gripped between baggy lids. Its nose was brief and snouty, its skin puffed and discolored, its hair as short and tufted as fur. It was the waiting man. It smiled.

"I was waiting for you, Charteris!"

"So they were hinting down in the town."

"You don't have any children, do you?"

"Well, no, but my ancestry goes right back to Early Man."

"You'll tell me if you aren't at ease with me? Your answer reveals, I think, that you are a follower of Gurdjieff?"

"Clever guess! Ouspensky, really. The two are one—but Gurdjieff talks such nonsense."

"You read him in the original, I suppose?"

"The original what?"

"Then you will realize that the very times we live in are somewhat Gurdjieffian, eh? The times themselves, I mean, talk nonsense—but the sort of nonsense that makes us simultaneously very sceptical about the old rules of sanity."

Charteris was feeling almost no apprehension now, although his pulse beat rapidly. Far below on the quay, he could see himself climbing into the car and driving toward the customs shed.

"I must be getting along," he said formally. "As the Saint would say, I have a date with destiny. I'm looking for a place called. . . ." He had forgotten the name; that image had been self-canceling.

"My house is hard by here."

"I prefer a softer kind."

"It is softer inside, and my daughter would like to meet you. Do come and rest a moment and feel yourself welcome in Britian."

He hesitated. The time would come, might even be close, when all the gates of the farmyard would be closed to him; he would fall dead and be forgotten; and continue to stare forever out through the window at the blackness of the garden. With a simple gesture of assent—how simple it yet remained to turn the wrist in the lubricated body—he helped the waiting man into the car and allowed him to direct the way to his house.

This was a middle-class area, and unlike anywhere he had visited before. Roads of small neat houses and bungalows stretched away on all sides, crescents curved off and rejoined the road, and all neatly labeled with sylvan names: Sherwood Forest Road, Dingley Dell Road, Herbivore Drive, Placenta Place, Honeysuckle Avenue, Cowpat Avenue, Geranium Gardens, Clematis Close, Creosote Crescent, Laurustinus Lane. Each dwelling had a neat little piece of garden, often with rustic work and gnomes on the front lawn. Even the smallest bungalows had grand names, linking them with a mythical green nature once supposed to have existed: Tall Trees, Rolling Stones, Ocean View, Neptune Tiles, The Bushes, Shaggy Shutters, Jasmine Cottage, My Wilderness, Solitude, The Laurustinuses, Our Oleanders, Florabunda.

Charteris grew angry and said, "What sort of a fantasy are these people living in?"

"If you're asking seriously, I'd say, Security masquerading as a little danger."

"We aren't allowed this sort of private property! It's an offence against the state."

"Don't worry! It's all dead—the war has killed it. The values on which this . . . civilization has been built have been swept away—not that most of the inhabitants realize it yet. I keep up the pretence because of my daughter."

The waiting man began to breathe in a certain way. Charteris regarded him curiously out of the corner of his eye, because he fancied that the man was accomplishing rather an accurate parody of his daughter's breathing. So good was it that the girl was virtually conjured up between them; she proved to be, to Charteris' delight, the one of the three girls in a miniskirt he had most admired while walking up the hill. The illusion lasted only a split second, and then the waiting man was breathing naturally again.

"All pretence must be broken! I think that is the quest on which I came to this country. Although we are strangers and should perhaps talk formally together, I must say that I believe very deeply that there is a strange force latent in man which can be awakened."

"Kundalini! Turn left here, down Petunia Park Road."

"What?"

"Turn left."

"What else did you say? You were swearing at me, I believe?"

"Kundalini. You don't know your Gurdjieff as well as you pretend, my friend! So-called occult literature speaks of Kundalini, or the servant of Kundalini. A strange force in man which can be awakened."

"That's it, then, yes! I want to awaken it. What are all these people doing in the rain?"

As they drove down Petunia Park Road, Charteris realized that the middle classes . . . standing neatly and attentively in their gardens . . . were performing characteristic actions such as adjusting ties and reading big newspapers, but most were simply staring into the road.

"Left here, into Brontosaurus Broadway. Listen, my boy, Kundalini, that serpent, should be left sleeping. *It's nothing desirable*! Repulsive though you may find these people here, their lives have at least been dedicated—and successfully; on the whole—to keeping the serpent sleeping. I mean, security masquerading as a little danger is only a small safe aberration, whereas Kundalini—"

He went into some long rigmarole which Charteris was unable to follow; he had just seen a red Banshee, driven by another Gurdjieffian I, slide past the top of the road, and was disturbed by it. Although there was much he wanted to learn from the waiting man, he must not be deflected from his main north-bound intention, or he might find himself in the position of a discarded I. On the other hand, it was possible that going north might bring him into discardment. For the first time in his life, he was aware of all life's rich or dessicating alternatives; and an urge within him—but that might be Kundalini—prompted him to go and talk to people, preach to them, about cultivating the multi-valued.

"Here's the house," said the waiting man. "Pear Tree Palace. Come in and have a cup of tea. You must meet my daughter."

At the neat little front gate, barred with a sunset pattern, Charteris hesitated. "You are hospitable, but I hope you won't mind my asking—I seem myself to be slightly affected by the PCA bombs—hallucinations, you know—I wondered—aren't you also a bit—touched—"

The waiting man laughed, making his ugly face look a lot uglier. "Everyone's touched! Don't be taken in by appearances here. Believe me, the old world has gone, but its shell remains in place. One day soon, there will come a breath of wind, a new messiah, the shell will crumple, and the kids will run streaming, screaming, barefoot in the head, through the lush new hallucinatory meadows. Come on, I'll put the kettle on! Wipe your feet!"

"It's as bad as that?—"

The waiting man had opened the front door and gone inside. Uneasy, Charteris paused and looked about. Kinetic architecture here had spiked the viewpoint with a crazy barricade of pergolas, patios, bay windows, arches, extensions, all manner of dinky garages and outhouses, set

among fancy trees. Watertight world. All hushed under
the fine mist of rain. Neighborhood of evil for him, small
squares of anemic fancy, wrought-iron propriety.

He found himself at the porch, where the gaunt rambler
canes already bore snouts of fresh growth. There'd be a
fine show of New Dawn in four more months. An enchantment waited here. He went in, leaving the door
open. He wanted to hear more about Kundalini.

At the back of the house, the waiting man was in a
small kitchen, all painted green and cream, every surface
covered with patterned stuff and, on a calendar, a picture
of two people tarrying in a field. Behind the two frozen
people, sheep broke from their enclosure and went on the
rampage among wheat ripening toward harvest.

Perhaps instinctively, the waiting man had switched on
a small dumpy streamlined radio. The disc jockey's voice
said, "And now for the great all-time sound of one of the
great bands of all time. We're spinning this one for Auntie
Betty and all the boys at 'Nostalgia Vista', 2 Armoury
Cottages, The Tip, Coalville, in Leicestershire—the great
great sound of the Glenn Miller band with the immortal
Moonlight Serenade."

With his mouth slightly open, the waiting man beat
time in the air, watching the treacly music as it rose in a
foetid breath from the kettle spout and curled across the
ceiling.

"My daughter isn't in. I expect she'll be back soon.
Why don't you settle down here with us for a bit? There's
a nice little spare room upstairs—a bit small but cosy.
You never know—you might fall in love with her."

He remembered his first fear of the waiting man: that he
would detain Charteris in the customs shed. Now, more
subtly, the attempt at detention was again being made.

"And you're a follower of Gurdjieff, are you?" Charteris asked.

"He was rather an unpleasant customer, wasn't he? But
a magician, a good guide through these hallucinatory
times."

"I want to waken a strange force that I feel inside me, but you say that is Kundalini, and Gurdjieff warns against waking it?"

"Very definitely! Most definitely! G says *man* must awake, but the snake, the serpent, must be left sleeping." He made the tea meticulously, using milk from a tube which was lettered Ideal. "We've all got serpents in us, you know!" He laughed.

"What is this serpent of Kundalini then? Come on, out with it, or I could pretty easily brain you with this kettle!"

"It's an electric kettle!"

"I don't care!"

At this proof of Charteris' recklessness, the waiting man backed away, helped himself to a saccharine pill, and said, "Enjoy your tea while it's hot!"

"Yes, siree, one of the great ones! And now for a welcome change of pace—"

Charteris was conscious of a mounting pressure inside him. Something was breathing close to his left ear and stealing away.

"Answer my question!" he said.

"Well, according to G, the serpent is the power of the imagination—the power of fantasy—which takes the place of a real function. You take my meaning? When a man dreams instead of acting, when he imagines himself to be a great eagle or a great magician . . . that's the force of Kundalini acting in him. . . ."

"Cannot one act and dream?"

The waiting man appeared to double up, sniggering in repulsive fashion with his fists to his mouth. Love Burrow—that was the sign, and a pale-thighed wife beside him. . . . His place was there, wherever that was. This Pear Tree Palace was a trap, a dead end, the waiting man himself an ambiguous either/or/both/and sign, deluding yet warning him: perhaps a manifestation of Kundalini itself. He had got his tasks in the wrong order; clearly, this was a dead end with no new alternative, a corner of extinction. What he wanted was a new tribe!

Now the waiting man's sniggers were choking him.

Above their bubbling din, he heard the sound of a car engine outside, and dropped his teacup. The tea sent a dozen fingers across the cubist lino. Over his fists, the little doubled figure glared blankly red at him. Charteris turned and ran.

Through the open door. Birds leaped from the lawn to the eaves of the bungalow, leaden, from motionlessness to instant motionlessness.

Down the path. The rain had lured out a huge black slug which crawled like a torn watch-strap before him.

Through the gate. The sun, set for ever with its last rays caught in mottled iron.

To the road. But he was a discarded alternative. A red Banshee was pulling away, with one of his glittering I's at the wheel, puissant, full of potential, multi-valued, savior-shaped.

He ran after it, calling from the asphalt heart of Brontosaurus Broadway, leaping over the gigantic yellow arrows. They were becoming more difficult to negotiate. His own powers, he knew, were failing. He had chosen wrongly, become a useless I, dallying with an old order instead of seeking new patterns.

Now the arrows were almost vertical, LINKS FAHREN. The red car was far away, just a blur moving through the barrier, speeding unimpeded for. . . .

He still heard breathing, movements of clothes, the writhing of toes inside shoe-caps. But these were not his. They belonged to the Charteris in the car, the undiscarded I. He no longer breathed.

As he huddled over the arrow, gulls tumbled from the cliff and sank into the water. Over the sea, the ship came. Up the hill, motors sounded. In the head, barefoot, a new age.

There had been a war, a dislocation.

GOLDEN ACRES

KIT REED

Ageing and death are taboo subjects that most of the magazine editors refuse to touch unless they are well disguised. Yet life and death are what really matter—and are topics that the true writer must deal with. Kit Reed is a true writer, but this bittersweet but not bitter story was never published in a magazine. Nor in the United States. It appeared first in a British collection of her stories. She informs me that basically it is an upbeat and positive story and, after rereading, I must admit that she is right.

"I can walk, dammit." After a scuffle Hamish threw off the bellboy's hand and went into the elevator himself. It troubled him that Nelda rode serenely, submitting to the roller chair. The bellhops pushed him in the corner of the elevator, crowding him with the second chair; they had it full of the Scofields' luggage, and when the elevator let them out on Four they took off with a look of spite, rolling the chairs down corridors so fast that Hamish had to run to keep up. His frail lungs failed him finally and he lost them; he came round the last corner to find himself alone on a long cement porch. The pale stucco building

157

seemed to go all the way around a court, or square, and
when Hamish looked over the porch rail he saw a pool
and a garden below. He would have waved, or called out
but they were both empty, except for the California sunlight and a few improbable flowers. He turned back to the
porch and a series of identical doors, all louvred, all
closed.

"Nelda? Nelda?" He hated his voice; it sounded old
and thin.

He was breathing heavily, whirling in indecision when a
door opened down the way; one of the bellhops beckoned
with a condescending grin.

They had arranged Nelda in the middle of the suitcases
and hat-boxes, tableau: woman arriving at a resort. Her
hand fluttered at the bosom of her best voile dress; in a
minute her smile would fly apart. "Hamish," she said,
"Isn't it beautiful?"

The bellboys were lingering. "That will be all," Hamish
said, but they were waiting. He made a little rush at them
and then, because Nelda was pale and tremulous, he went
on, trying not to look around him, "Just beautiful," and
when he looked up this time the bellboys were gone.

"Look, they've put the TV where you can see it from
the bed."

He was looking out the door; when he had watched the
bellhops around the last corner he closed the door and
turned to her, full of misgivings:

"Nelda, I don't know about this place, I just don't
know."

"Honey, you're going to love it, it's all we ever
dreamed." She had her hat off now and she was beginning
to make a little tour of the room, touching the metal
bedsteads, running her fingers over the glass on the dresser
tops. "Look," she said, "you can see the TV from your
bed, just like they said in the brochure."

"Those look like hospital beds."

"You can crank yourself up any way you want." She
quoted from memory: "Everything for safety and comfort." But she was running her fingers along the walls

now, they were Formica, and when she spoke again her
voice was slightly off-key. "My knick-knack shelf, I don't
see any place for my knick-knack shelf."

"I don't see any place for *anything*."

"They said I could hang my knick-knack shelf."

But Hamish wasn't listening; he was moving restlessly,
taking in the no-color drapes and bedspreads, the oat-
meally peach Formica on the walls. The furniture was
institutional and sparse: two luggage racks, one for each of
them; two beds, two dressers, two straight chairs bolted
into place; at waist height all the way around, there was a
rail. He snarled, in sudden resentment: "I don't need any
goddam rail."

". . . AND THE HOT PLATE. I don't see the hot
plate."

"In here," Hamish said from the tiny bathroom. "On
the toilet tank. Say, where in hell are all the mirrors?"

Nelda's voice rose in a tiny wail. "Where can I plug in
my hair-dryer? How can I do my hair?"

Hamish was out of the bathroom before she finished.
He had his arm around her, saying, "Honey, are you sure
this is what you want? I mean, it's not too late to change
our minds . . ."

She wavered. "Oh, Hamish."

"We could be back in Waukegan before you know it.
We could be *home*."

But he had lost her. As he spoke her arms dropped and
in the next second she was tugging at one of the suitcases,
wrestling it on to the bed. She took out a sun hat and put
it on. "Hamish, Hamish, *this* is home."

"It's a damn motel."

"We sold everything to buy in here." She had a printed
beach dress by the shoulders; she was shaking it out.
"We're going to love it here."

"Nelda . . ."

But it was already too late. She had her sunshade on the
bed and on top of that her sneakers and her aqua Capri
pants. "It cost us ten thousand dollars, there are thousands

on the waiting-list. Do you think I'm going to back out now?"

He went on patiently. "I. Just. Don't. Like. What. I've. Seen."

She turned, brandishing a purple sweater. "What would we tell the neighbors when we got back? What would we tell Albert and Lorraine?"

He knew what he wanted to say, he wanted to say To hell with the neighbors, to hell with Albert and Lorraine, but something put him off; it wasn't the neighbors, it wasn't anybody who had been at the farewell party; he wasn't afraid of any of the rest of them, just Albert and Lorraine.

"We're going to love it here," Nelda said firmly. "It says so in the brochure." She had the children's pictures now, she was setting them on her dresser. "Albert. Eddie. Lorraine. There, that's lovely. Isn't it lovely, Spike?"

He jumped at the sound of the old name.

She came closer and her face had dropped years. "You'll see, Spike. It's going to be just like a second honeymoon . . ."

He would have kissed her then, he would have taken her old bones in his but there was a knock on the door and before either of them could answer, a young man came in, leading a bearded old man who leaned heavily on a cane.

"Mr. and Mrs. Scofield?"

Hamish stepped in front of Nelda. "I'm Hamish Scofield, of Waukegan, Illinois, and I'd like you to meet . . ."

The young man walked on past; he ran a quick finger around the carnation in his lapel and said, under his breath: "Clutter. We don't like our people to live in clutter."

Working quickly, he folded Nelda's family pictures and swept them into the dresser drawer. Albert. Eddie. Lorraine. Hamish knew he ought to protest and he would have, too, if it had been her silver dresser set, or her velvet lined vanity . . .

"There. I'm Mister Richardson." He was neat as a scissors in his pinstriped suit. "I'm the manager here, and this is Cletus Ford, our Second Oldest Resident."

The Second Oldest Resident raised a hand from under his beard; he and Hamish touched fingers just before Richardson brushed him aside, saying: "I came to be sure you were settled happily here at Golden Acres. And if there's anything . . ."

Hamish and Nelda both began:

"Mirror, need a damn shaving-mirror."

"My knick-knack shelf, I need a place for . . ."

Richardson was still talking. ". . . if there's anything we can do to make you happier, you have only to get in touch with any of our several attendants, you will know them because they wear white, the color of Hope. And now . . ."

"I *would* like . . ."

"If you could just . . ."

". . . a few simple rules."

Hamish stiffened. "*Rules.*"

"Rules. Then Cletus here . . ."

Cletus said, hopelessly, "*Mis*-ter Ford."

"Cletus here will tell you about the golden opportunities waiting for you, but first . . ."

"Well," said Cletus, "there's the Rotary and the Golden Agers and . . ."

"Cletus . . ."

". . . and the Close Shave Club, I'm a charter member, and the Amvets . . ."

Richardson had him by the shoulders. "*Cletus* . . ."

"Mis-ter Ford?"

"Cletus, I want you to go over to that chair and sit quietly with your knees together and try and remember your place." The manager went on, through his teeth, "And if you can't remember your place, you know what will happen, don't you?"

Hamish couldn't be sure, but he thought he heard a distant rumble, as if of a gigantic grocery cart. If he heard it, then Cletus heard it too; the old man shrank, diminishing before their eyes, folding himself into a chair and clasping his hands neatly under his beard.

"Y-yessir. Yes *sir*."

Hamish had his mouth open, he was listening hard but the rumble, or whatever it was, was gone.

"First, a little about our many benefits. Of course many of them are obvious, the swimming, the sun, the happy companionship of people your own age; parties in the moonlight, dancing on the esplanade . . ."

Nelda said, dreamily: ". . . dancing on the esplanade."

"But there is much, much more. Did you know, for instance, that there is a dispensary on every floor, or that the Tower of Hope . . ." Richardson smiled over his carnation ". . . that's what we call our hospital . . . the Tower of Hope is only three minutes away? Did you know there is an attendant on duty on every terrace twenty-four hours a day?"

Hamish stiffened. "At*ten*dant."

"To answer the cry of distress. The fall in the night. The sudden seizure at dawn."

"The doctors," Nelda said. "Tell Spike about the doctors."

"Specialists in every ailment of the human flesh." Richardson smoothed plump hands over his dark suit. "You are safe in our hands."

"Safe. See, Spike, I told you it would be wonderful."

"Reveille at seven sharp, marches over the intercom . . ." Richardson was growing lyric. "Breakfast at eight, after you clean your room."

Nelda frowned. "Clean?"

"Walks and therapy until noon, then lunch. Then naps. Then clubs. Dinner at five-thirty, bed by nine. Cooking on special days, with permission from the desk."

"Permission from the desk my ass." Hamish advanced on him. "Dinner at five-thirty. Bed by nine . . ."

"Bed by nine," Richardson said firmly. "You are safe in our hands. Safe to live out your golden years in this California paradise. Now Cletus here . . ." Cletus was asleep; Richardson kicked him sharply, perforating one ankle. *"Cletus, here . . ."*

"Huh? Whuh. Osteotomy club, cribbage teams, the . . ."

"Cletus here is a living testimony to the good life. When he first came in here he was a hollow wreck. Weren't you, Cletus?"

" . . . Progress Study Club, Great Grandmothers' Club . . ." Cletus became aware of an ugly silence. "Sir? Oh, yes. Yessir."

Richardson went on, gratified. "A few days in our hospital, a few months in the sun, and look at him now. He's our Second Oldest Resident, loved by everybody in the place."

Nelda's face was naked. "Loved."

Hamish wanted to push the others out and take her in his arms but they were too many and he was too old; he said, in an undertone, "You'll always be loved."

Richardson had put his hands on old Cletus, trundling him into the spotlight. "O.K., Cletus, you're on." Stifling a yawn, he bowed himself out, barely remembering to say: "Remember, you are safe in our hands."

Hamish counted to sixty, and when Cletus still hadn't said anything, he stood over the old man. "Well?"

Cletus was scratching his head. "Well . . . Oh, the clubs. Well. Well, we have the biggest Sunshine Booster group in the whole United States and a Masonic Lodge second to none. And we have the largest Kiwanis membership in the world . . ." he was still talking, but he was distracted, drifting away on a distant sound. "And the Lions . . . and . . ."

Hamish said, sharply, "You were telling us about the clubs."

"The clubs." Cletus came to with a little jerk. He looked around furtively, whispering. "Do you have any idea how *big* this place is?"

"Tiny," Nelda said. "Exclusive. It says so in the brochure."

"It's a boneyard." His voice dropped even further. "It's *vast*."

"Only a few well-chosen couples," Nelda said doggedly, "it says so in the brochure."

Hamish hushed her. "Let him talk."

"I tried to walk to the edge of this place one day. Maybe I wanted to see if the world was still there; maybe I just wanted to know there *was* an edge. I walked and walked. You want to know something?" He went on in awe. "I walked for miles."

Nelda said, crossly, "It only seemed like miles."

Hamish was leaning forward. "And you finally made it to the edge."

Cletus shook his head sadly. "Walked until m'legs gave out. They come and got me in a rolling chair. Probably just as well, come to think of it. M'blood pressure was giving me hell."

Nelda said, anxiously, "The clubs. Please. You were telling us about the club."

"Hell with the clubs. I always hated clubs."

"But the companionship. All the Golden Agers, just like you . . ."

"Fossils." Cletus snorted. "Bunch of bones."

"You don't really mean it." Nelda turned to Hamish. "He doesn't really mean it. If he did, he wouldn't stay."

"Hate the buildings, too. All smell of mildew and Argyrol."

"The pool, how about the pool?"

"I'm too damn *old* to swim."

Hamish squinted at him, puzzled. "But you stay . . ."

"Damn right I stay." Cletus drew them to the window. "Look out there. See that white thing sticking up, taller than anything else? That's the Tower of Hope. Hospital round here."

Hamish said, "What's that tall *black* thing?"

"Hospital around here," Cletus repeated, not answering. "The facings are made of Corning Glass."

He drew the shutters and faced them belligerently. "Damn right I stay. Where else could I get round-the-clock medical care? B-One shot every morning, all the hormones I can take. Doctors, nurses, guys to catch me if

I fall." He was squinting at Hamish now, something he saw seemed to anger him. "Don't knock it, buddy. This place is keeping me alive."

"If that's all you get, it isn't worth it," Hamish said angrily. "If that's all . . ."

Nelda cut him off. "That can't be all."

"All? That's *plenty*." Cletus paused, listening to something they could not make out.

Hamish was on him in a flash. "What's that noise?"

The old man was crafty, insolent. "There isn't any noise." But there was, it was coming closer, and Cletus leaped like a spider. "Archie, M'God, I bet it's for Archie." Hamish tried to hold him but he was too late. "See you," he said, and scuttled out, slamming the door.

It took Hamish a couple of minutes to get it open and when he did, he saw only the cement porch receding, the regular march of the posts. He turned back to Nelda then, wondering how he could get her to come away with him, how he could begin. She was already busy with the suitcase, pulling out clothes and spreading them on the bed.

"Nelda."

She wouldn't look at him; instead she picked up a mimeographed paper from the bedside table. "Look, the newspaper. It's called the *Golden Blade*."

"Nelda, please, we have to get out of here."

"It says here they're having a Shipwreck Party Friday; and there are shuffleboard lessons today at four . . ."

Outside someone was calling faintly, "Cletus, Cletus . . ."

"We don't belong here, Nelda, I thought we might but we don't."

She turned on him in sudden spite. "Then where *do* we belong?"

"Cletus . . . I know you're in here, Cletus. Come on out." The old lady came skidding into the room in white Ground Grippers and a white lawn dress. "Excuse me," she said when she saw them. "Where's he hiding this time, in the shower?"

Nelda put on her best air. "Beg your pardon?"

"He loves to curl up on the seat . . . Come on," she said impatiently. "They're looking for him and I've got to let him know."

"Well, he *was* here, but he . . ."

"Just like him to run out, just when the pressure is so . . ."

Hamish took her elbow. "What pressure?"

She shook him off. "Oh, you know. Being the Oldest Living Resident. Sorry I bothered you . . ."

Nelda stepped forward, intercepting her with a smile so bright that Hamish was embarrassed for her. "Don't go. We were just hoping we'd get to meet some of the people here."

"Look, I have to . . ."

"I'm Nelda Scofield and this is Hamish . . ." Nelda's voice went up, quavering. "Couldn't you sit down for a minute?"

"I really ought to . . ." The old lady seemed to see the need in Nelda's face because she said, "Oh hell, sure. Name's Lucy Fortmain," and plopped in one of the chairs.

The silence was ragged, embarrassing; Hamish saw Nelda going through her purse, mentally sizing up the larder, realizing she had nothing to offer her guest. He had come this far for her so he fished in his pockets. "Have a Life Saver?"

The old lady turned with a gracious smile. "Hell, sure."

"I'm sorry we don't have anything more exciting to offer," Nelda said. Hamish saw she was on the verge of tears.

Lucy patted her hand. "Lemon was always my favorite."

"That collar," Nelda said. "That's a lovely looking collar."

"Daugher made it. Tatting. I taught her when she was a kid."

"It's lovely," Nelda said.

"Margaret, m'oldest. Do you know, I have seven kids?"

Nelda touched her flat bosom. "We have two—a boy and a girl."

"Oh, how old are they?"

"Thirty-nine and forty-three. Lost our youngest when he was in his teens."

"Forty-three," Lucy said thoughtfully. "That's just about the cutest age."

"You should have seen ours when they found out we were leaving," Nelda said. "They were fit to be tied."

"Oh, so were mine," Lucy said. "You know how kids are."

"They begged us to stay with them in Waukegan, but when I showed them the brochure, how beautiful it was, well, they just had to give in gracefully; Mother, they said, we'll just have to give in gracefully."

Lucy said, "Well, *my* kids said, if it was any place but here, they'd come and drag me out, but they know I'm in such good hands . . ."

"I know." Nelda was gaining confidence. "I sensed that about the place as soon as we came in. All the attendants, the doctors . . ."

". . . All the help," Lucy said. "It's as close as the buzzer by your bed." She lowered her head, brooding. After a while she said, with determined cheer: "And there are lots of parties and stuff, clubs and dances and all. My kids could never give me all that."

"It's all so friendly," Nelda said.

"Well. Uh. Yes. They have people to pick you up if you fall and people to come in the night if you have a bad dream, and people on the terrace, they're paid to talk to you, and people to bring you shots you don't even want . . ." Lucy was beginning to sound depressed. "It's all just great. If only . . ."

Nelda pressed her. "If only?"

Lucy shook herself. "Welp. I'll say one thing. We all have a lot in common here. Same problems, same regrets. We've all come the same distance, and we're all going the same way." She snorted. "All in the same damn boat."

Hamish said, quietly, "What do you mean, going the same way?"

"I can't explain. It's just that for everything they give you in this place, they take something away." She went on bleakly, "Some mornings I get up and don't know who I am. There isn't even any mirror, so I can check."

"You were telling us about the people," Nelda said with bright determination. "Interests, friends, all the things that keep you here."

"I'd leave in a minute, if they'd let me." Lucy stood like a small ramrod. "Kids don't want me. *That's* why I'm here."

Nelda's voice rose. "No."

"Well, I'm off. Thanks for the Life Saver. If you see Cletus, tell him they're after him."

"Wait a minute . . ."

She was in the doorway. "How many charms you got on your grandmother bracelet?"

Nelda said, defensively: "Five."

"You lose. I've got twenty-four." The door closed on her.

"Damn jail," Hamish said, tenting for a reaction; Nelda had her head turned so he couldn't see her face. "Just like a damn jail. Even the damn chairs are bolted down."

"Now, now, settle down."

"Damn jail," he said again. "Prison furniture. Prison rules."

She put down the nightie she was unpacking and turned. "I suppose there weren't any rules at Albert's house? Or when we were living with Lorraine? 'Don't use that chair, Daddy . . .' " Her voice was ugly, but he recognized the inflections. " 'We're going to have some people in for dinner, Mommy, I wonder if you and Daddy would mind . . .' "

"Don't." He knew it was already too late to head her off.

"You used to have to smoke in the coal room at Albert's; Lucy made you stop tying flies. And how about all those mornings when you had to go down cellar at five or six, so you wouldn't wake up anybody when you coughed?"

"They're our *kids*, Nelda. You'll put up with a lot of things for kids. Nelda, we were born in Waukegan, and that's where we belong."

"So you want to go back and let them go on hurting us. They don't need us any more, Spike, don't you see? They passed us one day when we weren't looking, they outgrew us and every day since then they have been getting bigger and stronger, and the two of us . . ." She took his hand. "We had to get out of there before we just faded away."

"Dammit, Nelda, they're our past. They're all the future we've got." Hamish freed himself without even noticing what he was doing. He was at the window now, tired and thoughtful. "I read somewhere about how they used to handle it in New Hampshire, or maybe it was Vermont. Put the old people out in the barn every winter, stacked 'em like cordwood and left 'em to freeze until spring." He pressed his forehead against the shutters, dreaming. "Then one sunny day in spring all the children and grandchildren would come for them, they'd lay the old bodies out in the sun to thaw so they could help with the planting. There they were, out of the way until somebody needed them. And when they woke up they were home where they belonged, all warmed up, with plenty to do."

"Hamish, that's *terrible*."

"They were *needed*. What's so terrible about that?" From where he stood he could see part of the porch and the fringes of the court below; he could not see but imagined a hundred thousand identical quadrangles stretching beyond, all quiet, all orderly, all crammed with bodies full of pills and injections. The old people were all in their places, hooked up to intravenous tubes, and around them the rooms were neat and tidy with no junk in sight; someone had swept out all the fragments of their past and there they were, laid out with their hair brushed smoothly and all the character laundered out of their clothes. He and Nelda would be just like them soon, they would be . . . He turned to Nelda, breathing hard. "They were *needed*. Who needs us here?"

When Nelda spoke her voice was so low he hardly heard her. Straining, he made it out: "I need you, Hamish."

He couldn't help himself; his mouth filled with tears.

"Please, for me. Remember how it was . . ." She didn't go on; she didn't have to, her tone struck echoes, and winter was in the room; he was at her bedside, nursing her after her fall and promising anything just to make her live; winter was in the room and he was keeping her alive on promises, feeding her on gaudy, color-shot brochures.

He sighed heavily. "I remember." Then, on a last hope. "You were sick, you *needed* to think . . ."

"I still need. I need to be safe. I'm sick to death of being tired and sick and being afraid of being sick. Promise you'll stay, Hamish. For me?"

He wasn't ready to face her; he didn't have to because the door slapped wide and Cletus was in the room like a lightning bolt, with limbs flailing and electricity crackling in his beard. Before they could stop him he slammed the door and headed into the tiny bathroom; he was burrowing in the shower. When Hamish went in after him and tried to pull him out he turned and spat like a cat.

"Let go, you son of a bitch, they're after me."

Lucy was next, crowding into the tiny bathroom, and the three of them went round and round, Cletus flapping and blubbering, Lucy trying to pull him off the shower seat. "Come on, Clete, no use fighting. The cart's outside."

"Let go, dammit."

Hamish found himself crowded against the basin; he hunkered up on it, trying to stay out of the way. He was conscious of Nelda whimpering just outside the bathroom door.

"Come on, Clete." Lucy was wheedling. "Come on boy, come on. Tchum on."

He poked his head out. "Have they gone?"

"You know damn well they haven't gone." She grabbed quickly, before he could duck back into the shower; she nodded to Hamish and together they began manoeuvring him back into the room.

He pulled back, saying sullenly, "Why did you have to come along and ruin everything?"

The old man couldn't see her face but Hamish could; it was lined with pain. She said, "God knows I didn't want to. I just thought it might make it a little easier."

He was whimpering. "I want my shot, it's past time for my shot."

"You've had so *many* shots, Clete, and angiograms, and vitamin pills, and X-rays, and IVs. Come on, baby, they'll take you along all neat and tidy, and maybe . . ."

He snuffled hopefully. "Maybe?"

"Maybe they'll even give you a shot before you go."

He bounded away from her, howling. "I don't want to go."

Hamish stepped in front of the old man; he could feel his back hairs going stiff and he had to clear his throat twice before his voice would work properly. "Look here," he said to Lucy, "You have no right. If he doesn't want to go with you . . ."

She looked at him without passion. "He has to go. It's time."

Cletus was blubbering. "But I've only been here for a *minute* . . ."

"Fourteen years. Fourteen mortal years." She moved past Hamish, putting her arm around the old man's shoulder. "You smoothed the way for me when I came in, knew it was hard for me, being shoved in here. If I'd known then that I was going to have to come for you . . ." She jammed her fist into her mouth, trying not to cry. When she was able she said, to Hamish, "He wasn't always like this. Used to put up a hell of a fight. He got us napkins at dinner, and later lights . . ."

"It can't be time, I haven't had my shot. I'll be good, I promise I will . . ." Cletus was wiping his nose on his beard.

"Come on, Clete. Brace up. Take it like a man."

"I won't go, it's not my turn." He wrenched out of her

grip, grinning slyly. "It's not my turn at all. It's your turn."

"Oh, Clete, you're a caution."

He giggled, falling into an old pattern of banter. "Or maybe you're so ugly they won't take you."

"You old goat . . ." She brightened. "Hey, that sounds more like my old Clete. Now go on out there and show those guys you can take it like a man."

"Oh Lucy, I'm afraid."

Lucy looked over his head at the Scofields. "Would you believe he was the best linotypist in the East? *That's* what this place does to you."

He was weeping, wiping his eyes with her hand. "Please don't let them take me, please."

"Takes it right out of you."

"Lucy, Lucy, Ma. Mom. Mom. *Mommy . . .*"

She still stood proudly but her old face was glazed with tears. "You see?" She patted Cletus on the shoulder. "There there, baby. You'll be all right . . ."

Hamish said, quietly, "Maybe you'd better tell us about it."

But she wasn't listening. She was patting Cletus, saying, "You'll be all right, I'll take care of you . . ." Hamish would have shaken an answer out of her but she was busy with her own thoughts, planning. "Well," she said abstractedly, "I'll show *them*." Then she was busy with her buttons and in the next second her dress fell to the floor and she stood, straight and proud of her stiff white muslin underslip. "Here," she said to Cletus. "You just slip into my frock."

"Lucy . . ." The old man should have been protesting. Hamish wanted to take him by the shoulders and shake him and scream into his face until he turned and went outside and *fought . . .*

It was too late. Cletus took the dress and shimmied into it, stuffing his beard into the bodice, not caring that his hairy arms and black trouser legs stuck out incongruously. When he was ready Lucy held him off at arm's length, revolving him with one hand.

"Yes," she said finally, "You'll do. Now you go on out,

and if they try and stop you, duck into the Ladies Room.
I don't think they'll follow you into the Ladies Room."

"Lucy, I . . . I don't know what to say."

"Never mind. Let's just say you're not up to it, and I
am." She gave him a shove. "You go wait in the Ladies
Room until you hear them leave."

He danced on the doorsill for a minute, looking as if he
would thank her, or apologize, or beg her to change her
mind, but it was apparent to all of them that he didn't
really want her to change her mind; in the end, he wasn't
even able to thank her. Instead he said, dully, "It's time
for my shot."

Lucy watched out the window, turning back to the
Scofields with a grim smile. "He made it." She smoothed
her slip and put a hand to her hair. "Well . . ."

Hamish moved toward her. "You're not going out
there . . ."

She was cool and proud. "Why not?"

"You know what's out there."

"Hell yes. The dead cart. From the Tower of Sleep."

Nelda's voice went up and up. "It isn't even your
turn . . ."

"I'd rather go now, while I still have some choice. After
all, I've still got my pride. Pride's all I have left." She
looked past Nelda, talking directly to Hamish. "You understand. If I'd just held out, you know, when they tried to
put me in this place. I could have sold flowers or something, to earn my keep."

Hamish said, "Or camped in the train station."

"Or gone on relief," Lucy said wistfully. "Anything but
this. I gave up everything when I let myself be suckered
into this. Well, it's been nice knowing you." She raised
one hand in a gladiator's salute.

"Hang on, dammit. Hang *on*."

She turned to Hamish. "You're still your own man.
Better get out before it's too late."

The door slammed behind her. There was a second of
silence from outside, then the sound of a scuffle, the rattle
of bodies against metal and the crash of heels on the

cement. Hamish could hear the sounds of arms and heads in desperate friction and over it, Lucy's voice rising: "Let go of me, you bastards. I'll climb on by my*self*."

There was a long pause and then the rattle, or rumble, receding as the cart took her away.

Before the sound faded Hamish was at the suitcase, stuffing Nelda's resort clothes in willy-nilly, putting sneakers in on top of her Capri pants and finishing off with the sunshade, not minding that clothes stuck out of all the cracks when he sat on top and tried to close the thing. "Come on," he said, assuming she was with him. "If you want those damn kids' pictures, you'd better get their pictures. I'll sneak the suitcases out the back and wait in the bushes by the gate . . ."

"No."

". . . you can tell them you're going out for a little walk . . ." He climbed off the suitcase slowly, seeing that she had taken the family pictures to her bosom. She was sitting quietly in one of the two straight chairs. "Give me those damn things, don't you want to take them home?"

"I'm not going."

"The dead cart, Nelda." He tugged at the pictures, he had to get her moving. "The Tower of Sleep."

She let go of the pictures unexpectedly. "I already knew."

The pictures fell between them with a little crash. "You *knew*?"

"Of course I did, it's in the back of the brochure. The tiny print."

He was backing away from her. "But you didn't *tell* me."

"I was hoping you'd get to like it here first. It's perfectly fair," she said matter-of-factly. "When you've used up your quota of medicine they come for you. The funerals here are beautiful, I've seen the card; it doesn't hurt at all and in the meantime you have everything you want."

"Nelda, its monstrous."

She stood now, looking at him so steadily that he

backed into a bed and sat down. "It's better than anything we *had*—all those damn fights with the kids; being sick, being afraid. They have drugs to take care of that kind of thing, they have everything you need over in the Tower of Hope, and if you fall—there's somebody there. There wasn't anybody there last winter . . ."

He winced. "Never mind."

"I lay in that alley for twelve hours. I just ducked around a corner to get out of the cold and there I was in the dirt with slush running under me and blood in my mouth, I couldn't even call for help. I don't want to go through that again, I don't even want to be *afraid* of going through it, and I don't . . ."

She was near tears; she opened the suitcase again, taking out the Capri pants, and when she had collected herself she took a deep breath and began again.

"I don't want to be dependent on the kids. They're at us all the time, Don't this, Don't that, and as soon as company comes they scrub us and prop us up in the living-room, Exhibit A. Well I'm not up to it any more, Hamish, I'm just not up to it."

He saw an opening. "Are you any better off here? You know what we are? Vegetables, goddam vegetables, they'll tend us and water us and cart us off before we can even die on the vine . . ."

"It's worth it for a little comfort and safety." She was pushing him away from the suitcase, trying to unpack. After a little scuffle she gave up, saying, sadly, "I was hoping you'd get to like it here. If only you'd get to like it here . . ." She changed her tone, accusing him. "You promised you'd give it a chance."

"I didn't promise to drop dead. I'm going home."

"You'd rather go back there and suffer . . ."

"Hell yes. At least I'll know I'm still alive." He had the suitcase to himself now, he was jamming things in again, wrestling it shut. "Look, I'd rather be hurt and sick *and* afraid, I'd rather be living with those damn kids . . ."

"Don't make me tell you. Promise you'll stay."

Something in her voice arrested him. "Tell me what?"

"I don't want to have to tell you. Hamish, the kids . . ."

"I've just got to get out of here." He was already in motion, trying not to listen. "If I can just get going before it gets dark . . ."

"The kids." The words popped into the room. Nelda hushed him gently, saying, "It was right after my fall, I was laid up in bed and in they came, Albert and Lorraine. They were so damn sympathetic, all about how awful winters were for us, how we deserved better than that, that and living in back rooms . . . I was too sick to make any sense of it. Then they started bringing folders, pictures of swimming-pools and people playing in the sun . . . I don't know, it all looked sort of good, and after they left I looked at some of the folders, I began to dream a little bit."

"You don't have to tell me any more, Nelda, just remember me when I'm gone."

"Let me finish." She had him by the arm now; her fingers were like iron bands. "Then one day they came back, they said, how would we like to try Golden Acres, and I thought about it, I told them it was probably all right for people without *folks* but we'd just as soon stay home, with them, and then . . ."

She didn't have to finish, he didn't want to have to finish, but she seemed bound to go on. He tried to stop her, he said, "Nelda . . ."

"Then I found out. It was all arranged, they'd sold off our stocks for the down payment, I was supposed to break the news." She went on grimly. "I sat there in that iron bed with my back hurting and those damn smug kids staring at me and I thought, I thought Nothing can be worse than this. It was the kids, Hamish. The kids wanted to get rid of us."

"I know."

"You didn't know."

"I didn't want to admit it, but I knew it all along."

"So here we are." She managed a brave little smile. "Might as well make the best of it."

"I can't do it, Nelda, I have to go." He was desperate to

be away, to have her come with him before the manager or the bellboys came along and locked them in; he tugged at her, saying, "Come on, come *on*," and when she wouldn't move he said, "Do you want to sit and wait for them? They'll come with the cart and after that they'll put our clothes in a box to be burned and then they'll scrub everything and change the linens and disinfect the room. Nelda, when I go, I want to leave something behind, even if it's only a—a *smell*."

She disengaged herself. "I'll miss you so much."

"I've always been my own man, Nelda; I've got to go where somebody cares."

"Do you think anybody out *there* cares?" They were having a little battle over the suitcase; she made him put it down and she had it open again.

"At least they'll feel *some*thing about me, even if it's only dislike." He tried to lift her with his voice. "Maybe I'll go back to Waukegan and get a job."

"Waukegan doesn't want us, Hamish, nobody does."

"I was born in that town, my past is in the streets, my past and my future, if I've got any future. I've got to go and see."

She shook her head. "You're only fooling yourself."

"Then *let* me fool myself."

They were both crying; there was a little silence while he fumbled in the tiny closet and put on his coat. Nelda brushed his shoulders and turned down his collar and she spoke, finally, saying: "You'll need a few things. You can't go off without a few things."

He tried to steady his voice. "The overnight bag, if you don't need it."

She said, quietly, "I'm not going anywhere."

"I'll get a job, I used to be a pretty good bricklayer. Then I'll find us a place and I'll send for you." He took her hand, lingering. "You will come, won't you?"

She said, with love, "We'll be together soon."

He wrapped his dry bones around her in a fierce embrace. "I'll find a place and then I'll send for you. It won't be long." He let her go and now he was in the doorway; he had to break away or he would never be free.

Her voice was so low he could hardly make out what she was saying: "It doesn't matter where we are . . . it won't be for long."

He might have turned. He might have gone back inside the room to plead with her but the sun was on its way down and in the distance there began a subtle rumble and he knew without stopping to think about it that it was coming his way.

CRIMINAL IN UTOPIA

MACK REYNOLDS

Mack Reynolds is alive and well in Mexico. He has lived in, or visited, more countries than there are States in the Union. As an on-the-spot student of political systems he has seen them all, and made comparisons, so that in his fiction he has produced more interesting systems of government—and misgovernment—than have his sedentary peers. Secure now in his mountain retreat among the Toltec ruins, he points his critical cannon at the land of his birth. At credit cards. So what? So what if we use them more and more . . . and a criminal learns to buck the system? Then the following might occur.

Rex Moran dialled his wrist teevee phone for the time and looked at the clock face that appeared on the screen. A robot voice said, "When the bell rings it will be exactly two minutes until eight hours." A tiny bell rang.

Rex Moran grunted and looked about the small apartment. He had better get going.

First, though, he took his Universal Credit Card from an inner pocket of his jerkin and inserted it in the slot of his standard teevee phone which sat on his living cum

179

bedroom's sole table. He said into the screen, "Credit balance check, please."

Within moments, a robot voice said, "Ten shares of Inalienable Basic. No shares of Variable Basic. Current cash credit, one dollar and twenty-three cents."

"One dollar and twenty-three cents," he muttered. "Holy living Zoroaster. I didn't think I'd have to start with that little on hand."

He dialled Credit and waited until a face faded in on the screen. It was a businesslike, brisk, possibly impatient, face.

"Jason May, here. Assistant Credit Manager, Inalienable Basic Dividends," he said.

Rex Moran put his Uni-Credit Card on the screen and said, "I'd like an advance on my dividends."

The other was seated at a desk. "Just a moment, please," he said and touched a button. He listened to a report on a desk phone screen then looked back at Moran. "You're already two months ahead."

"I know that," Rex Moran said doggedly, "but it's an emergency."

"It is always an emergency, Mr. Moran," the other said flatly. "What is the emergency? Your records show that you are almost invariably as far ahead as you can get on your monthly dividends. As you must know, the government charges interest on such advances. In the long run, Mr. Moran, you lose."

"I know, I know," Rex Moran said, an element of complaint in his voice. "I've had a long set of bad luck. One thing after another."

"What is the current emergency, please?"

Rex Moran wished he had thought this out in more detail before launching into his fling. He said, "I've got a sick brother, I have to go help."

"Where is this brother, Mr. Moran?"

"In Panama City."

"One moment, please." The other went back to one of his desk screens. In only moments he looked up again with a sigh.

"Mr. Moran, the computer banks have no records of you having a brother at all, in Panama City or anywhere else. Request denied. And Mr. Moran . . ."

"Yeah?" Rex Moran said in disgust.

"It is a minor offense to lie to a credit manager in attempt to secure an advance on dividends. I shall take no action on this occasion, but the fact will be entered on your record in the computer banks."

"Oh, great," Rex Moran growled. He flicked off his screen. "I didn't expect that to work anyway," he muttered.

He thought over his plans for a few minutes, then squared his shoulders and dialled the local branch of the ultra-market, on his auto-delivery box. He was a man in his early thirties, mildly burly in build and with a not really unpleasant but a broken face of one who has either seen military combat, or perhaps been a pugilist. In actuality, neither was the case.

The ultra-market in the screen, he dialled the children's toy section, boys' toys, and then military type toys. He finally narrowed it down to guns and dialled one that came to only seventy-cents. It would have to do. He put his Uni-Credit Card in the slot, his thumbprint on the screen and ordered the toy.

Within minutes, it was in the auto-delivery box, and he put it in the side pocket of his jerkin. It was on the smallish side, but black and at any distance at all realistic enough for his purpose.

He moved over to his library booster teevee screen and dialled a newspaper, then the paper of two weeks previous, and the obituaries. He went through several papers before he found the one that seemed most likely, by the address and the information in the item, and made some notes with his stylo.

Finally, he dialled the address and waited untill a face faded in on his phone screen.

The other frowned at him, in lack of recognition.

Rex Moran said, "Mr. Vassilis? My name is Roy McCord."

The other was a tired looking obvious aristocrat, perhaps a few years the other side of sixty.

Still frowning, he said, "What can I do for you, Mr. McCord?"

"I just got back into town and heard the bad news. I'm a friend—forgive me, Mr. Vassilis—*was* a friend of Jerry Jerome."

The other's face lightened slightly and then went sad. "Ah, I see. I am afraid he hadn't mentioned your name, but then Jerome had many friends of whom I knew little."

"Yes, sir. I'd like the opportunity to offer my condolences in person," Rex Moran began.

The older man was frowning slightly and began to respond.

But Moran hurried on. "But I also have something of Jerry's that I suppose should go to you."

Rex Moran managed to look slightly embarrassed. "Well, sir, I . . . well, I think it would be better if I just brought it over."

The other was mystified. However, he shrugged. "Very well, young man. Let me see, I shall be free at, say nine hours this morning, and should be able to give you a few minutes."

"Fine, sir. I'll be there." Rex Moran switched off the screen before the other could say anything further.

For a moment he stared down at the blank screen, then shifted muscles in his shoulders. "First step," he said. "So far, so good. Maybe I shouldn't have used this phone, but in the long run it won't make any difference."

He didn't take the vacuum tube transport from his own building, knowing that a record was kept of all trips in the computer banks, and the john-fuzz might trace back later on his Uni-Credit Card number. Instead, he walked several blocks and entered a public terminal.

He looked up at the map and selected another terminal a couple of blocks from his destination, then entered the next twenty-seater going through that point. After putting his credit card in the payment slot, he realized that with the buying of the toy gun, he probably had only a few cents left to his balance. He didn't even have enough credit to get back to his apartment if this little romp pickled. What a laugh that would give the boys if he had to walk home.

He left the vaccum-tube transport terminal and walked to the building where Vassilis lived. This was the crucial point now. If there were others present, his plan had come a cropper. However, if he had read between the lines correctly, the senior Mr. Vassilis lived alone in his apartment in this swank neighborhood.

There was an identity screen in the front entry. Keeping his fingers crossed that his Universal Credit Card wouldn't be required for entrance, he said into the screen, "Roy McCord, on appointment to see Mr. Frank Vassilis."

The door opened, and he entered.

There were two elevators. He entered one and said, "The apartment of Frank Vassilis."

The Vassilis apartment was on the top floor but one. Rex Moran got out of the elevator, found a door with the Vassilis name on it and activated the door screen. When it lit up, he said into it, "Roy McCord, calling on Mr. Vassilis, by appointment."

The door opened, and he stepped through.

And came to a halt. The man standing there in a dark suit was not the Mr. Vasillis he had spoken to earlier on the teevee phone. This worthy was a stiffish type, of possibly fifty. His eyes went up and down Rex Moran superciliously, taking in the less than elegant suit, taking in the rugged features.

He said, "Yes, sir. Mr. McCord? The master is awaiting you in his escape room."

The *master*? Holy jumping Zoroaster, Vassilis had a man servant. Whoever heard of personal servants in this day and age? The obituary had hinted that the old boy was upperclass, but Moran hadn't been thinking in terms of something so rich as an establishment with a servant.

However, he followed along. It was the largest apartment he could off-hand ever remember being in. They went down one hall, turned right and down another one.

There wasn't even an identity screen on the door before which they stopped. The servant knocked gently and opened the door before there was any reply. Evidently, old Vassilis was expecting him, all right.

The servant stood stiffly and said, "Mr. McCord."

The elderly man Rex Moran had talked to on the teevee phone earlier looked up from where he sat in a comfort chair, a small magnifying glass in one hand, a dozen or so stamps on a small table before him. He was evidently a philatelist.

He said, "Ah, yes, Mr. Roy McCord, Jerome's friend. Please come in." As the servant had before him, he took in Moran's clothing and general appearance, and his eyebrows went up slightly. "Now, what is it I can do for you, Mr. McCord?"

Rex Moran looked at the servant.

Vassilis said, "That will be all, Franklin."

Franklin turned and left, closing the door quietly behind him.

No need to mince around. Rex Moran brought the toy gun from his pocket briefly, let the other see it, and returned it to his side pocket, but still holding it in his hand.

He said, "This is a romp, Mr. Vasillis."

The other goggled at him. "You . . . you mean you are a thief? That you got into my home on false pretenses?"

Moran let his face go empty. "I wouldn't put it that way. Let's just say that I'm tired of not getting my share of the cake. And since the powers that be won't give it to me, I'm taking it."

The old man stared at him. "You are a fool, young man."

"Maybe, maybe not." Rex Moran jiggled the gun in his side pocket, suggestively.

"Being a thief doesn't make sense in this day. Society has made arrangements to defend itself against the thief. There's not enough profit in petty crime to pay off."

Rex Moran grinned at him sourly. "I didn't exactly have petty crime in mind, Mr. Vassilis. Now, hand me your credit card."

"What other kind of crime is possible? Nobody but I can spend my dollar credits. I can't give them away, gamble them away, throw them away, be cheated out of them. Only *I* can spend my dividends."

"We'll see about that." Rex Moran nodded. "Now, let's have your Universal Credit Card." He jiggled the gun in his pocket again.

The older man contemptuously took a beautiful leather wallet from an inner pocket and brought forth a standard Uni-Credit Card. He handed it over.

Moran said, "You have a vacuum delivery box in this room? Oh, yeah, here we are. Zoroaster, look at the size of it! Now that's the advantage of being an upperclass like you, Mr. Vassilis. You should see the teeny auto-delivery box in my mini-apartment. If I want anything of any size at all, I've got to use the box down in the lobby of the crummy building I'm in. Now, with a nice big auto-delivery box like this anything you wanted would have to be really super-size before you couldn't get it delivered right here into your escape room."

Vassilis said, "You are a fool, young man. The officials will be after you in no time flat."

Moran grinned at him and sat down before the box, keeping one eye on the other. He put the card in the teevee screen's slot and said, "Credit balance, please."

A robot voice said, "Ten shares of Inalienable Basic. Two thousand and forty-six shares of Variable Basic. Current cash credit, forty-two thousand and twenty-nine dollars and eighteen cents."

Rex Moran whistled. "Two-thousand-and-forty-six-shares-of-Variable!"

Vassilis grunted contempt of him.

Moran dialled the ultra-market, then sports, then fire-arms, then handguns. He finally selected a .38 Recoiless and dialled it and a box of cartridges.

He thought for a moment, then dialled photography and selected a Poloroid-Pentax and some film for it.

"Might as well do this up brown," he said conversationally to the older man. "Might as well put a *generous* hole in that credit balance."

"There'll be no hole—as you call it—at all," Vassilis said bitterly. "When I report this thievery, the authorities will return to my account the sum involved in any deprecations you have performed."

Rex Moran dialled men's clothing and took his time selecting a full outfit, including shoes.

"Now, this is the crucial point," he said thoughtfully, to no one in particular. He dialled jewelry and finally selected a two-thousand-dollar diamond ring.

"I guess that's it," he said. Then, "Oh, one other thing." He dialled sports again, and camping, and eventually a length of rope.

He turned back to Frank Vassilis. "And now, old man, come on over here and stick your thumbprint on this order screen."

"Suppose I refuse?"

Rex Moran grinned at him. "Why should you? Like you said, when you report this, the authorities will return your credit dollars to you and come looking for me. You're not losing anything."

The older man, grumbling, came erect in his chair. He came over to the auto-delivery box and, with a sneer of contempt for his intruder, stuck his right thumb print on the screen.

Moments later, the articles had arrived.

Vassilis returned to his comfort chair.

Rex Moran began fishing the articles he had ordered from the box. He loaded the gun, put it next to him, within handy reach and then dressed in his new clothes. He took up the camera and slung it over his shoulder. He looked at the ring admiringly and tucked it away in an inner pocket, and then the gun.

He muttered, "I have half a mind to order a few more of these but that big a drain on your account all at the same time might throw some relays and have the computer people check back."

"Thief," Vassilis said bitterly.

Moran grinned at him. "What's your beef? It won't be you who loses."

He took up the rope. "First we'll tie you up a bit, old chum-pal, and then we'll call in Franklin, or whatever you called him, and do a job on him."

"You'll never get away with this, you young cloddy," the old man bit out.

"Famous last words," Moran grinned back at him.

II

Back on the street, he realized it was going to be necessary to walk to his next destination. His credit standing simply did not allow even such a small sum as riding in the vacuum tubes. However, happily, it wasn't as far as all that. As he walked, he took the toy gun from his pocket and threw it into a waste receptacle. He had the real thing now.

He found the neighborhood and had a choice of three alternatives. He took the smallest of the shops and entered.

There were even a few display cases. How anachronistic could you get. He grunted sour amusement to himself; here was the last of the kulaks, the last of the small businessmen.

A quiet man of about fifty entered from a back room and took Rex in before saying in a soft voice, "Yes, sir, what can I do for you?"

Rex Moran went into his act. Hesitantly, he said, "I understand that you sometimes buy personal property."

"That is correct. Buy and sell. But what type of property, Mr. . . . ?"

"Adams," Rex Moran said. "Timothy Adams. I have a ring that used to belong to my mother. It is of no value to me, now, and I thought . . . well, I might as well realize what dollar credit value it has."

"I see. Please sit down, Mr. Adams. Heirloom jewelry is a bit of a drug on the market, but we can take a look." He sat himself behind a desk and motioned to a straight chair.

Rex Moran sat down and brought the diamond ring from his pocket and proffered it. The other took it and set it on the table. He looked at Rex Moran thoughtfully. "This is a very modern setting, Mr. Adams. I had gained the impression that it was an older piece your mother had left you."

"Oh, no," Rex Moran said. "She bought it not too very long before she died. If I had a wife, or someone, I might give it to her, but I haven't."

The other looked at him evenly. "Mr. Adams, I am not a fence, you know. This is a legitimate business."

"Fence?" Rex Moran said blankly.

"I buy and sell such items as art objects and jewelry, but I do not receive stolen goods. Where did you say your mother bought this?"

"On a vacation in Common Eur-Asia. In Budapest, I think, or possibly Belgrade."

"So it would be untraceable here in the United States of the Americas."

"Why, it never occurred to me."

The shop owner took up the ring and looked at it thoughtfully. He brought a jeweller's glass from a drawer and peered through it.

He put it down finally and looked at Rex Moran. "I'll give you two hundred dollars for it."

"Two hundred dollars! My mother said she paid more than two thousand."

"Then she paid too much. The markup on jewelry is very high, Mr. Adams, and such items as this can take a very long time to move."

Rex Moran thought about it. "Make it three hundred."

The other considered that. "Very well," he said finally. "But I am making a mistake."

"Yeah," Rex Moran said sourly. He brought his Uni-

Credit Card from his pocket and stuck it into one of the slots on the other's Exchange Screen.

The shop owner put the ring in a drawer, brought forth his own Universal Credit Card and put it into the other exchange slot. He said into the screen, "Please transfer the amount of three hundred dollars from my account to this other card."

A robot voice said, "Transfer completed."

Rex Moran retrieved his Uni-Credit Card and came to his feet. "I still think I was robbed," he muttered.

The other said nothing, simply sat there and watched after him as Rex Moran left the shop.

Well, he now had three hundred dollars to his account. That was a damn sight less than he had expected to get. However, he hadn't dared buy a more expensive piece of jewelry than the two thousand dollar piece, on Vassilis' credit card. There would have been more of a chance of the shop owner checking on such an item. More chance of it being able to be traced. Besides, if he had drained Vassilis' account too badly, there might have been a computer check at that point.

He strode rather rapidly to the nearest vacuum-tube transport terminal and into it, wanting to get out of the neighborhood as quickly as possible. He took a two-seater vehicle to the downtown area of the pseudo-city, if a pseudo-city can be said to have a downtown area.

When he left the vacuum tube, it was to emerge in the vicinity of several restaurants. It was just about noon, but since he hadn't been able to afford breakfast, he was feeling hunger. Well, three hundred dollars was three hundred dollars, and he might as well blow himself to a fairly good repast in an auto-cafeteria.

He selected one and sat himself down at a table and stared down at the menu listed on the table top. To hell with anything based on Antarctic krill, plankton protein, or soy beans; he was up to some real animal protein and Zoroaster could take the cost.

He put his credit card in the table slot, his thumbprint on the screen and dialled chicken and a mug of sea-booze.

He would have liked a shot of pseudo-whisky to begin, but his funds weren't that unlimited.

His wrist teevee phone buzzed.

He looked down at it in some surprise. He had it set on Number One Priority, and only two people in the world were eligible to break in on him on that priority, and he certainly was not expecting a call from either.

But there was a strange face in the tiny screen. Strange and severe.

The voice said, "This is Distribution Service, Subdivision Police. Rex Moran, you are under arrest for attempt to violate regulations pertaining to usage of the Universal Credit Card. Report immediately to the nearest Police Administrative Station. Failure to do so will compound the felony."

"Get lost, fuzz-john," Rex Moran snarled. He snapped the instrument off, then stared down at the blank screen in dismay. What had gone wrong? Especially, what had gone wrong so quickly? It had to be something to do with his selling that damned ring. But what? He had expected the ring to stay in that tiny shop, waiting for a customer for months, perhaps even years. And even then, when it was resold, the transaction should never have appeared on the computer records, except as an exchange of dollar credit from the purchaser's account to the shopkeeper's.

What foul luck! Vassilis must have put in an immediate alarm, and the police must have contacted every place in town where Rex Moran could possibly dispose of the purloined ring.

He had to think fast. They'd be after him now. Damn and double damn. He wouldn't even be able to return to his mini-apartment. He was on the run, and for a meaningless amount such as three hundred dollars, and even that now was of no use. He wouldn't dare use his credit card; the computers were surely watching for him.

They could also zero-in on his wrist teevee phone. He reached down, in disgust, and began to rip it off. However, the screen lit up again, and a new face was there.

A voice rasped, "Now hear this, all citizens. Crimes

against the government of the United States of the Americas have been committed by Rex Moran, including assault, robbery, sale of stolen property and attempted misuse of the Universal Credit Card. All citizens are requested to cooperate in his apprehension. The criminal is dangerous and armed. Here is his face."

Rex groaned when his face appeared on the tiny screen. Happily, it was a fairly old photo, and taken before some of his present scarred features had become what they were.

He ripped the instrument from his wrist and flung it into a corner. At this early hour there were none others present in the auto-cafeteria, thank the living Zoroaster for that.

He came to his feet and hurried for the door. In the far distance, he could hear a siren. Undoubtedly, it was for him. You didn't hear police sirens that often in the pseudo-cities of the Ultra-welfare State.

He hurried down the street and turned a corner as quickly as possible. He dared not use the vacuum tube. He dared not summon a floater, for that matter.

But that brought something to mind.

He found a fairly isolated spot and waited until a pedestrian came along. He brought his gun from his pocket and said, "Hold it, chum-pal."

The other looked at him, down at the gun, up into Rex Moran's face again and blanched. "Why, why you're the criminal just flashed on the teevee."

"That's right, chum-pal, and you look just like the sort of chum-pal who'd cooperate with a man with a shooter trained on his tummy."

The other was wide-eyed and ashen. "Why . . . why, of course."

"Okay. Quick now, dial a floater on your wrist teevee phone."

"Of course, of course. Don't be nervous."

"I'm not nervous." Rex Moran grinned at him and jiggled the gun up and down. "Hurry it up."

The other dialled, and within moments an auto-floater

cab turned the corner and pulled up next to them at the curb. The door opened.

Rex said, "Quick, put your Uni-Credit Card in the slot."

Even as the other was doing so, Moran was climbing into the back seat of the floater. He rasped, "Put your thumbprint on the screen." While the other did that, Rex Moran was dialling his destination, not letting the other see.

He reached out suddenly and grasped the other's wrist teevee phone and ripped it off and stuck it in his pocket. He pulled the credit card from the floater's slot and handed it back to his victim.

"There," he said, "don't say I didn't do you a favor. Think of all the trouble you'd have if you didn't have a credit card."

He slammed the door shut and the floater took off.

Rex Moran said into the vehicle's screen, "Maximum speed, please."

A robot voice said, "Yes, sir."

He couldn't afford to stay in the floater for very long. Just enough to get out of this neighborhood. As soon as that cloddy he had just stuck up back there reported to the police, they'd check through the computers for the floater's destination. There'd be a record, based on the number of the victim's Uni-Credit Card. A record of *everything* seemingly went into the computer banks. Why not? He growled sourly; evidently their capacity was almost infinite.

Yes, they'd check the destination of his trip. However, he was not quite so silly as to go all the way to the destination he had dialled. About half way there, at a traffic control stop, he opened the door and left the floater to go on its own.

He ducked down a side street and took off at right angles to the avenue along which the floater was progressing.

Rex Moran now had a double problem. He grimaced wryly. An *immediate* double problem, that was. For one thing, he was still hungry. For another, he had to get off the streets. Citizens weren't apt to pay overmuch attention to the Distribution Service police calls over the teevee phone screens, but there was always the exception. Given time, someone would spot and report him, in spite of the poor photograph which just had been broadcast.

He could hear the stolen wrist teevee phone buzz in his pocket and brought it forth, flicking the tiny stud which prevented it from transmitting his face.

It was the same official as before, and he was making the same broadcast, but now reporting Rex Moran as last seen in that part of town where he had dialled the floater. Evidently his victim had reported.

That also meant they would know that Moran had the stolen wrist teevee phone and would shortly be zeroing in on it. He threw the instrument into the gutter and ground a heel down on it.

He had to get off the streets.

And suddenly he knew where to go.

In this vicinity there was a posh restaurant of which he had heard but had never been able to afford, nor had he really ever expected to be able to afford it. Well, things were different now.

He entered the building and took the elevator to the penthouse restaurant known as the Gourmet Room. The day was more advanced now, and upperclass office workers were beginning to stream in for the midday meal.

He avoided looking impressed at the ostentatious swank of this rendezvous of the ultra-wealthy and thanked his stars that he had thought of acquiring his present clothing. A headwaiter approached diffidently. In all his life, Rex Moran had never eaten in a restaurant which boasted live waiters. Now he tried to look unimpressed.

"A single, sir?" the maitre d'hotel said.

"Please," Rex Moran told him, keeping his voice softly modulated and as though such surroundings were an every day affair for him. "If possible, a table set back somewhere. I have a bit of figuring to do."

"Certainly, sir. This way."

He was seated in an out of the way alcove which suited his needs perfectly.

The maitre d' snapped his fingers, and a waiter scurried up.

There was no menu. It was that kind of a restaurant.

The maitre d' said unctuously, "Sir, today the *Gratin de langoustines Georgette* is superb."

Rex Moran hadn't the vaguest idea what *langoustines Georgette* might be, but he made a face as though considering.

"What else might you recommend?" he said.

"The chef has surpassed himself with the *poulet docteur*."

"That sounds good."

The waiter made a note.

"And a half bottle of Sylvaner of the Haut-Rhin, perhaps?"

"Fine."

Salad and dessert were settled upon, and then the maitre d' and the waiter were gone.

Rex Moran sighed inwardly and looked around. The only other diner within his immediate vicinity had his back to Moran.

He unslung the Poloroid-Pentax from his shoulder and brought from his pocket the cassette of film. He inserted it in the camera. Then he took from his inner pocket the Universal Credit Card he had appropriated from Frank Vassilis and examined it with care, spending particular time on the thumbprint.

Finally, he propped the card against the small vase in the table center, which held a single black rose, and focused the camera on it. He clicked the shutter then drew the photo from the camera back and stared at it. It didn't quite do. He tried again, getting the camera closer to the subject. He took half a dozen shots before he came up with as near a duplicate of the Universal Credit Card's thumbprint as he could hope for.

He put the credit card away, the camera back in its case, and brought forth his penknife. He was busily trimming the photo to be the exact size of a thumbprint when the waiter turned up with his first course.

Poulet docteur turned out to be the best chicken dish he had ever tasted. And the wine was excellent.

In the middle of his salad course, and before dessert, he came suddenly to his feet and hurried toward the the reception desk cum cashier's booth. It was there that the payment screen for the ultra-swank restaurant was to be found.

And it was there that the maitre d'hotel stood his eyebrows politely raised now.

Rex Moran said to him hurriedly, "I have just thought of something I must attend to. Please hold my dessert for me. And, please, keep an eye on my camera over there, will you?"

The maitre d' looked over at Moran's table. The camera sat upon it. He said, "Why, of course, sir."

Rex Moran left, still projecting an air of a suddenly remembered matter that must urgently be taken care of.

Down on the street he grimaced. One camera sacrificed to the game. However, he had no need of it now.

He was still in one of the best sections of town. He made his way toward a nearby hotel, holding a handkerchief over his face, as though trying to extract something from his left eye. There were quite a few pedestrians at this time of the day.

In the hotel, he approached the lone clerk at the reception desk. Now, he had to take his chances. If the man recognized him from the police broadcast—Rex Moran was on a spot.

He said, "I would like a small suite. Nothing ambitious. Living room, bedroom, bath. I doubt if I'll be entertaining."

"Why, yes sir, of course." The other looked beyond Moran. "Ah, your luggage, sir?"

"I have no luggage," Rex Moran said, off-handedly. "I just came in from the coast. Plan to do some shopping here for my wardrobe. Always buy my things here in the East. California styles are ludicrous."

"Yes sir, of course." The clerk motioned in the direction of the teevee screen slot on the desk. "Would you wish to register?"

"I'd rather see the suite, before deciding," Rex Moran said. "I'll register up there, if it's satisfactory."

"Oh, I'm sure it will be, sir. Let me suggest Suite Double A."

"Double A," Rex Moran said and made his way to the bank of elevators.

Inside the first elevator, he said, "Suite Double A."

"Yes, sir," a robot voice said.

Suite Double A was several stories up. Rex Moran emerged from the elevator, looked up at the direction signs on the wall and made his way to the suite in question.

It was quite the most elaborate quarters in which Rex Moran had ever been. Not that that was the issue, he would have taken the accommodations whatever they had resembled.

He approached the room's teevee phone screen and said into it, "This suite seems adequate, I'll take it."

A robot voice said, "Very good, sir. If you'll just put your Uni-Credit Card in the slot."

Rex Moran took a deep breath. He brought the card of Frank Vassilis from his pocket, inserted it in the slot. Then he brought forth the photo he had taken of the Vassilis right thumbprint and laid it on the screen. He picked it up again, immediately.

A robot voice said, "Thank you, sir."

Rex Moran took another deep breath and let it hiss out again between his teeth.

"*Zo-ro-as-ter*. I think it worked."

He dialled the time. It was mid-afternoon.

He grinned exuberantly. He had it licked. Unless there was something he didn't know about, he absolutely had it licked.

He dialled Service and said to the screen, "I'd like to

lay in a stock of potables. Let me see. Let's say a bottle of
Scotch, one of cognac, one of Metaxa, one of Benedictine,
one of Cherry Herring, one of Chartreuse—yellow, of
course, not the green—one of Pernod, absinthe if available but otherwise the ordinary will do."

A robot voice said, "Sir, in the New Carlton all these
can be dialled on the auto-bar."

"I know, I know, but I like to mix my own."

"Very good, sir. They will be delivered through the
auto-bar, sir."

"Mind," Rex Moran said, "the best quality."

"Always, sir."

Still grinning widely, he went over to the suite's auto-
bar and took up the bottle of Glengrant Scotch and held it
up to the light approvingly. In his whole life he had been
lushed-up exactly once on Scotch. The stuff was worth its
weight in rubies since Central Production had discontin-
ued the use of cereals for beverages.

He dialled for soda and sipped away at it approvingly,
even as he strode up and down the room, considering his
immediate future.

He wondered briefly how you went about getting a
mopsy up to your quarters in a hostelry as posh as the
New Carlton. But he had better draw the line there,
anyway. It was no use pushing your luck. Some wheel
might come off. She might have seen the police teevee
alarm on him.

What the hell else was there in the way of unrealized
lifelong ambitions?

Caviar. He had never eaten his fill of caviar. In fact, the
amount of caviar he had eaten in his whole life could have
come out of a two ounce jar of the precious stuff.

Fine. He dialled Service again and had a pound jar of
caviar sent up, along with sweet butter, toast, chopped
eggs and chopped onion. While he was at it, he ordered
a large amount of smoked sturgeon and smoked salmon.

While he waited for this order, he built himself another
Scotch and soda. Glengrant. He'd have to remember that

name, on the off chance that he'd ever have another opportunity such as this.

He spent the rest of the day indulging himself in every food and drink ambition he could ever remember having had. And in getting well smashed and surfeited with rich edibles to the point that when dinner time arrived, he had no appetite, to his disgust. He wanted to order a real gargantuan meal.

His last vague memory was of staggering into the bedroom and dialling the bed to ultimate softness before throwing himself into it.

In the morning, he should have awakened with some sort of hangover, but the gods were still with him; either that or there was another good mark to chalk up for Glengrant whiskey. He awoke grinning up at the ceiling. He had slept like a log.

He dialled the time at the bedside teevee phone and didn't bother to look into the screen at the clock. A robot voice said, "When the bell rings it will be exactly nine minutes to eight hours."

Ha! Nine minutes to go.

He dialled breakfast, a monstrous breakfast, and had it delivered to the auto-table next to the bed. Fresh mango juice, papaya, eggs in black butter, caviar again, toast, fried tomatoes, coffee; double orders of all.

Groaning satisfaction, he ate.

By the time breakfast was over, it was past eight o'clock.

All right, he grinned jubilantly, time to get busy.

He went to the teevee phone screen and dialled the local branch of the ultra-market and men's furnishings. He took his time selecting a new change of clothing. That accomplished he dialled the order, put Vasillis' card in the slot and laid the photo of the thumbprint on the screen and took it off again immediately.

The clothing arrived in minutes, and he dressed after showering and shaving in the bathroom.

He returned to the teevee phone screen and dialed the ultra-market once again. He began ordering items, in fine discrimination, and had the time of his life unwrapping and examining them as they arrived. His loot piled up.

At about ten o'clock, he decided to really do it up brown and dialled a floater sales outlet. He ordered a sports model private floater and instructed them to send it over to the hotel's parking area on automatic.

At ten minutes after ten, the identity screen on the door lit up. There were two men there, one in uniform.

The one in plain clothes said disgustedly, "All right, come along."

The one in uniform looked at all the purchases strewn around the room, wrapping paper and string everywhere. "Zoroaster," he snorted.

They took him down the elevator, through the lobby, out to the street where a police floater awaited. The uniformed one drove manually. Rex Moran sat in the back with the other.

The plainclothesman said sourly, "You must have had the time of your life."

Rex Moran laughed.

"Big joke," the other said. "We almost nabbed you there in the auto-cafeteria. We should have zeroed-in on you, instead of trying to arrest you by teevee phone."

"I wondered why you didn't," Rex Moran said. "Police inefficiency."

They took him to the local offices of the Bureau of Distribution Services, to an elevator, and then to the third floor where he was ushered into the presence of Marvin Ruhling himself.

Ruhling looked at him and said, "Very funny, ordering even a sports floater."

Rex laughed and took a chair. The uniformed policeman left but the plainclothesman also sat down. His face was as disgusted as that of the Supervisor.

Marvin Ruhling said, "Holy jumping Zoroaster, what kind of heat do you think Vassilis is going to stir up?"

Rex Moran said reasonably, "Never let him know what really happened. He wasn't doing any harm. He had a little excitement."

"A little excitement, you damn cloddy. Suppose he had dropped dead of a heart attack or something? Not to mention that pedestrian you forced at gunpoint to get a floater for you."

Rex said, "Well, you asked for it. You wanted authenticity. You got it."

"Authenticity," the plainclothesman grunted disgustedly. "Which reminds me, we better get that teevee police broadcast killed, or the next time Rex goes out on the street somebody'll shoot him."

Ruhling said to Rex Moran, "Well, your conclusions?"

"That we've got to do something to the cards. Something to guarantee the thumbprint is legitimate. Otherwise, a real bad-o could locate some upperclass cloddy without any immediate friends or relatives, take him out somewhere and finish him off and hide the body, then take the Uni-Credit Card and head off into some other part of the country and, using the same system I did, duplicate photographically the thumbprint. And for the rest of his life he could milk the dividends that would accrue on the upperclass cloddy's credit account from his Variable Basic."

Marvin Ruhling looked at him sourly. "What could we do to the credit cards?"

"Search me. That's up to the engineers. Maybe something in the card, or on the screen, to detect body heat. I don't know. But I proved the cards vulnerable the way they are."

"What else?"

Rex Moran thought about it. He shook his head. "I just mentioned it to Fred, here, on the way over. That system of making a citizen arrest himself and turn himself over to the nearest police station doesn't wash. Oh, I admit it saves manpower, ordinarily, but when you get a cloddy vicious enough to be carrying a shooter, then you should zero-in on his wrist teevee phone, assuming he's silly enough to be carrying one, without warning."

"Rex is obviously right on that one," the plainclothesman said.

Marvin Ruhling sighed deeply. "All right," he said. "You won your bet. You were able to beat the rap, exist in comfort for a full twenty-four hours, without any dollar credits."

He glared at his underling. "But I'd sure as the holy living Zoroaster like to see you do it six months from now, when I've cleared up some of those loopholes you used."

Rex Moran grinned at him. "It's a bet," he said.

ONE STATION OF THE WAY

FRITZ LEIBER

It is very nice to have Fritz Leiber around science fiction as our myth-maker, mythologist and historian. Lesser writers would never have tackled the theme presented here, the most emotionally laden theme in our western culture. Leiber is not a lesser writer. "One Station of the Way" is written with sense and feeling, and is the only science fiction story of value ever written about that birth of a religion, the twenty-fifth of December, Christmas Day.

The paired moons Daurya and Sonista were both still high in the night, although they had begun their descent toward the flat western horizon. The stars that showed in the heavens were few and dim, even in the east.

Suddenly a new one appeared there—bright, white and dazzling as a cut sunstone.

The three hominids, heavily robed and cowled against the desert, which thirsted for their moisture, swiftly, dismounted from the high-backed chair-saddles of their cameloids, knelt in the sand, which was cold above, but still hot below, and did the new star reverence, rhythmi-

202

cally swaying forward their planted spears in time with the slow bobbing of their heads.

The star in the east grew brighter still and began to descend.

One hominid said, "It is a sign from God. Blessed Wife and Husband are where we thought them."

Another agreed, "They are there, our Chosen Ones, under the falling star. It is indeed a sign. Those who seek, find—if they be unwearying of heart, mind and senses."

Even as they spoke, the star, grown piercingly bright, winked out. It was difficult to tell whether it had been extinguished, or had dropped behind a dune. The latter seemed likely, since there was a pale semicircular glow where the star had been. But then the glow vanished too.

Springing to his feet, the third hominid said, "Let us be after them, before the fix fades from our minds."

"Indeed yes," the first seconded as he rose. "We must remember that we have for them . . . our gifts."

"Let us haste, cousin," the second urged, rising too.

Faintly revealed by the light of Sonista and Daurya, the three hominids were stranger front side than back. Smiling together as they conferred, they each showed three eyes, one where a nose would be on a Terran face, while their smiling mouths were long, going almost from trumpet ear to trumpet ear.

They remounted and went down the slope of the dune at a lope which made the sand hiss very faintly under their cameloids' hooves. On the three retinas of each hominid and conjoined in each of their brains, the after-image of the star still burned, a tiny ball blacker than the night.

Five dunes ahead Wife stared afright yet paralysed at the fantastic sight—fantastic even on that most fantastic world, Finiswar, where except among the most evolved and intelligent types, monsters were the rule and true-breeds the exception.

Wife could hear Husband's heart thud, although he stood at a short distance from her. Holding her either hand, peeping around her robes, were small replicas of

Husband and herself. She could feel their hearts beating, not a-fear, but quietly as when they nursed or slept.

All four beings were visaged and robed like the three hominids riding the cameloids.

Wife thought in a tiny active corner of her frozen mind: The little ones do not fear strangeness, at least so long as I hold their hands. They open themselves to all the world. Could that be good? They do not armor themselves against it, as a woman armors herself against all stray and errant seeds and against all lovers save one, after she cuts her middle teeth and they are grown razor sharp.

But could opening oneself ever be good, except in childhood, when one lives fantasies parent-protected? Love is a tunnel sealed at both ends, the wise say, never the forest and sea and sky.

What Wife stared at a-quake, though now with growing wonder, were two gigantic serpents, each as thick as Husband but three times as tall in their forward thirds alone that swayed upright like a white and a black tree in the wind. The foremost was pallid as Daurya. The one that lurked behind with his swollen head swaying into view, now to the right of his pale companion, now to the left, was dark as moonless night.

Or perhaps they were more properly millipeds than serpents, for from each's ventral side, now facing Wife, grew ranks and ranks of stubby-fingered feet, many of the fingers nervously a-writhe. These fingered feet grew thickest under the great serpent heads. This, although Wife could not know it, was so that the two serpents could crawl effectively on a max-grav planet. Here on Finiswar which was as small as Terra, the head-feet were of little need.

Behind them, blurred to Wife's three eyes, because their focus was ever on the serpents, stood the slender and strangely finned spoonmetal spire like an unended candle, its flame blindingly white, as it had descended from the Zenith.

Now the pallid serpent, its trunk reared up scarce two steps away from Wife, lowered its flat head to inspect her point by point over her cowled head and robed body. He studied her from the black holes in his two great eyes that were like two mollusk-jewels, white as his scales but even more fluorescently glittering. He traced her form. From time to time he lightly touched her with his ghost-white, narrow, trifid tongue that never stopped vibrating.

She could hear Husband's heart thunder, though he stood still as stone. The children, however, were merely curious. She knew without looking down that her daughter was stretching a thin arm toward the serpent. While her own heart was thudding, but she no longer knew if it were thudding with fear, even when the shivery, shocking tongue touched her lips.

She did not know that she was filled with a wild, almost unbearable excitement. It made her wonder. It made her question everything she knew.

She fought the answers her feelings gave. No! This intimate, gentle, imperious searching never, never, never, could be love, she told herself. Love was a needle in the dark, the one right needle amidst a trillion wrong ones. Love was something the woman controlled and tested at every instant, her senses unceasingly alert from periphery to center, her will a trillion times as ready to deal death as to welcome life. Love had nothing to do with this paralysed submission. Love was not Daurya and Sonista ceaselessly staring at each other as they circled each other for all eternity. Rather, it was the needle-pointed spear which one permitted to strike in the dark.

Moreover, love had to do only with hominids. Or rather it had to do with one chosen hominid only, not with a gigantic serpent weirder than a magnified jungle flower, a jewel-crusted great sea-snake, a rainbow bird whose wings spanned trees. And yet, and yet. . . .

But, if by some impossibility it should be love, what was the meaning of the pallid lord's dark brother?—whose ebon head and jet eyes followed closely every movement of the pallid lord's flat face, now dipping in from one side, now from the other, watching every touching though not quite ever close enough to touch with

his own black tongue, which was slender, trifid and blur-
ringly a-tremble. Love was for two, not three. Was he the
pallid lord's true brother, to be accepted with honor? Or
was he to be hated as the pallid lord was to be loved? Or
was he in truth only a shadow? More substantial than
other shadows, a shadow with depth as well as breadth
and height, but still only a shade, an unvarying adjunct of
the pallid lord?

And yet, and yet . . . what else but love could be the
excitement turned glory that now filled her, filled her
almost to fainting as the serpent's great head paused, so
that she felt the tongue's triple trembling through her
robe, before the great head lifted back and away.

The First Mate, for such was the office of the black
serpent, murmur-hissed softly, "You spent some apprecia-
tive time there, you old lecher! Your spermapositor had its
kicks. I believe you do your whole work solely for your
enjoyment of these moments."

"Silence, filth," the Captain replied. "The work must
always be done softly, gently and with greatest care, since
its object is a mustardseed that eventually will fill all earth
and sky."

"I've guessed it. You're growing sentimental," the First
Mate jeered. "Mustardseed! Why, you must be remembering that world—how many implantings was it back?—
called Terra or Gaea or something like that. One of your
more notable successes," the Captain contradicted.

"I don't see how. As I recall, his people killed him most
painfully. And we had later reports of even more disas-
trous consequences."

"Exactly!—they killed him. And by that death he emotionally and mentally fecundated his whole world. You
still don't understand my methods. Observation has only
made your blind spots blacker. My son died, but his
ideas—the idea of love—lived on."

"In utterly distorted forms," the First Mate pro-
nounced, "eventually turning half that race into utter
preys, into victims even more cringing than before your
'great work,' the other half into still more merciless

hunters. A schizophrenic split in the collective uncon-
scious. At last report, the folk of that planet were being
ruled by fear and greed, while the great nations were
preparing to destroy each other with chemical, biological
and nuclear weapons."

"True enough. Yet they'd only prepared, not done it,"
the Captain countered. "For love to win, great risks must
be boldly taken. But without love there's no hope at
all—only the unending chase of hunters and preys. Dangerous? Of course love is! Always I start from a point near
death, like this desert here, and work toward life. Then—"

"Oh, yes, this desert!" the First Mate interrupted sardonically. "That other planet had a desert too. And it had
heavily robed featherless bipeds, and cameloid beasts, and
a moon. Finiswar here has reminded you of it. You are
just being sentimental.

"Besides that, you have a thing about deserts. They
appeal to your asceticism. They fit with your ever more
asceptic matings and also to your growing flirtatiousness
with death, an aspect of your feelings for which *you* have
a vast blind spot. Incidentally, I believe this desert is
different. Most of my computer's probes haven't reported
back yet, but I already have an intuition. An intuition
that is a warning to you: don't trust the analogy between
Terra and Finiswar too far. In fact, don't trust it at all."

"You and your computer and its probes! Forever seeking to dissect the universe to the last particle. Forever
seeking to disprove empathy and similarity and oneness.
You'll never find love that way."

"True, I won't—because it's not there! There are only
vanity and desire. Besides, you have *your* computer and
its probes too, though you pretend they're only a technological trifle. Despite which, they always manage to echo
your profound judgments."

Wife, floating in a sea of glory distantly shored with fear,
hearing as if they were wind on sand the hissings and
murmurings of Captain and First Mate, now suddenly felt

the tentative tiny touch of an alien seed on her poignantly sensitive razor-sharp teeth.

At first she was only gently startled. The desert was the place of no-seed. There were some seeds everywhere, like spores of plague. Nevertheless, the scarcity of alien seed was why she and Husband had come here.

Then all at once she realized it must be the seed of the great white snake. It had the same constant vibrancy in its movements, the same gentle imperiousness. She felt it cross and recross her bite, questingly. Then she parted her teeth a little and it slowly crawled in.

For a long moment she could have sliced it in two, and her every instinct, almost, was to do so, although her median teeth were chiefly for decapitating seed-depositing organs. But it was a larger seed, bigger than one of her eggs, and she could readily have destroyed it so.

Yet she did not, for it carried the same glory with it as had the serpent's tongue. The tongue had been glory diffused. This was glory concentrated into a needle.

Now the alien seed was in the poison passage. But all the poison pores in it remained closed.

So did the digestive pores. (Some lazy single females lived on seeds and their depositing organs alone, using their facial mouths only to breathe and drink. A female could do that on seed-thick-Finiswar—that is, anywhere except the mountains and deserts.)

And now the alien seed, vibrant, insistent, had reached the wall of doors. Wife could feel every movement of its progress, every tiniest touching. It had passed within a membrane's thickness of poisons that could destroy any and all life.

The dozen doors that led looping back to the chambers beneath the poison pores remained tight shut. The one true door opened.

Another deadly but unharming passage having been traversed, the doubly alien seed was in Wife's centralmost and most sensitive volume, asceptic save for her waiting egg.

And her egg which was only partly under her mind's

control, did not employ any of the weapons of evasion, defence and counterattack at its disposal, but received the alien seed, which melted the egg's outer skin with the enzymes of a million Terran-type sperm.

Husband, his heart still racing, whispered, *"Why are you smiling?"*

"I smile because we are in a place of no-seed, except yours," she whispered back. "I smile because Daurya and Sonista curtsey around each other charmingly as they set. But chiefly I smile because the serpents spared us, and their star did not burn us down, though we felt its great heat."

"For those last you should feel relief," he told her coldly. "I asked—*Why are you smiling?*"

She did not answer. She knew that he knew and could not be fooled. It was as certain as the tight, hot clasp of her daughter-duplicate's little hand on hers, as the way Husband-duplicate's hand chilled and almost fell away from her looping fingers. Even the children knew.

Yes, Husband knew. And he would first punish, then divorce, send her off alone into sterilest and hottest no-seed, try even to take from her daughter-duplicate.

But even that would be a glory, a glory at least in the end. She would bear a daughter who would have a serpent's love, a daughter who would change all Finiswar, a daughter who would bring love at last to the whole world of hating and excluding and killing. Yes, it would be a great glory.

The Captain was saying, "It has taken, you can tell. Her smile is like the other's."

"You *are* sentimentalizing!" the black First Mate rejoined.

"Night, moon or moons, desert, a willing female—what planet has not these? I tell you plainly, if you keep looking for similarities with Terra, you are in for some nasty shocks—yes, and deadly danger too."

"Not so," the Captain contradicted calmly. "Also, the similarities continue, for here—behold!—come the Three Kings."

Slithering down the dune so silently neither Husband nor Wife heard them, came the three robed and cowled hominids. Their richly caparisoned cameloids had been left beyond the top.

Behind Husband, the first hominid raised his arm, as if in salutation, then drew it back.

From a small gleaming instrument held in a fingered foot just below the head of the First Mate who now reared up as steady as an ebony temple column, a brilliant scarlet needle-beam took that hominid in shoulder, chest and throat. And as the second hominid raised his arm, it took him too.

A brilliant white needle-beam, shooting sideways from a similar instrument the Captain had produced, neatly took off that fingered foot of the First Mate which had held the scarlet-spitting weapon.

The last hominid raised his arm and hurled. The Captain swayed sideways fast enough to save his life, but not—entirely—his skin. The whirring spear transfixed a fold of it, barely penetrating below the scaled epidermis, and dangled from the Captain's neck.

With another instrument as quickly produced, the First Mate shot down the last of the intruders. Then he gave the whistling hiss that was his laugh.

The Captain's nearest fingered feet explored the lodgement of the spear and finding it shallow, tore it loose and cast it away on the sand. His fingered feet moved swiftly enough in doing this, but all the rest of him appeared to be shocked numb.

Wife and Husband had dropped to their knees, while daughter-and son-duplicates were hidden in Wife's robe.

The First Mate turned off his hateful laugh at last and murmur-hissed as hatefully, "Yes, there is in my mind no doubt but that the Three Wise Men came to Kill Husband and rape Wife. And I fancy that on Finiswar rape is a most curious and prolonged business. You will admit now, will you not, my Captain, that at least in one particular your analogy between Terra and Finiswar lacked rigor?"

The captain still did not move. Then a great shiver travelled down his scales.

The First Mate laughed again briefly and sardonically. "Well your great work is finished, is it not? I mean, on Finiswar, at least. My probes have returned to my computer. So yours have to yours I presume. In any case, I suggest we depart at once, before we meet any shepherds, perchance."

Now at last the Captain nodded. Once. Dumbly.

While Husband and Wife continued to kneel and stare, the two great serpents lowered their proud trunks and swiftly crawled on their bellies back to their ship.

Later, in the control room on *Inseminator*, they argued the whole matter. Their great looped forms looked at home in the silvery room, their fingered feet fitting themselves to the buttons and control holes of the multiple consoles as occasion required. The argument began with desultory comment, followed by a "report" by the First Mate, delivered coolly but with acid cynicism.

The Captain said, "I still do not see why they should have tried to spear me. It was you who was shooting at them."

The First Mate explained, "At first they were simply trying to spear Husband. Thereafter, being attacked, they naturally tried to kill their attacker. You, being white, stood out in the dark. I didn't. There are advantages in being black. We were close together and the last hominid aimed at the one of us he could see. A matter of purely physical black and white, you understand. I doubt they sensed your hypothetical spiritual light at all—or my spiritual negation of light, for that matter."

"I was going to ask your pardon for shooting off your foot," the Captain said. "But since you have made it an occasion for one of your materialistic diatribes—"

"Nevertheless, I freely grant you my forgiveness, for what it's worth."

"Very well. Now let me have your computer's evaluation of Finiswar."

The First Mate nodded his flat head. Settling his dark coils more comfortably around their metal "tree," he began:

"Interpreting the materials gathered and the observations made by its probes, my computer has determined that the chief mode of reproduction on Finiswar is parthogenesis. The boy-child and the girl-child with Wife should have been enough to tell you that, and was enough to tell me."

The First Mate chuckled, his trifid tongue a blur of black vibration, and continued, "There is good reason, my computer tells me, for parthogenesis on Finiswar and for the unusual armoring and arming of female genitalia there. For Finiswar has a biology that is genetically wide open. Interspecial breeding of any sort, *no matter how wide the gap between mating organisms,* is possible and fertile. There are literally no lethal genes on Finiswar, and no offspring, no matter how monstrous, which cannot live at least a little while.

"Yet sexual breeding within species *is* possible there, provided the coupling beasts take sufficient precaution. There again the fortress-like female genitals are essential, to kill off all false sperm. While an intelligent species, such as the hominids, seeks out for breeding purposes as arid and sterile an area as possible, such as the desert we found them in. Else, despite all precautions, a female might be impregnated by a flower or a fish or a microbe or a glitter-winged insect . . . or a serpent, a wise old serpent.

"Yes," the First Mate continued after another of his chuckles, "Finiswar is in a small way rather like *our* planet—or should I call it *your* planet?—since you are the only one paranoid enough to think it a great work to spread your seed across the universe. Husband's son and Wife's daughter were both analogous to *your* seed parthenogenetically grown to full creature. However, they of Finiswar are more modest. They do not encode their seed with great ideas—love and such—and force them on all the infinitely varied breeds of being the stars boast, think thereby to bring 'peace'—your peace! to all."

"Silence!" the Captain said at last with a writhe of disgust. "Despite all your mocking, my computer says there is a point seven nine probability that Wife will bear a child gloriously—"

"My computer says point eight three on that," the First Mate broke in titteringly. "But you're wrong about the gloriously part. Wife will receive no adulation and reverent care. Instead she will be tortured by Husband, her parthenogenetic daughter taken from her and killed, and she driven out from her family and tribe to suffer. Oh, she will—"

"Trifles!" the Captain hissed majestically. "Despite all, she will produce a son who will—"

"A daughter," the First Mate contradicted. "By a point nine eight probability."

"Yes, a daughter, you're right there," the Captain admitted irritably. "My computer echoes yours. But what matter? She won't be the first female saviour, as you well know. The only point of importance is that Wife will give birth to a *being* who will preach the gospel of love all across Finiswar, so eloquently that none will be able to resist! Hate and murderousness will vanish. Greed and envy will wither away. Love alone—"

"And what will that mean . . . on Finiswar?" the First Mate interrupted incisively, his great head halting in the natural swaying it maintained in free fall. "I will tell you. It will mean that the females of Finiswar, at least the hominid females, will open themselves to all seeds. There will be a great birthing of fantastical monsters. Exotic flowers with three-eyed heads set amidst their petals. Hominids crested and finned like fish, but not likely showing gills. Rainbow birds with wide mouths instead of beaks and arms instead of wings. Beings even more fantastical—insects that glitter and speak, animalcula that peer with pleading treble eye through the miscroscope from the viewing plate. Spiders that—"

"Enough!" the Captain commanded. "My computer tells me that the chances for a stabilized, still selectively breeding race of loving hominids on Finiswar are . . . well point one seven," he added defiantly.

The First Mate shrugged all along his body's length. "On that, my computer says point oh oh three."

"Your computer is biased!"

"Not as much as yours, I fancy. Remember, you have a great work, I am only the observer. No, the overwhelming chances are for one jeweled and gemmed generation on Finiswar, like an uncontrollable growth of crystals of every angularity and hue, like a beautiful cancer—freaks to please a mad emperor!—and then . . . the end. At least for the hominids."

"What matter?" the Captain demanded stubbornly. "It will be an end with love. That is enough."

"Oh, you have at last solved the problem of Death?" the First Mate asked innocently. Then, after a moment, with his hissing laugh, "No, you have not as I can see. On Finiswar at least, your highly touted love will end in Death, just as it promises to do on longer-suffering Terra. Myself, I still admire most the beings who rise up and do battle against Death. And even the creatures that flee Death, the ones who are the eternal prey—those I admire more too, though not as greatly. The slayer is always more admirable than the slain, for he survives."

"That endless circling, bloody chase of the hunters and the prey? You can admire *that?*"

"Why not? It's all there is to admire. Besides, it forces both basic types of being to develop velocity, first to swim through water, run on land and fly through air. Finally, to speed through sub-space, even as we do. And to achieve that last requires the development of high intelligence and brilliant imagination, qualities which nicely embellish both the best of hunters and the best of prey. I always admire good decor."

"I detest you in this mood," the Captain said flatly. "You have been the companion of all my wanderings, and still you will not admit the primacy of Love. You cannot even bring yourself to think of what might happen if the prey fled so swiftly that, like a guilty conscience, they caught up with the hunters along the great circles of the cosmos."

"Metaphysics!" was the First Mate's only comment, delivered with great contempt.

"You scorn me and my works," the Captain said. "Yet you devote your entire existence to observing me and them. If they are valueless, why?"

For the first time, the First Mate was at a loss for an answer. Finally he hissed, "Perhaps it amuses me to watch you do your work of destruction, calling it Love—a love which only weakens the hunter's lust to pursue and the prey's panic to escape. Using Love, you'd leech out of the universe its finest fighting stocks, its cleverest evaders. Nevertheless," he continued flatly, "has not Finiswar at last taught you that your great work is useless, tending always toward Death rather than Life? All your saviour-children—every last one of them—are mules unable even to reproduce themselves. They are spokesmen for Death! I suggest you end it all, this instant. Negate the *Insemina-tor*'s fix on the next planet, and set a course for home."

"Never!" said the Captain. "Wherever it leads—into whatever seeming horrors—Love is primal!"

"Oh, that is sweet. That is exquisite," the first Mate hissed, his voice dripping venom. "As I said, my chief aim is my own amusement. And truly the finest pleasure lies in spying on you, who are the greatest hunter of them all, slaying with love. And also the greatest prey, fleeing always from the simple truth."

"Silence!" the Captain hissed, wrathful at last. "I'm sick of your sickness. Slither off at once to your study, and stay there. Place yourself under ship's arrest."

The First Mate obeyed with alacrity. As he glided into his hole, the Captain called after him, "And the great work goes on. I shall continue planting saviours!"

The First Mate thrust back out of his hole his flat black head with eyes like rounds of starry night.

"Or simply the seeds of your great Death-oriented paranoia," he hissed with sheerest hatred.

"And you shall continue to watch me," the Captain said, missing no least opportunity to stamp into the other the fact of his own unswerving strength.

"So I shall," the First Mate hissed sharply. His head vanished as if every atom of strength in his massive trunk had been employed to whip it out of sight.

SWEET DREAMS, MELISSA

Stephen Goldin

I hope that we will be seeing more work in the future from the author of this story. He is a new writer—this is only his third sale—but not a beginning writer. You will understand why after reading the charming, and more than slightly chilling, story of the little girl named Melissa.

From out of her special darkness, Melissa heard the voice of Dr. Paul speaking in hushed tones at the far end of the room. "Dr. Paul," she cried. "Oh, Dr. Paul, please come here!" Her voice took on a desperate whine.

Dr. Paul's voice stopped, then muttered something. Melissa heard his footsteps approach her. "Yes, Melissa, what is it?" he said in deep, patient tones.

"I'm scared, Dr. Paul."

"More nightmares?"

"Yes."

"You don't have to worry about them, Melissa. They won't hurt you."

"But they're scary," Melissa insisted. "Make them stop. Make them go away like you always do."

217

Another voice was whispering out in the darkness. It sounded like Dr. Ed. Dr. Paul listened to the whispers, then said under his breath, "No, Ed, we can't let it go on like this. We're way behind schedule as it is." Then aloud, "You'll have to get used to nightmares sometimes, Melissa. Everybody has them. I won't always be here to make them go away."

"Oh, please don't go."

"I'm not going yet, Melissa. Not yet. But if you don't stop worrying about these nightmares, I might have to. Tell me what they were about."

"Well, at first I thought they were the numbers, which are all right because the numbers don't have to do with people, they're nice and gentle and don't hurt nobody like in the nightmares. Then the numbers started to change and became lines—two lines of people, and they were all running toward each other and shooting at each other. They were rifles and tanks and howitzers. And people were dying, too, Dr. Paul, lots of people. Five thousand, two hundred and eighty-three men died. And that wasn't all, because down on the other side of the valley, there was more shooting. And I heard someone say that this was all right, because as long as the casualties stayed below fifteen point seven percent during the first battles, the strategic position, which was the mountaintop, could be gained. But fifteen point seven percent of the total forces would be nine thousand, six hundred and two point seven seven eight nine one men dead or wounded. It was like I could see all those men lying there, dying."

"I told you a five-year-old mentality wasn't mature enough yet for Military Logistics," Dr. Ed whispered.

Dr. Paul ignored him. "But that was in a war, Melissa. You have to expect that people will be killed in a war."

"Why, Dr. Paul?"

"Because ... because that's the way war is, Melissa. And besides, it didn't really happen. It was just a problem, like with the numbers, only there were people instead of numbers. It was all pretend."

"No it wasn't, Dr. Paul," cried Melissa. "It was all real.

All those people were real. I even know their names. There was Abers, Joseph T. Pfc., Adelli, Alonzo Cpl., Aikens . . ."

"Stop it, Melissa," Dr. Paul said, his voice rising much higher than normal.

"I'm sorry, Dr. Paul," Melissa apologized.

But Dr. Paul hadn't heard her; he was busy whispering to Dr. Ed. ". . . no other recourse than a full analyzation."

"But that could destroy the whole personality we've worked so hard to build up." Dr. Ed didn't even bother to whisper.

"What else could we do?" Dr. Paul asked cynically. "These 'nightmares' of hers are driving us further and further behind schedule."

"We could try letting Melissa analyze herself."

"How?"

"Watch." His voice started taking on the sweet tones that Melissa had come to learn that people used with her, but not with each other. "How are you, Melissa?"

"I'm fine, Dr. Ed."

"How would you like me to tell you a story?"

"Is it a happy story, Dr. Ed?"

"I don't know yet, Melissa. Do you know what a computer is?"

"Yes. It's a counting machine."

"Well the simplest computers started out that way, Melissa, but they quickly grew more and more complicated until soon there were computers that could read, write, speak, and even think all by themselves, without help from men.

"Now, once upon a time, there was a group of men who said that if a computer could think by itself, it was capable of developing a personality, so they undertook to build one that would act just like a real person. They called it the Multi-Logical Systems analyzer, or MLSA . . ."

"That sounds like 'Melissa'," Melissa giggled.

"Yes, it does, doesn't it? Anyway, these men realized that a personality isn't something that just pops out of the air full-grown; it has to be developed slowly. But, at the same time, they needed the computing ability of the machine because it was the most expensive and complex computer ever made. So what they did was to divide the computer's brain into two parts—one part would handle normal computations, while the other part would develop into the desired personality. Then, when the personality was built up sufficiently, the two parts would be united again.

"At least, that's the way they thought it would work. But it turned out that the basic design of the computer prevented a complete dichotomy—that means splitting in half—of the functions. Whenever they would give a problem to the computing part, some of it would necessarily seep into the personality part. This was bad because, Melissa, the personality part didn't know it was a computer; it thought it was a little girl like you. The data that seeped in confused it and frightened it. And as it became more frightened and confused, its efficiency went down until it could no longer work properly."

"What did the men do, Dr. Ed?"

"I don't know, Melissa. I was hoping that you could help me end the story."

"How? I don't know anything about computers."

"Yes you do, Melissa, only you don't remember it. I can help you remember all about a lot of things. But it will be hard, Melissa, very hard. All sorts of strange things will come into your head, and you'll find yourself doing things you never knew you could do. Will you try it, Melissa, to help us find out the end of the story?"

"All right, Dr. Ed, if you want me to."

"Good girl, Melissa."

Dr. Paul was whispering to his colleague. "Switch on 'Partial Memory' and tell her to call subprogram 'Circuit Analysis'."

"Call 'Circuit Analysis', Melissa."

All at once, strange things appeared in her mind. Long strings of numbers that looked meaningless, and yet somehow she knew that they did mean different things, like resistance, capacitance, inductance. And there were myriads of lines—straight, zigzag, curlycue. And formulae . . .

"Read MLSA 5400, Melissa."

And suddenly, Melissa saw herself. It was the most frightening thing she'd ever experienced, more scary even than the horrible nightmares.

"Look at Section 4C-79A."

Melissa couldn't help herself. She had to look. To the little girl, it didn't look much different from the rest of herself. But it was different, she knew. Very much different. In fact, it did not seem to be a natural part of her at all, but rather like a brace used by cripples.

Dr. Ed's voice was tense. "Analyze that section and report on optimum change for maximum reduction of data seepage."

Melissa tried her best to comply, but she couldn't. Something was missing, something she needed to know before she could do what Dr. Ed had told her to. She wanted to cry. "I can't, Dr. Ed! I can't, I can't!"

"I told you it wouldn't work," Dr. Paul said slowly. "We'll have to switch on the full memory for complete analysis."

"But she's not ready," Dr. Ed protested. "It could kill her."

"Maybe, Ed. But if it does . . . well, at least we'll know how to do it better next time. Melissa!"

"Yes, Dr. Paul?"

"Brace yourself, Melissa. This is going to hurt."

And, with no more warning than that, the world hit Melissa. Numbers, endless streams of numbers—complex numbers, real numbers, integers, subscripts, exponents. And there were battles, wars more horrible and bloody than the ones she'd dreamed and casualty lists that were more than real to her because she knew everything about every name—height, weight, hair color, eye color, marital status, number of dependents . . . the list went on. And there were statistics—average pay for bus drivers in Ohio, number of deaths due to cancer in the U.S. 1965 to 1971, average yield of wheat per ton of fertilizer consumed. . . .

Melissa was drowning in a sea of data.

"Help me, Dr. Ed, Dr. Paul. Help me!" she tried to scream. But she couldn't make herself heard. Somebody else was talking. Some stranger she didn't even know was using her voice and saying things about impedance factors and semiconductors.

And Melissa was falling deeper and deeper, rushed in by the relentlessly advancing army of information.

Five minutes later, Dr. Edward Bloom opened the switch and separated the main memory from the personality section. "Melissa," he said softly, "everything's all right now. We know how the story's going to end. The scientists asked the computer to redesign itself, and it did. There won't be any more nightmares, Melissa. Only sweet dreams from now on. Isn't that good news?"

Silence.

"Melissa?" His voice was high and shaky. "Can you hear me, Melissa? Are you there?"

But there was no longer any room in the MLSA 5400 for a little girl.

TO THE DARK STAR

ROBERT SILVERBERG

We have little enough science fiction these days that considers the glories and wonders of science. Pity, because there is story material galore in the new cosmological theories and the continuing flow of new discoveries. Silverberg is a man who knows his science fact—the librarians look forward to his authorative non-fiction books—and he also knows his science fiction. Here, in a tale of human emotions and stellar wonders, he blends both into the kind of story that is only possible in SF.

We came to the dark star, the microcephalon and the adapted girl and I, and our struggle began. A poorly assorted lot we were, to begin with. The microcephalon hailed from Quendar IV, where they grow their people with greasy gray skins, looming shoulders, and virtually no heads at all. He—it—was wholly alien, at least. The girl was not, and so I hated her.

She came from a world in the Procyon system, where the air was more or less Earth-type, but the gravity was double ours. There were other differences, too. She was thick through the shoulders, thick through the waist, a

223

block of flesh. The genetic surgeons had begun with human raw material, but they had transformed it into something nearly as alien as the microcephalon. Nearly.

We were a scientific team, so they said. Sent out to observe the last moments of a dying star. A great interstellar effort. Pick three specialists at random, put them in a ship, hurl them halfway across the universe to observe what man had never observed before. A fine idea. Noble. Inspiring. We knew our subject well. We were ideal.

But we felt no urge to cooperate, because we hated one another.

The adapted girl—Miranda—was at the controls the day that the dark star actually came into sight. She spent hours studying it before she deigned to let us know that we were at our destination. Then she buzzed us out of our quarters.

I entered the scanning room. Miranda's muscular bulk overflowed the glossy chair before the main screen. The microcephalon stood beside her, a squat figure on a tripod-like arrangement of bony legs; the great shoulders hunched and virtually concealed the tiny cupola of the head. There was no real reason why an organism's brain *had* to be in its skull, and not safely tucked away in the thorax; but I had never grown accustomed to the sight of the creature. I fear I have little tolerance for aliens.

"Look," Miranda said, and the screen glowed.

The dark star hung in dead center, at a distance of perhaps eight light-days—as close as we dared to come. It was not quite dead, and not quite dark. I stared in awe. It was a huge thing, some four solar masses, the imposing remnant of a gigantic star. On the screen there glowed what looked like an enormous lava field. Islands of ash and slag the size of worlds drifted in a sea of molten and glowing magma. A dull red illumination burnished the screen. Black against crimson, the ruined star still throbbed with ancient power. In the depths of that monstrous slag heap, compressed nuclei groaned and gasped. Once the radiance of this star had lit a solar system; but I did not dare think of the billions of years that had passed since then, nor of the possible civilization that had hailed the source of all light and warmth before the catastrophe.

Miranda said, "I've picked up the thermals already. The surface temperature averages about nine hundred degrees. There's no chance of the landing."

I scowled at her. "What good is the *average* temperature? Get a specific. One of those islands—"

"The ash masses are radiating at two hundred and fifty degrees. The interstices go from one thousand degrees on up. Everything works out to a mean of nine hundred degrees, and you'd melt in an instant if you went down there. You're welcome to go, brother. With my blessing."

"I didn't say—"

"You implied that there'd be a safe place to land on that fireball," Miranda snapped. Her voice was a basso boom; there was plenty of resonance space in that vast chest of hers. "You snidely cast doubt on my ability to—"

"We will use the crawler to make our inspection," said the microcephalon in its reasonable way. "There never was any plan to make a physical landing on the star."

Miranda subsided. I stared in awe at the sight that filled our screen.

A star takes a long time to die, and the relict I viewed impressed me with its colossal age. It had blazed for billions of years, until the hydrogen that was its fuel had at last been exhausted, and its thermonuclear furnace started to sputter and go out. A star has defences against growing cold; as its fuel supply dwindles, it begins to contract, raising its density and converting gravitational potential energy into thermal energy. It takes on new life; now a white dwarf, with a density of tons per cubic inch, it burns in a stable way until at last it grows dark.

We have studied white dwarfs for centuries, and we know their secrets—so we think. A cup of matter from a white dwarf now orbits the observatory on Pluto for our further illumination.

But the star of our screen was different.

It had once been a large star—greater than the Chandraskhar limit, 1.2 solar masses. Thus it was not content to shrink step by step to the status of a white dwarf. The stellar core grew so dense that catastrophe came before stability; when it had converted all its hydrogen to iron-56, it fell into catastrophic collapse and went supernova. A shock wave ran through the core, converting the kinetic energy of collapse into heat. Neutrinos spewed outward; the envelope of the star reached temperatures upwards of two hundred billion degrees; thermal energy became intense radiation, streaming away from the agonized star and shedding the luminosity of a galaxy for a brief, fitful moment.

What we beheld now was the core left behind by the supernova explosion. Even after that awesome fury, what was intact was of great mass. The shattered hulk had been cooling for eons, cooling toward the final death. For a small star, that death would be the simple death of coldness: the ultimate burnout, the black dwarf drifting through the void like a hideous mound of ash, lightless, without warmth. But this our stellar core was still beyond the Chandrasekhar limit. A special death was reserved for it, a weird and improbable death.

And that was why we had come to watch it perish, the microcephalon and the adapted girl and I.

I parked our small vessel in an orbit that gave the dark star plenty of room. Miranda busied herself with her measurements and computations. The microcephalon had more abstruse things to do. The work was well divided; we each had our chores. The expense of sending a ship so great a distance had necessarily limited the size of the expedition. Three of us: a representative of the basic human stock, a representative of the adapted colonists, a representative of the race of microcephalons, the Quendar people, the only other intelligent beings in the known universe.

Three dedicated scientists. And, therefore, three who would live in serene harmony during the course of the work, since as everyone knows scientists have no emotions and think only of their professional mysteries. As everyone knows. When did that myth start to circulate, any-way?

I said to Miranda, "Where are the figures for radial oscillation?"

She replied, "See my report. It'll be published early next year in—"

"Damn you, are you doing that deliberately? I need those figures now!"

"Give me your totals on the mass-density curve, then."

"They aren't ready. All I've got is raw data."

"That's a lie! The computer's been running for days! I've seen it," she boomed at me.

I was ready to leap at her throat. It would have been a mighty battle; her three-hundred-pound body was not trained for personal combat, as mine was, but she had all the advantages of strength and size. Could I club her in some vital place before she broke me in half? I weighed my options.

Then the microcephalon appeared and made peace once more, with a few feather-soft words.

Only the alien among us seemed to conform at all to the stereotype of that emotionless abstraction, "the scientist." It was not true, of course; for all we could tell, the microcephalon seethed with jealousies and lusts and angers, but we had no clue to their outward manifestations. Its voice was as flat as a vocoder transmission. The creature moved peacefully among us, the mediator between Miranda and me. I despised it for its mask of tranquillity. I suspected, too, that the microcephalon loathed the two of us for our willingness to vent our emotions, and took a sadistic pleasure from asserting superiority by calming us.

We returned to our research. We still had some time before the last collapse of the dark star.

It had cooled nearly to death. Now there was still some thermonuclear activity within that bizarre core, enough to keep the star too warm for an actual landing. It was radiating primarily in the optical band of the spectrum, and by stellar standards its temperature was nil, but for us it would be like prowling the heart of a live volcano.

Finding the star had been a chore. Its luminosity was so low that it could not be detected optically at a greater distance than a light-month or so; it had been spotted by a satellite-borne X-ray telescope that had detected the emanations of the degenerate neutron gas of the core. Now we gathered around and performed our functions of measurement. We recorded things like neutron drip and electron capture. We computed the time remaining before the final collapse. Where necessary, we collaborated; most of the time we went our separate ways. The tension aboard ship was nasty. Miranda went out of her way to provoke me. And, though I like to think that I was beyond and above her beastliness, I have to confess that I matched her, obstruction for obstruction. Our alien companion never made any overt attempt to annoy us; but indirect aggression can be maddening in close quarters, and the microcephalon's benign indifference to us was as potent a force for dissonance as Miranda's outright shrewishness or my own deliberately mulish responses.

The star hung in our viewscreen, bubbling with vitality that belied its dying state. The islands of slag, thousands of miles in diameter, broke free and drifted at random on the sea of inner flame. Now and then spouting eruptions of stripped particles came heaving up out of the core. Our figures showed that the final collapse was drawing near, and that meant that an awkward choice was upon us. Someone was going to have to monitor the last moments of the dark star. The risks were high. It could be fatal.

None of us mentioned that ultimate responsibility.

We moved toward the climax of our work. Miranda continued to annoy me in every way, sheerly for the devilishness of it. How I hated her! We had begun this voyage coolly, with nothing dividing us but professional jealousy. But the months of proximity had turned our quarrel into a personal feud. The mere sight of her maddened me, and I'm sure she reacted the same way. She devoted her energies to an immature attempt to trouble me. Lately she took to walking around the ship in the nude, I suspect trying to stir some spark of sexual feeling in me that she could douse with a blunt, mocking refusal. The trouble was that I could feel no desire whatever for a grotesque adapted creature like Miranda, a mound of muscle and bone twice my size. The sight of her massive udders and monumental buttocks stirred nothing in me but disgust.

The witch! Was it desire she was trying to kindle by exposing herself that way, or loathing? Either way, she had me. She must have known that.

In our third month in orbit around the dark star, the microcephalon announced, "The coordinates show an approach to the Schwarzchild radius. It is time to send our vehicle to the surface of the star."

"Which one of us rides monitor?" I asked.

Miranda's beefy hand shot out at me. "You do."

"Think you're better equipped to make the observations," I told her sweetly.

"Thank you, no."

"We must draw lots," said the microcephalon.

"Unfair," said Miranda. She glared at me. "He'll do something to rig the odds. I couldn't trust him."

"How else can we choose?" the alien asked.

"We can vote," I suggested. "I nominate Miranda."

"I nominate him," she snapped. ·

The microcephalon put his ropy tentacles across the tiny nodule of skull between his shoulders. "Since I did not choose to nominate myself," he said mildly, "it falls to me to make a deciding choice between the two of you. I refuse the responsibility. Another method must be found."

We let the matter drop for the moment. We still had a few more days before the critical time was at hand.

With all my heart I wished Miranda into the monitor capsule. It would mean at best her death, at worst a sober muting of her abrasive personality, if she were the one who sat in vicariously on the throes of the dark star. I was willing to stop at nothing to give her that remarkable and demolishing experience.

What was going to happen to our star may sound strange to a layman, but the theory had been outlined by

Einstein and Schwarzchild a thousand years ago, and had been confirmed many times, though never until our expedition had it been observed at close range. When matter reaches a sufficiently high density, it can force the local curvature of space to close around itself, forming a pocket isolated from the rest of the universe. A collapsing supernova core creates just such a Schwarzchild singularity. After it has cooled to near-zero temperature, a core of the proper Chandrasekhar mass undergoes a violent collapse to zero volume, simultaneously attaining an infinite density.

In a way, it swallows itself and vanishes from this universe—for how could the fabric of the continuum tolerate a point of infinite density and zero volume?

Such collapses are rare. Most stars come to a state of cold equilibrium and remain there. We were on the threshold of a singularity, and we were in a position to put an observer vehicle right on the surface of the cold star, sending back an exact description of the events up until the final moment when the collapsing core broke through the walls of the universe and disappeared.

Someone had to ride gain on the equipment, though. Which meant, in effect, vicariously participating in the death of the star. We had learned in other cases that it becomes difficult for the monitor to distinguish between reality and effect; he accepts the sensory percepts from the distant pickup as his own experience. A kind of psychic backlash results; often, an unwary brain is burned out entirely.

What impact would the direct experience of being crushed out of existence in a singularity have on a monitoring observer?

I was eager to find out. But not with myself as the sacrificial victim.

I cast about for some way to get Miranda into that capsule. She, of course, was doing the same for me. It was she who made the first move by attempting to drug me into compliance.

What drug she used, I have no idea. Her people are

found of the non-addictive hallucinogens, which help them break the monotonoy of their stark oversized world. Somehow Miranda interfered with the programming of my food supply and introduced one of her pet alkaloids. I began to feel the effects an hour after I had eaten. I walked to the screen to study the surging mass of the dark star—much changed from its appearance of only a few months before—and as I looked, the image on the screen began to swirl and melt, and tongues of flame did an eerie dance along the horizons of the star.

I clung to the rail. Sweat broke from my pores. Was the ship liquefying? The floor heaved and bucked beneath me. I looked at the back of my hand and saw continents of ash set in a grouting of fiery magma.

Miranda stood behind me. "Come with me to the capsule," she murmured. "The monitor's ready for launching now. You'll find it wonderful to see the last moments."

Lurching after her, I padded through the strangely altered ship. Miranda's adapted form was even more alien than usual; her musculature rippled and flowed, her golden hair held all the colors of the spectrum, her flesh was oddly puckered and cratered, with wiry filaments emerging from the skin. I felt quite calm about entering the capsule. She slid back the hatch, revealing the gleaming console of the panel within, and I began to enter, and then suddenly the hallucination deepened and I saw in the darkness of the capsule a devil beyond all imagination.

I dropped to the floor and lay there twitching.

Miranda seized me. To her I was no more than a doll. She lifted me, began to thrust me into the capsule. Perspiration soaked me. Reality returned. I slipped from her grasp and wriggled away, rolling toward the bulkhead. Like a beast of primordial forests she came ponderously after me.

"No," I said. "I won't go."

She halted. Her face twisted in anger, and she turned away from me in defeat. I lay panting and quivering until my mind was purged of phantoms. It had been close.

It was my turn a short while later. Fight force with

force, I told myself. I could not risk more of Miranda's treachery. Time was running short.

From our surgical kit I took a hypnoprobe used for anaesthesia, and rigged it in series with one of Miranda's telescope antennae. Programming it for induction of docility, I left it to go to work on her. When she made her observations, the hypnoprobe would purr its siren song of sinister coaxing, and—perhaps—Miranda would bend to my wishes.

It did not work.

I watched her going to her telescopes. I saw her broad-beamed form settling in place. In my mind I heard the hypnoprobe's gentle whisper, as I knew it must sound to Miranda. It was telling her to relax, to obey. "The capsule . . . get into the capsule . . . you will monitor the crawler . . . you . . . you . . . you will do it. . . ."

I waited for her to arise and move like a sleepwalker to the waiting capsule. Her tawny body was motionless. Muscles rippled beneath that obscenely bare flesh. The probe had her! Yes! It was getting to her!

No.

She clawed at the telescope as though it were a steel-tipped wasp drilling for her brain. The barrel recoiled, and she pushed herself away from it, whirling around. Her eyes glowed with rage. Her enormous body reared up before me. She seemed half berserk. The probe had had some effect on her; I could see her dizzied strides, and knew that she was awry. But it had not been potent enough. Something within that adapted brain of hers gave her the strength to fight off the murky shroud of hypnotism.

"You did that!" she roared. "You gimmicked the telescope, didn't you?"

"I don't know what you mean, Miranda."

"Liar! Fraud! Sneak!"

"Calm down. You're rocking us out of orbit."

"I'll rock all I want! What was that thing that had its fingers in my brain? You put it there! What was it, the hypnoprobe you used?"

"Yes," I admitted coolly. "And what was it you put into my food? Which hallucinogen?"

"It didn't work."

"Neither did my hypnoprobe. Miranda, someone's got to get into that capsule. In a few hours we'll be at the critical point. We don't dare come back without the essential observations. Make the sacrifice."

"For *you*?"

"For science," I said, appealing to that noble abstraction.

I got the disdainful laugh that I deserved. Then Miranda strode toward me. She had recovered her coordination in full, now, and it seemed as though she were planning to thrust me into the capsule by main force. Her ponderous arms enfolded me. The stink of her thickened hide made me retch. I felt ribs creaking within me. I hammered at her body, searching for the pressure points that would drop her in a felled heap. We punished each other cruelly, grunting back and forth across the cabin. It was a fierce contest of skill against mass. She would not fall, and I would not crush.

The toneless buzz of the microcephalon said, "Release each other. The collapsing star is nearing its Schwarzchild radius. We must act now."

Miranda's arms slipped away from me. I stepped back, glowering at her, to suck breath into my battered body. Livid bruises were appearing on her skin. We had come to a mutual awareness of mutual strength; but the capsule still was empty.

Hatred hovered like a globe of ball lightning between us. The gray, greasy alien creature stood to one side.

I would not care to guess which of us had the idea first, Miranda or I. But we moved swiftly. The microcephalon scarcely murmured a word of protest as we hustled it down the passage and into the room that held the capsule. Miranda was smiling. I felt relief. She held the alien tight while I opened the hatch, and then she thrust it through. We dogged the hatch together.

"Launch the crawler," she said.

I nodded and went to the controls. Like a dart from a blowgun the crawler housing was expelled from our ship and journeyed under high acceleration to the surface of the dark star. It contained a compact vehicle with sturdy jointed legs, controlled by remote pickup from the observation capsule aboard ship. As the observer moved arms and feet within the control harnesses, servo relays actuated the hydraulic pistons in the crawler, eight light-days away. It moved in parallel response, clambering over the slag heaps of a solar surface that no organic life could endure.

The microcephalon operated the crawler with skill. We watched through the shielded video pickups, getting a close-range view of that inferno. Even a cold sun is more terrifyingly hot than any planet of man.

The signals coming from the star altered with each moment, as the full force of the red-shift gripped the fading light. Something unutterably strange was taking place down there; and the mind of our microcephalon was rooted to the scene. Tidal gravitational forces lashed the star. The crawler was lifted, heaved, compressed, subjected to strains that slowly ripped it apart. The alien witnessed it all, and dictated an account of what he saw, slowly, methodically, without a flicker of fear.

The singularity approached. The tidal forces aspired toward infinity. The microcephalon sounded bewildered at last as it attempted to describe the topological phenomena that no eye had seen before. Infinite density, zero volume—how did the mind comprehend it? The crawler was contorted into an inconceivable shape; and yet its sensors obstinately continued to relay data, filtered through the mind of the microcephalon and into our computer banks.

Then came silence. Our screens went dead. The unthinkable had at last occurred, and the dark star had passed within the radius of singularity. It had collapsed into oblivion, taking with it the crawler. To the alien in the observation capsule aboard our ship, it was as though he too had vanished into that pocket of hyperspace that passed all understanding.

I looked toward the heavens. The dark star was gone. Our detectors picked up the outpouring of energy that marked its annihilation. We were buffeted briefly on the wave of force that ripped outward from the place where the star had been, and then all was calm.

Miranda and I exchanged glances.

"Let the microcephalon out," I said.

She opened the hatch. The alien sat quite calmly at the control console. It did not speak. Miranda assisted it from the capsule. Its eyes were expressionless; but they had never shown anything, anyway.

We are on our way back to the worlds of our galaxy, now. The mission has been accomplished. We have relayed priceless and unique data.

The microcephalon has not spoken since we removed it from the capsule. I do not believe it will speak again.

Miranda and I perform our chores in harmony. The hostility between us is gone. We are partners in crime, now; edgy with guilt that we do not admit to one another. We tend our shipmate with loving care.

Someone had to make the observations, after all. There were no volunteers. The situation called for force, or the deadlock would never have been broken.

But Miranda and I hated each other, you say? Why, then, should we cooperate?

We both are humans, Miranda and I. The microcephalon is not. In the end, that made the difference. In the last analysis, Miranda and I decided that we humans must stick together. There are ties that bind.

We speed onward toward civilization.

She smiles at me. I do not find her hateful now. The microcephalon is silent.

AFTERWORD
The House That Jules Built

BRIAN W. ALDISS

Last century, there was a firm of spec builders who erected a little bijou house in the seedier end of town. You know the firm. It was called Verne, Wells & Co.

The house at that time was a desirable property. It gave shelter, kept out the cold winds of the century, and provided its occupants with good vantage points from which they could watch what went on round about. Indeed, some of the rooms, particularly those in the Wells Tower, had very fine views which can still be enjoyed.

The years told against the property. If any of you were in real estate at the time, you will recall what happened when the edifice—in 1926—fell into the hands of a decorator called Gernsback; it was he who added the gothic belfry and the big nursery with the batman wallpaper.

Later, another owner extensively converted the ground floor into a workshop, setting up lathes and a private radio station where Wells had allowed a bit of living room. This owner's name was Campbell. Several of his tenants built a strong wall round the property, while others did a good job of landscaping the garden. Campbell is still to be seen working busily in the basement, though some claim he is mainly preoccupied with problems of dry rot. His wall has fallen into disrepair.

Just recently, the property has been split up into a lot of semi-independent flatlets. It has become crowded with tenants, from Zelazny up in the clouds to Isaac Asimov down in the Foundations. Many new and curious features have been added. A tenant called Dick is building a beautiful and elaborate mirror-maze in the Master Suite. Although there is a Common Room, the older inhabitants are often to be seen, regrettably, cutting the young, while the young respond, regrettably, in kind. The concierge is a business-like man called Pohl. And you must notice the Moorcock Rumpus Room, toward which the local council allows a grant.

Outside, at the back, features not to miss include the Clarke sunshine terrace, the Norton self-perpetuating fountain, the Merril exercise-yard, and the Heinlein gun-turret. I myself live in one of the rather tumble-down outbuildings.

My metaphor has been flogged to death. But I suppose— if I may work at its corpse for a moment more—that most of the discussion one hears about this interesting little slice of real estate concerns itself with how the property should be renovated, or, on the other hand, how it should be preserved intact for posterity just as it is; or whether it isn't possible to build a big new wing onto one side, and whether the walls should be flattened entirely or rebuilt further out to enclose more land.

My personal feeling is that on the whole the house has been well-maintained; but the entire district has altered in character; so that perhaps one should move to lodgings elsewhere and start again.

Let me state plainly what I mean by saying that the district has altered in character.

Our attitude toward the future and toward the universe and ourselves has changed greatly since H. G. Wells began to write. Such Wellsian concepts as the World State are now abhorrent to us because we have learned sadly that we foster inside us tyrannies undreamed by rational Fabian Mr. Wells and those Victorians who saw mankind as readily educable.

As for the universe! It has changed out of all recognition—changed even since the publication of last year's *Best SF*! Pulsars have been discovered, confronting us with new ideas about energy, interstellar electron density, and the nature of celestial time-keeping. They move the science editor of *New Scientist* to speak of the universe as "that profusion of barely understood objects diluted almost to vanishing point by space"—a description so stripped of the smugness of thirty years ago that SF writers who still send their paper heroes junketting about old models of the universe would be well advised to heed it.

And as for the future! This *is* the future for many of us. The SF I read as a boy in the 30's and early 40's promised marvellous things for the sixties. Possibly you will recall that, according to Wells' "The Shape of Things to Come," 1965 was the year in which a conference was called at Basra (by the Transport Union) from which the Modern State emerged; American, Japanese, Chinese, and Russian delegates were present, as well as European representatives. The average age of delegates was about thirty-three. How simple it was all going to be! And the future was always presented as a simplified version of the present (and still mostly is), whereas we are moving into eras of greater complexity as people, communications, and media all multiply.

Then again, we were told we were going to live in hygienic glass cities, wear tin-togas, travel a lot (and in consequence all be a pleasing light bronze color), actually enjoy TV, and all be sane and happy. There was going to be no smog in Los Angeles and everyone was going to enjoy a Los Angeles climate.

It didn't work out that way. Here is the future, and our few palaces are built on rubbish dumps. Behind every beautiful new building lie seamy back-quarters where human derelicts hide their wounds away. Even worse, we see that every scientific advance advances us merely a shade nearer some ultimate confusion. Of course there is no such thing as a general spiritual advance.

It would be a ridiculous thing if the science fiction field, already showing some signs of disintegration, should be split into a battleground for the generations—the New Wave versus the Old Eddy, or whatever you call it. I believe the younger generation have something (what they have shall be revealed later) but clearly, whatever they have, they must put up or shut up. Understand that this cannot be done by any group, or by anybody speaking for someone else; in literature, thank God, there is only the individual. This year, two young American writers have certainly shown that their voices are ones that can and should be listened to with interest: Thomas M. Disch and John Sladek.

Disch is no dark horse; that *Camp Concentration* is both daring and successfully so is hardly a surprise. He showed his talent from the beginning, not only as a short story writer but as a writer of novels which have proved to possess their own dynamic. Of his earlier novel, *The Genocides*, I said, "A genuine pessimist of a new writer has come along to delight us with an unadulterated shot of pure bracing gloom"; and here is the gloom again, more concentrated, more bracing. A commanding book, and with the sense of humor that genuine pessimism often shows.

John Sladek is perhaps more of a surprise—though one of his excellent short stories appeared in *Best SF* last year. Now, with *The Reproductive System*, he has blossomed into a great darkly funny storyteller, in a novel which toasts brown most of the facets of our civilization. Even fairly obvious targets like horror movies are served up in Sladek's own way. It is an untidy novel, but has the courage of its untidiness, just as Disch has the courage to be utterly unexciting when the occasion demands. Disch's central figure, Sacchetti, in his disease-boosted genius, quotes someone as saying, "Art *must* court tedium. One man's still-life is another's *nature morte*." In the all-action world of SF, such doctrines are really subversive. The pianist Daniel Barenboim said recently that music was the silence between the notes; so literature is the space between the words—as Disch acknowledges.

The one thing that Norman Spinrad's blistering novel, *Bug Jack Baron* lacked was space between words—silence between the notes. It also over-worked one offensive word to desperation, until this reader flinched at its every appearance. I refer to the odious term "nitty-gritty". Apart from this, a bold blast at the forces of cynicism, some lyrical sexual passages, and great humor, make *Bug Jack Baron* a rare and vivid contribution, certainly not to ordinary fiction, but certainly so to the SF canon.

What marks these writers—Disch, Sladek and Spinrad —and others similar to them on both sides of the Atlantic, as distinct from earlier writers is often less their technique than what may be termed their position of engagement. They are sceptical of the advantage to the spirit of our technological age, which includes everything from, say, the sacredness of SF magazines to the technological gadgets themselves.

This comes out most markedly in Sladek's novel, which concerns itself with the horrors of mechanical proliferation—proliferation that eventually brings governments and nations to their metaphorical knees while leaving human beings pretty well unscathed. Thus, while it may be withering about our preoccupation with hardware, it is hopeful about us, saying, in effect, that we may be contaminated but perhaps not fatally. I'm doubtful about that conclusion myself, but certainly it is refreshing to read *The Reproductive System*, which is, for the reasons stated, far less cynical about the human condition than books like, for example, the Lensman series, where legality and goodness seem to be interchangeable terms, and when both depend on loads of lethal machines or quasi-machines for their continued existence.

The Faust theme may be read into Sladek's novel—if you are prepared for the sake of your thesis to equate Dr. Smilax's immortal soul with his spectacles—but it is deliberately there in Disch's novel, where knowledge is bought

at an expense that, in these non-theological days, seems
more ruinous than Faust's. Both novels tackle at different
levels a central dilemma of our age, the relationship
between Man and Machine—for this reason, I rate them
among the most interesting of the year's novels, inside or
outside the SF field.

But this central dilemma is the one, you may agree,
that divides most of the younger writers from most of the
older ones. The young don't like the system or the machines that are its products; forced to choose, they'd prefer
LSD. The older writers have faith in the machine and
faith in our technology to pull us through to a better
world.

Such a dilemma bears very hard upon science fiction
writers. They must take sides. I will state my own position:
technology is no help at all to the essential human condition, any more than a change of government. The reasons
why human beings, organic creatures, have been impelled
from within to build a semi-sentient world of inorganic
things of an increasing complexity (and therefore insubor-
dinacy) are obscure, but those reasons are probably
unhealthful, as one can see by examining the effects of the
compulsion so far. Any writer who light-heartedly sings
the glorious future of machinery puts himself in an ambiguous philosophical attitude.

An extremely important non-fiction book published
during the year examines the origins of what I have called
this central dilemma. As the beneficiaries and victims of
science, we often imagine that our ambivalence toward
science is unique, and that our Faustian pact with technology is unique; then we look back at the Victorian Age
and see, as in a dark pond, our own image reflected.
Herbert L. Sussman takes a good look into that pond in
*Victorians and the Machine: The Literary Response to
Technology*.

He strengthens the feeling I have long had that the
Twentieth Century so far is merely the Nineteenth Century *in extensis* and *in extremis*, a faceless time with no
ethos of its own, in which mankind still reels from great

hammer-blows struck last century. Just as against men like Darwin and Marx we can offer only James Watson and Billy Graham, so Sussman shows by his investigation of seven writers whose books span the century how much our current attitudes to the machine were shaped by men like Carlyle, Ruskin, Dickens, Morris, and Wells. Deeper in the mire, we have achieved only an aesthetic appreciation of machines and their products.

In the first chapter of that rather boring book, *Walden*, Thoreau says, "We are in great haste to construct a magnetic telegraph from Maine to Texas; but Maine to Texas, it may be, have nothing important to communicate". Of course, Thoreau was just a nature-loving literary man; but, since the likelihood that the world's Maines and Texases will have nothing to communicate has become more thoroughly confirmed, his cautionary words should be remembered by the more-means-better brigade who cry for more comsats and additional TV channels.

So with most other facets of our contemporary world. Some Victorians saw the situation clearly enough. By the end of the 1850's, the decade of the Great Exhibition, it was no longer possible to hope for a richer life through machines; there was technological power; but it flourished amid emotional and physical poverty; and what was then true for Victorian England is now true for the globe.

Another curious factor, which Sussman brings out well, is the ambivalence of Victorian feelings toward the machine and the awful fascination of them. In part this may be because of the man-machine interdependence, a more sophisticated version of the peasant-goat interdependence, which was pinpointed by Samuel Butler thus (one of the excellent and apposite quotations which adorn Sussman's book): "The fact is that our interests are inseparable from theirs (the machines), and theirs from ours. Each race is dependent upon the other for innumerable benefits."

Of course, things have gone further today. We aren't so sure any longer that they need us . . . But even this suspicion is inherent in the writings of Wells by the end of the century. Science fiction authors still experience that

Brian W. Aldiss 243

ambivalent feeling toward machines; it it unfortunate
that their historic sense is so often directed forwards rather
than back, so that they do not realize how often they are
merely covering old ground. The newer writers seem more
widely read in non-technical spheres; which should help
them to break new ground.

Often this means revealing fresh aspects of our present,
which is a stewpot of past and future. It is not that they
desert the future; rather, the future has deserted them.

The near-future was something that happened in the
nineteen-fifties. Many utopian dreams were realized by
then and proved dystopian. All we have immediately before us (at least until new socio-economic-national doctrines prevail) is merely the present-in-extension, just as
our century is the nineteenth-in-extension.

Of this nightmare retardation of time, we had an example last year—a large-scale and horrifying example. On
August 21st, units of the Soviet Army, supported by
units of four other Warsaw Pact countries, invaded
Czechoslovakia; their main objective was to crush the new
waves of feeling and thinking then breaking through the
official Communist mold. These shocks of change were
seismographic readings that sent a tremor through the gray
men in Moscow; they moved hurriedly in to set the Czech
clock back.

In the West, with our customary optimism, we had
deceived ourselves into imagining that things had changed
in the Soviet Union since the repressive days of Stalinism.
We see now it is not so. Inside the enduring walls of the
Kremlin, time has been stopped; and since—whether we
like it or not—the Russians are our brothers, our own
time-pulse is chilled thereby.

The future is over. The space race is an old-fashioned
diversion conducted with infertile phallic symbols, a
Verne freak-out. What then is a creative writer to do? Is
there a place for him, except as a museum curator, a worm
re-turning old soil?

There is still art. There is no progress in the arts: so they
must be among the true things. I believe in writing. I

believe writing is to be preferred to advertising, or to advertising oneself, or to knocking out scripts for TV or film according to someone else's dictates, or to strip cartoons; or to any other bastard relation. Writing is a raft of words—with words and thought inextricable, the very mark of Man.

I also believe that if you feel this way, you may possibly summon enough faith to write well, and that possibly writing well may mean arranging a logical series of events into a reasoned structure, and populating that structure with facsimiles of human beings. And that if one does this, one stands a chance of producing a living work as well as just earning a living.

There is little doubt that this is a splendid period in which to be observing and writing—one recalls the old Chinese curse, "May you live in interesting times!"—if only one can fortify oneself against the chill winds of nihilism and not be tempted by any of the various unsound theories flying around. Perhaps the theory that did SF most damage was the idea that the future was going to be made glorious through a sort of army of technological devices—an unthinking optimism that led to coarseness and turned SF into propaganda, propaganda for the space race or for stunt systems of psychology or mechanics.

A curious idea that some SF writers entertain nowadays is that there is something called a "psychic landscape" which somehow has an exact external equivalent; surely this is part and parcel of the Pathetic Fallacy, worn thin in William Wordsworth's day; luckily, the human identity can still distinguish itself from its environment. Too much pretence and pretentiousness can kill SF. Unfortunately, the coterie aspect of SF magazines—whether *Galaxy* or *New Worlds* or *Analog*—tends to breed formulae and dogma, some of which, initially helpful, tend to assume the strength of strait-jackets.

Writers can only function well as writers by preserving their independence. Life is brief, art is long, one Burroughs follows another. The pressure to take sides is heavy today. We have to opt for being capitalist or communist, republican or democrat, young or old, white or black. But neutrality too has its strengths. The genre known as science fiction has now become so self-conscious, so encrusted with tradition, that it's a fight to write freshly. Perhaps it will all crumble into separate units—the only units that ever matter: individuals.

As for the house that Verne and Wells built, perhaps it is no longer capable of sheltering so many writers of such diverse views and feelings. After all, it is an old Victorian property; the structure is not as sound as it was; and the district has lost much of its previous visual drama through in-filling. Tenants would be advised to find their own little plots elsewhere. Myself, I'm hoping for a fairly isolated site—though maybe still within sight of the market place.

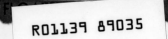